W9-DES-307

DISNEY · PIXAR

FINDING NEMO

Disney · PIXAR
FINDING NEMO

THE STORY OF THE MOVIES IN COMICS

DARK HORSE BOOKS

DARK HORSE BOOKS

PRESIDENT AND PUBLISHER **MIKE RICHARDSON**

COLLECTION EDITOR **SHANTEL LAROCQUE** COLLECTION ASSISTANT EDITOR **BRETT ISRAEL**

DESIGNER **JEN EDWARDS** DIGITAL ART TECHNICIAN **JOSIE CHRISTENSEN**

NEIL HANKERSON Executive Vice President • TOM WEDDLE Chief Financial Officer • RANDY STRADLEY Vice President of Publishing • NICK McWHORTER Chief Business Development Officer • DALE LaFOUNTAIN Chief Information Officer • MATT PARKINSON Vice President of Marketing • VANESSA TODD-HOLMES Vice President of Production and Scheduling • MARK BERNARDI Vice President of Book Trade and Digital Sales • KEN LIZZI General Counsel • DAVE MARSHALL Editor in Chief • DAVEY ESTRADA Editorial Director • CHRIS WARNER Senior Books Editor • CARY GRAZZINI Director of Specialty Projects • LIA RIBACCHI Art Director • MATT DRYER Director of Digital Art and Prepress • MICHAEL GOMBOS Senior Director of Licensed Publications • KARI YADRO Director of Custom Programs • KARI TORSON Director of International Licensing • SEAN BRICE Director of Trade Sales

DISNEY PUBLISHING WORLDWIDE GLOBAL MAGAZINES, COMICS AND PARTWORKS

PUBLISHER Lynn Waggoner • EDITORIAL TEAM Bianca Coletti (Director, Magazines), Guido Frazzini (Director, Comics), Carlotta Quattrocolo (Executive Editor), Stefano Ambrosio (Executive Editor, New IP), Camilla Vedove (Senior Manager, Editorial Development), Behnoosh Khalili (Senior Editor), Julie Dorris (Senior Editor), Mina Riazi (Assistant Editor), Gabriela Capasso (Assistant Editor) • DESIGN Enrico Soave (Senior Designer) • ART Ken Shue (VP, Global Art), Manny Mederos (Senior Illustration Manager, Comics and Magazines), Roberto Santillo (Creative Director), Marco Ghiglione (Creative Manager), Stefano Attardi (Illustration Manager) • PORTFOLIO MANAGEMENT Olivia Ciancarelli (Director) • BUSINESS & MARKETING Mariantonietta Galla (Senior Manager, Franchise), Virpi Korhonen (Editorial Manager)

Library of Congress Cataloging-in-Publication Data

Names: Bazaldua, C. (Charles), author. | Sciarrone, Claudio, illustrator. | Matta, Gabriella, colourist. | Baldoni, Davide, colourist. | Calabria, Dario, colourist. | Ferrari, Alessandro, 1978- author. | Sammarco, Nicola, illustrator. | Greppi, Andrea, 1970- penciller. | Damiani, Mara, colourist. | Dickey, Chris, letterer. | Walt Disney Productions. | Pixar (Firm)
Title: Finding Nemo and Finding Dory : the story of the movies in comics!
Other titles: At head of title: Disney/PIXAR | Finding Nemo (Motion picture)
Description: First edition. | Milwaukie, OR : Dark Horse Books, 2020. | Audience: Ages 10+ | Summary: "Marlin, a clownfish, teams up with a forgetful but friendly Blue Tang named Dory to find his son Nemo in this collection of the films retold as comics! Along the way they'll meet new friends and they'll discover just how much Dory is capable of in this heartwarming undersea adventure that brings DisneyPixar's Finding Nemo and Finding Dory from the screen to your fingertips!"-- Provided by publisher.
Identifiers: LCCN 2019053288 | ISBN 9781506717593 (hardcover) | ISBN 9781506717623 (epub)
Subjects: LCSH: Graphic novels. | BISAC: JUVENILE FICTION / Comics & Graphic Novels / Media Tie-In.
Classification: LCC PZ7.7.B394 Fi 2020 | DDC 741.5/973--dc23
LC record available at https://lccn.loc.gov/2019053288

Published by Dark Horse Books
A division of Dark Horse Comics LLC
10956 SE Main Street | Milwaukie, OR 97222

DarkHorse.com

To find a comics shop in your area, visit comicshoplocator.com

First edition: October 2020
Ebook ISBN 978-1-50671-762-3 | ISBN 978-1-50671-759-3

1 3 5 7 9 10 8 6 4 2
Printed in China

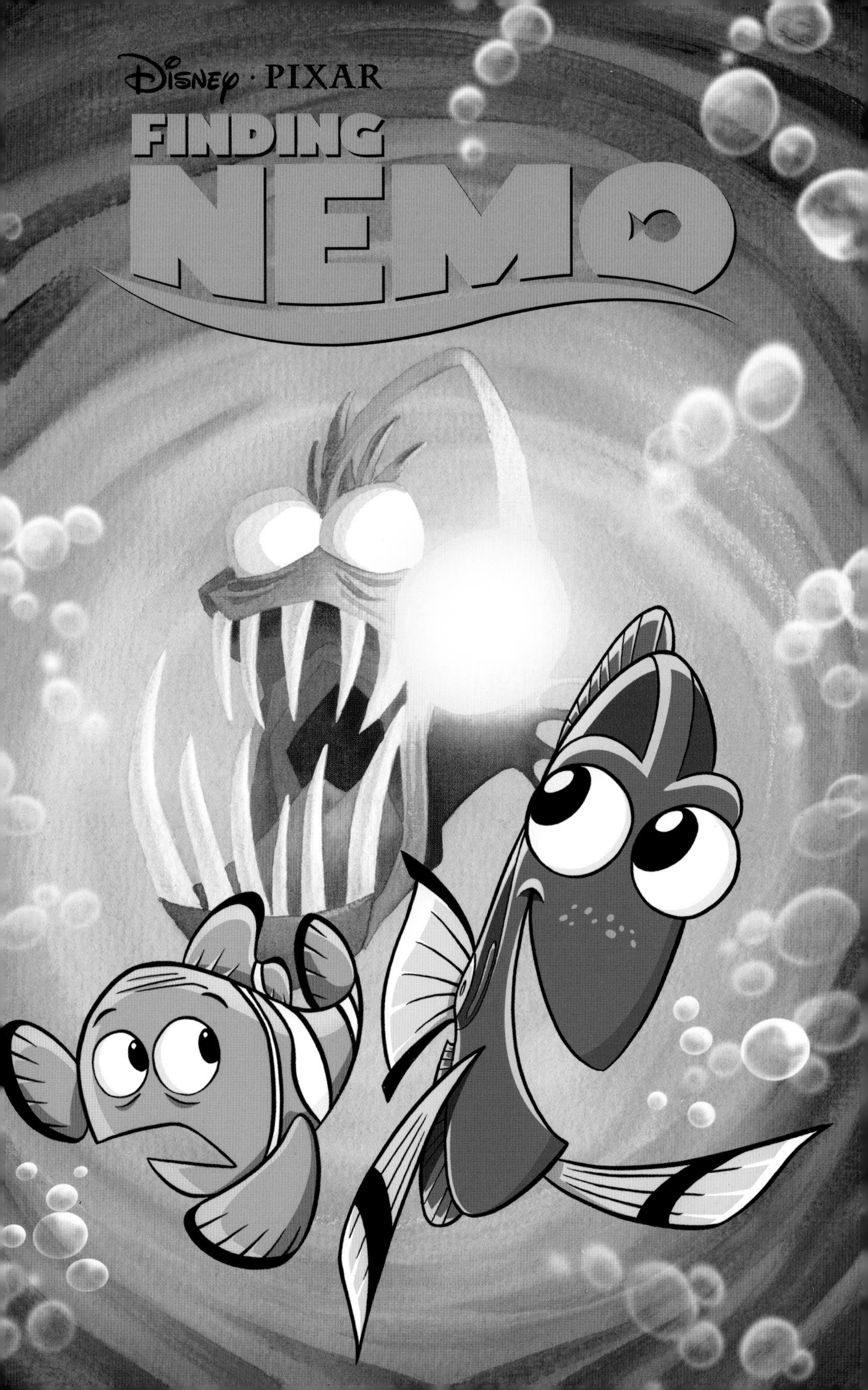
Disney · PIXAR
FINDING
NEMO

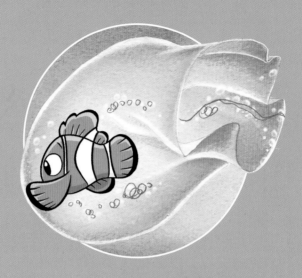

Script adaptation
CHARLES BAZALDUA

Layouts, Pencils, & Inks
CLAUDIO SCIARRONE

Color
**GABRIELLA MATTA,
DAVIDE BALDONI, DARIO CALABRIA**

Cover
Layouts, Pencils, & Inks
CLAUDIO SCIARRONE

Colors
GABRIELLA MATTA, DAVIDE BALDONI

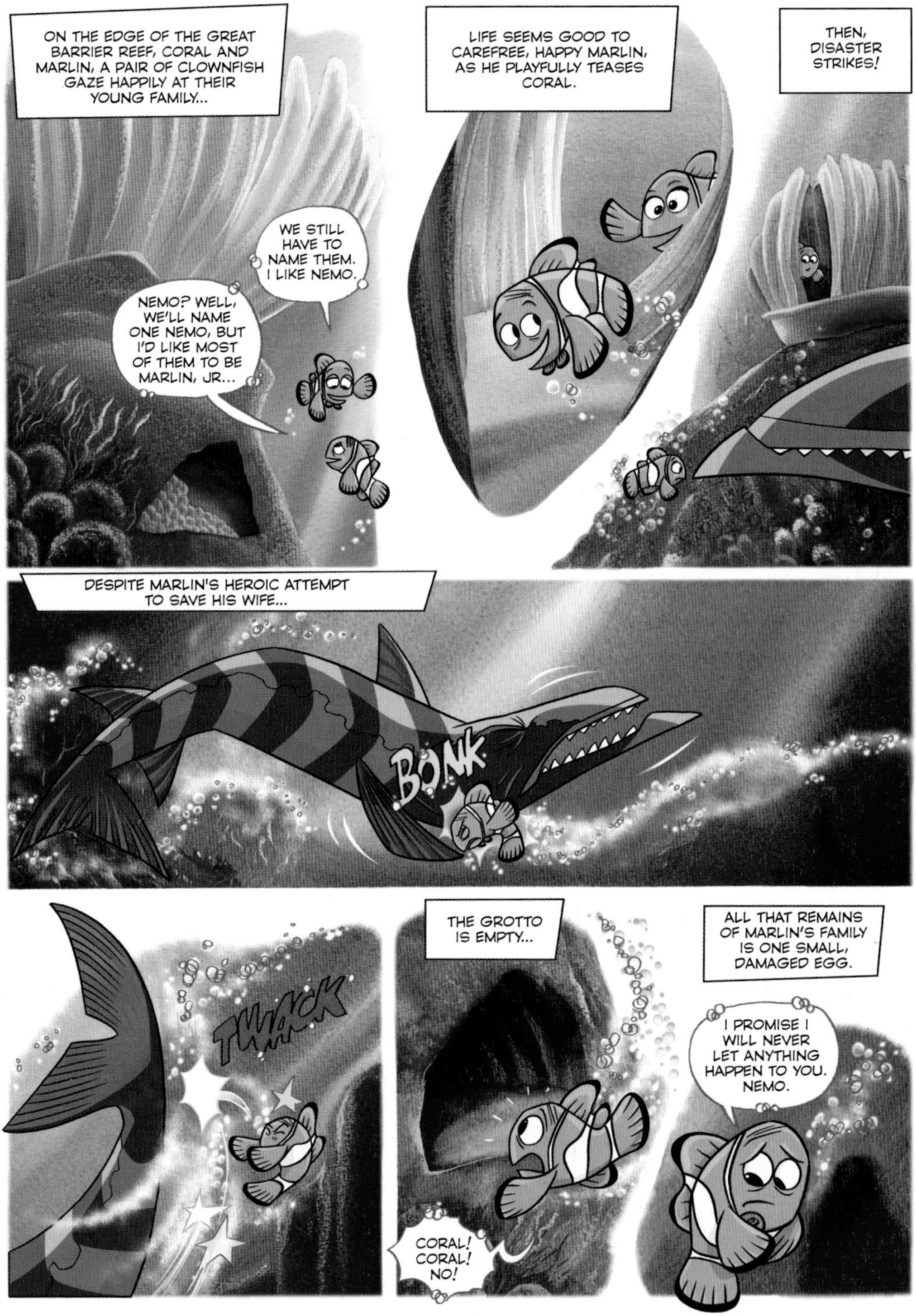
ON THE EDGE OF THE GREAT BARRIER REEF, CORAL AND MARLIN, A PAIR OF CLOWNFISH GAZE HAPPILY AT THEIR YOUNG FAMILY...
WE STILL HAVE TO NAME THEM. I LIKE NEMO.
NEMO? WELL, WE'LL NAME ONE NEMO, BUT I'D LIKE MOST OF THEM TO BE MARLIN, JR...
LIFE SEEMS GOOD TO CAREFREE, HAPPY MARLIN, AS HE PLAYFULLY TEASES CORAL.
THEN, DISASTER STRIKES!
DESPITE MARLIN'S HEROIC ATTEMPT TO SAVE HIS WIFE...
BONK
TWACK
THE GROTTO IS EMPTY...
CORAL! CORAL! NO!
ALL THAT REMAINS OF MARLIN'S FAMILY IS ONE SMALL, DAMAGED EGG.
I PROMISE I WILL NEVER LET ANYTHING HAPPEN TO YOU. NEMO.

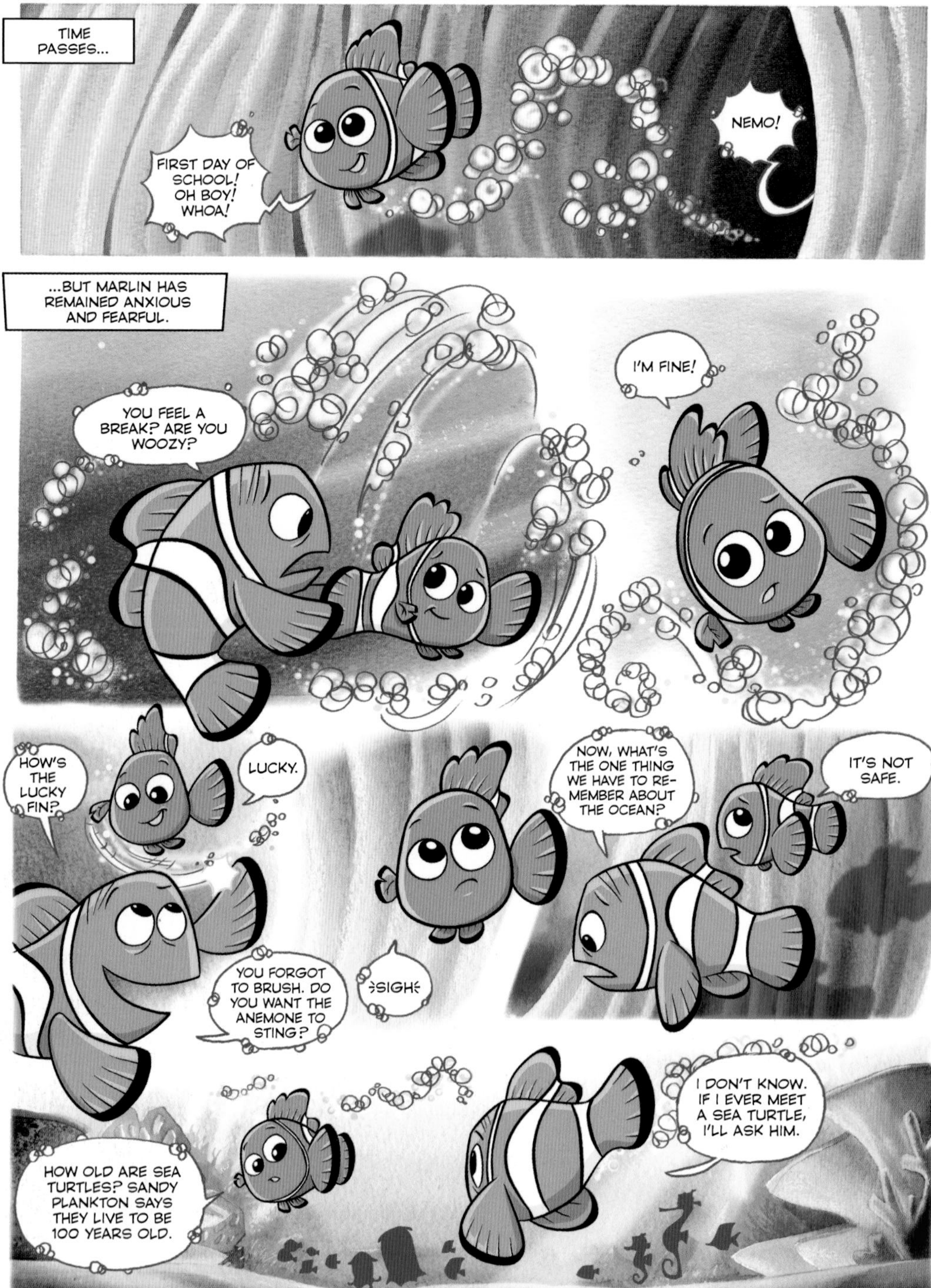
TIME PASSES...
FIRST DAY OF SCHOOL! OH BOY! WHOA!
NEMO!
...BUT MARLIN HAS REMAINED ANXIOUS AND FEARFUL.
YOU FEEL A BREAK? ARE YOU WOOZY?
I'M FINE!
HOW'S THE LUCKY FIN?
LUCKY.
YOU FORGOT TO BRUSH. DO YOU WANT THE ANEMONE TO STING?
SIGH
NOW, WHAT'S THE ONE THING WE HAVE TO RE-MEMBER ABOUT THE OCEAN?
IT'S NOT SAFE.
HOW OLD ARE SEA TURTLES? SANDY PLANKTON SAYS THEY LIVE TO BE 100 YEARS OLD.
I DON'T KNOW. IF I EVER MEET A SEA TURTLE, I'LL ASK HIM.

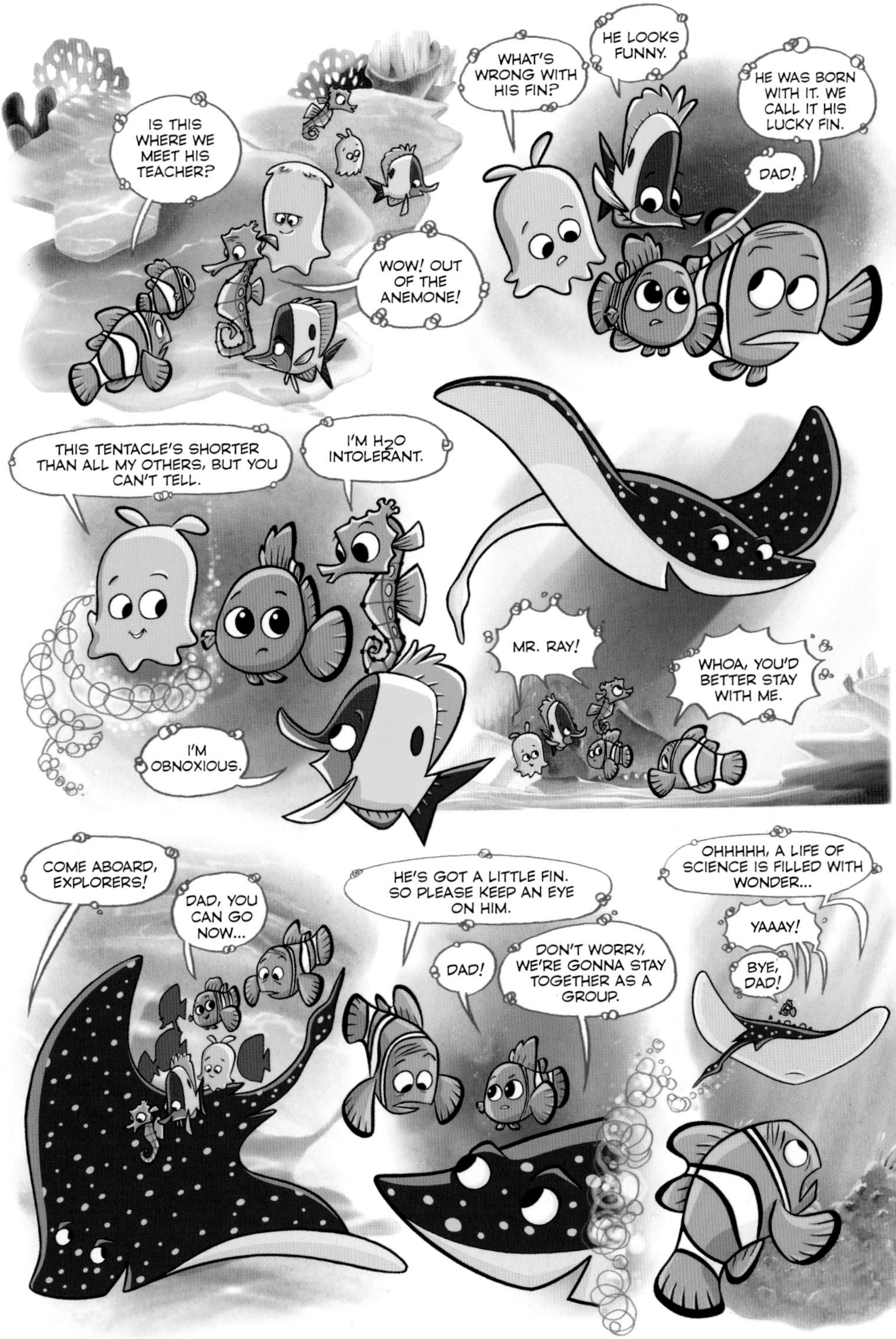
IS THIS WHERE WE MEET HIS TEACHER?
WOW! OUT OF THE ANEMONE!
WHAT'S WRONG WITH HIS FIN?
HE LOOKS FUNNY.
HE WAS BORN WITH IT. WE CALL IT HIS LUCKY FIN.
DAD!
THIS TENTACLE'S SHORTER THAN ALL MY OTHERS, BUT YOU CAN'T TELL.
I'M H_2O INTOLERANT.
I'M OBNOXIOUS.
MR. RAY!
WHOA, YOU'D BETTER STAY WITH ME.
COME ABOARD, EXPLORERS!
DAD, YOU CAN GO NOW...
HE'S GOT A LITTLE FIN. SO PLEASE KEEP AN EYE ON HIM.
DAD!
DON'T WORRY, WE'RE GONNA STAY TOGETHER AS A GROUP.
OHHHHH, A LIFE OF SCIENCE IS FILLED WITH WONDER...
YAAAY!
BYE, DAD!

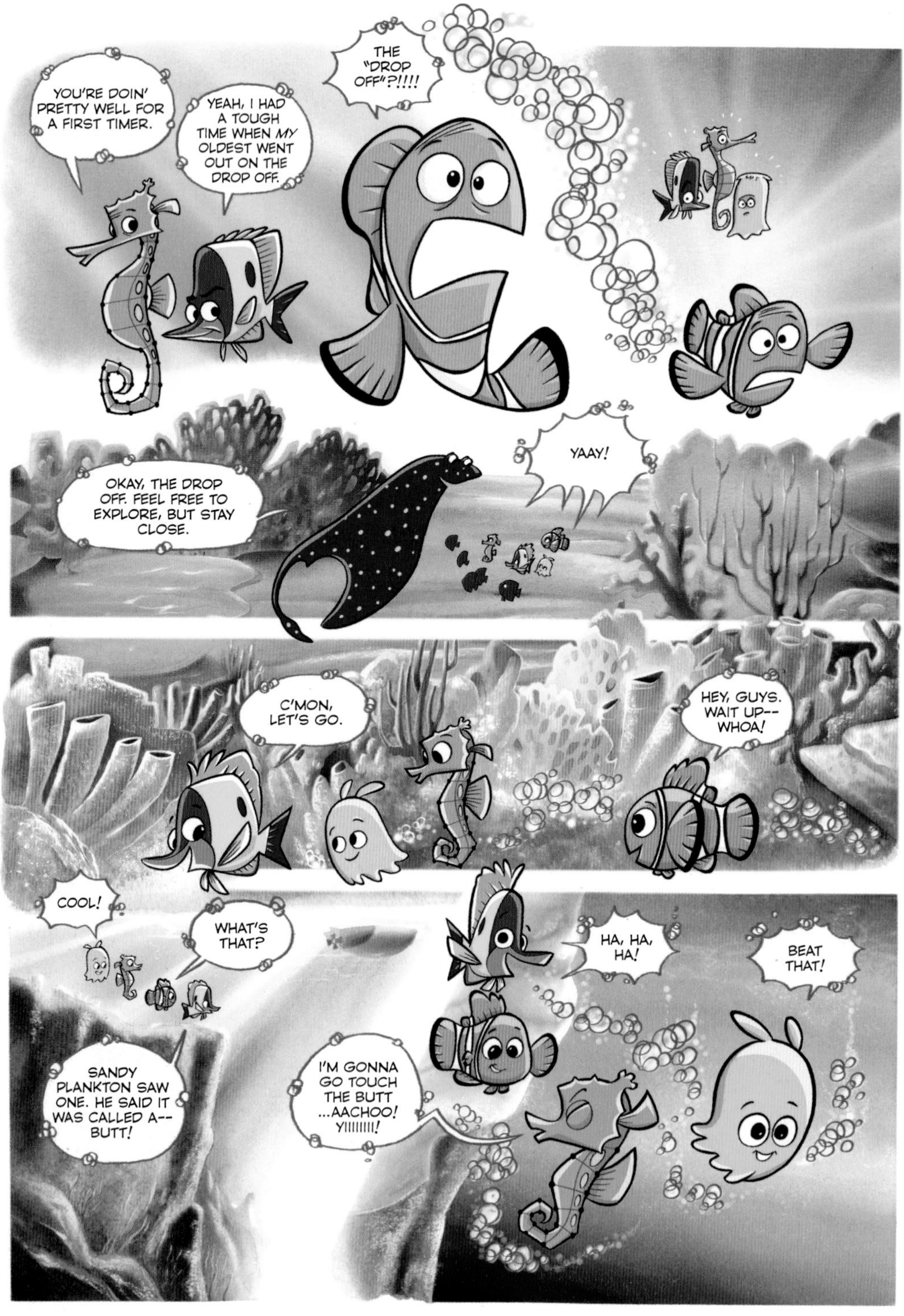
YOU'RE DOIN' PRETTY WELL FOR A FIRST TIMER.
YEAH, I HAD A TOUGH TIME WHEN *MY* OLDEST WENT OUT ON THE DROP OFF.
THE "DROP OFF"?!!!!
OKAY, THE DROP OFF. FEEL FREE TO EXPLORE, BUT STAY CLOSE.
YAAY!
C'MON, LET'S GO.
HEY, GUYS. WAIT UP-- WHOA!
COOL!
WHAT'S THAT?
SANDY PLANKTON SAW ONE. HE SAID IT WAS CALLED A-- BUTT!
HA, HA, HA!
BEAT THAT!
I'M GONNA GO TOUCH THE BUTT ...AACHOO! YIIIIIII!

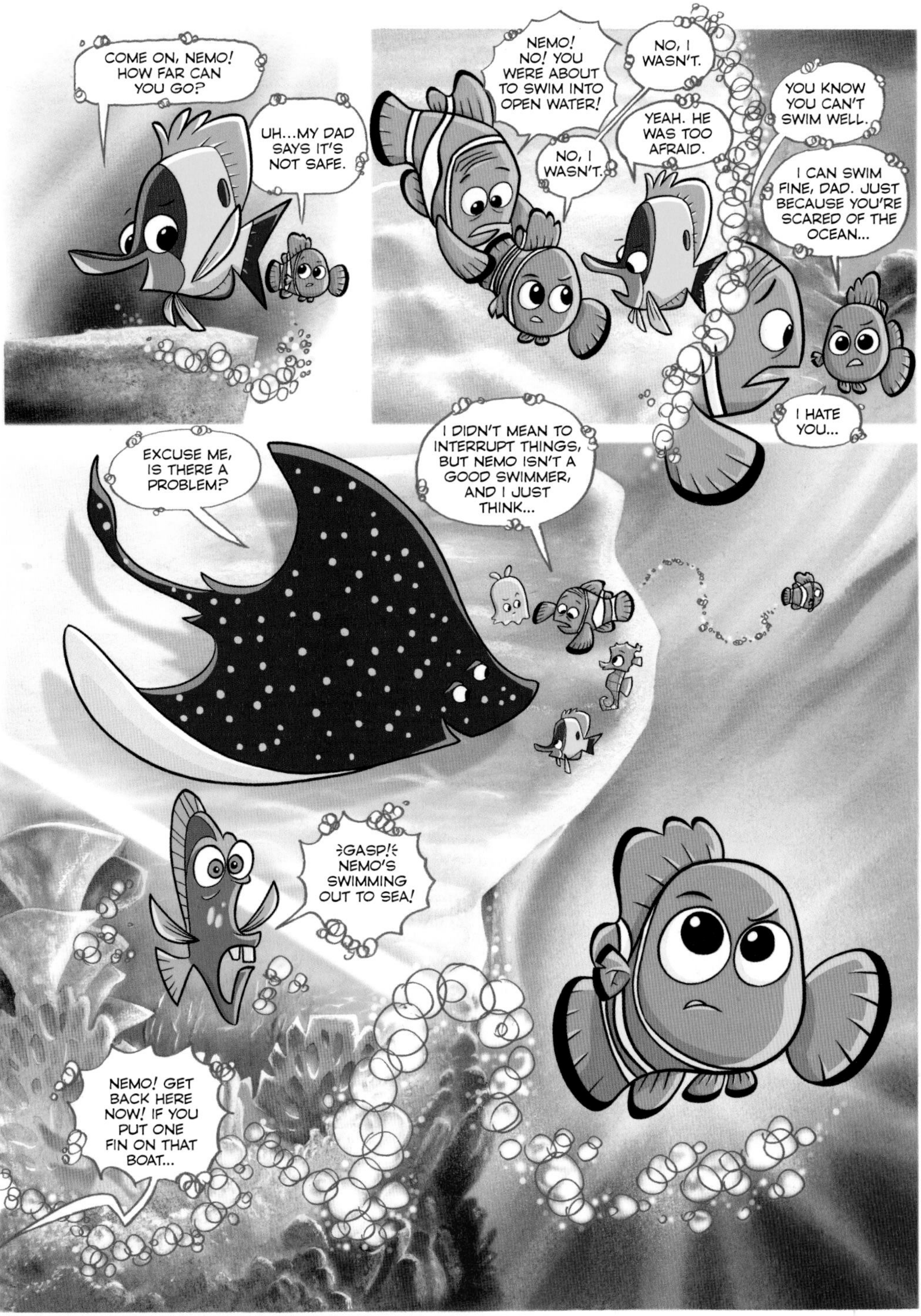
COME ON, NEMO! HOW FAR CAN YOU GO?
UH...MY DAD SAYS IT'S NOT SAFE.
NEMO! NO! YOU WERE ABOUT TO SWIM INTO OPEN WATER!
NO, I WASN'T.
NO, I WASN'T.
YEAH. HE WAS TOO AFRAID.
YOU KNOW YOU CAN'T SWIM WELL.
I CAN SWIM FINE, DAD. JUST BECAUSE YOU'RE SCARED OF THE OCEAN...
I HATE YOU...
EXCUSE ME, IS THERE A PROBLEM?
I DIDN'T MEAN TO INTERRUPT THINGS, BUT NEMO ISN'T A GOOD SWIMMER, AND I JUST THINK...
GASP! NEMO'S SWIMMING OUT TO SEA!
NEMO! GET BACK HERE NOW! IF YOU PUT ONE FIN ON THAT BOAT...

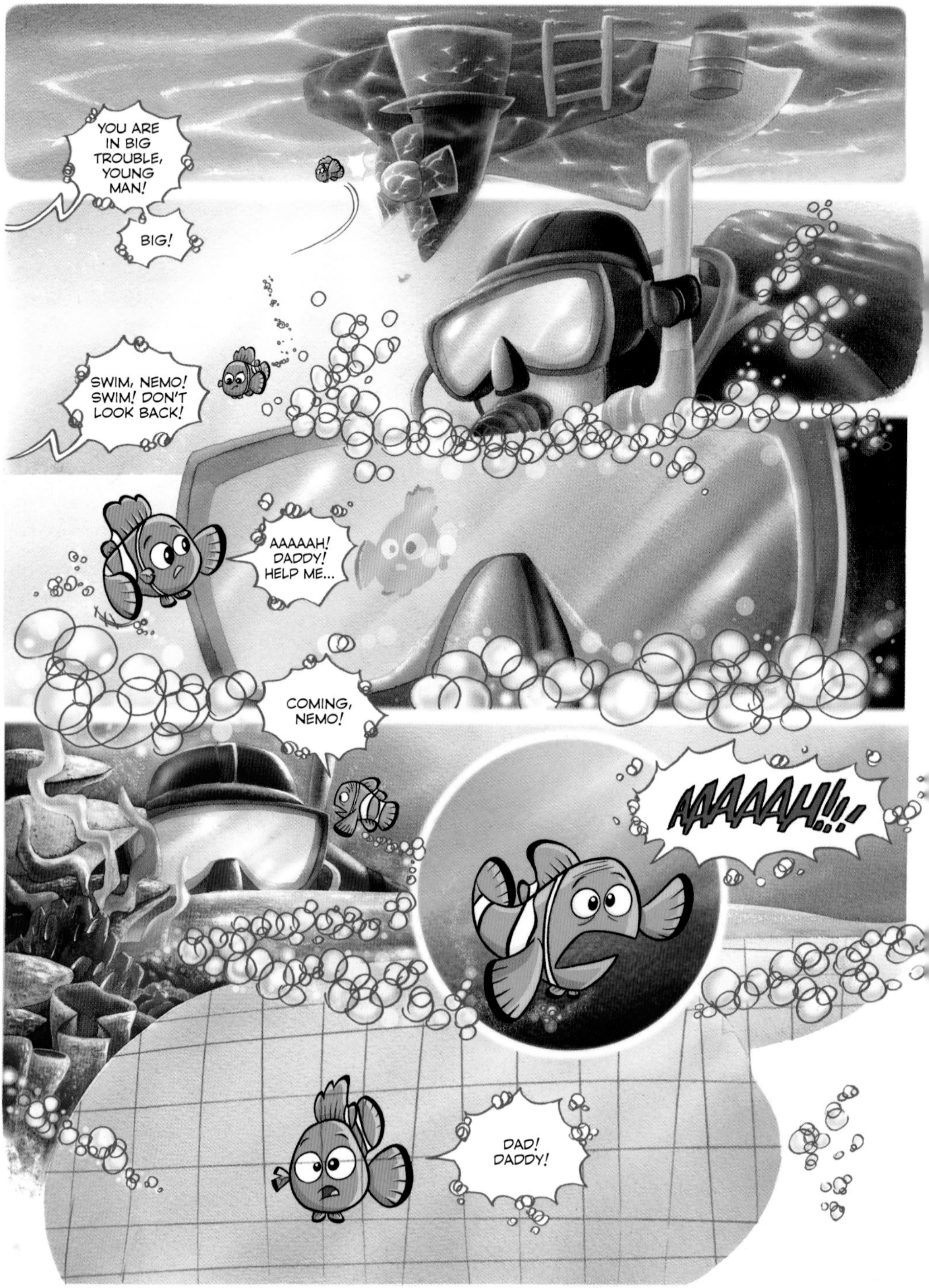
YOU ARE IN BIG TROUBLE, YOUNG MAN!
BIG!
SWIM, NEMO! SWIM! DON'T LOOK BACK!
AAAAAH! DADDY! HELP ME...
COMING, NEMO!
AAAAAH!!!
DAD! DADDY!

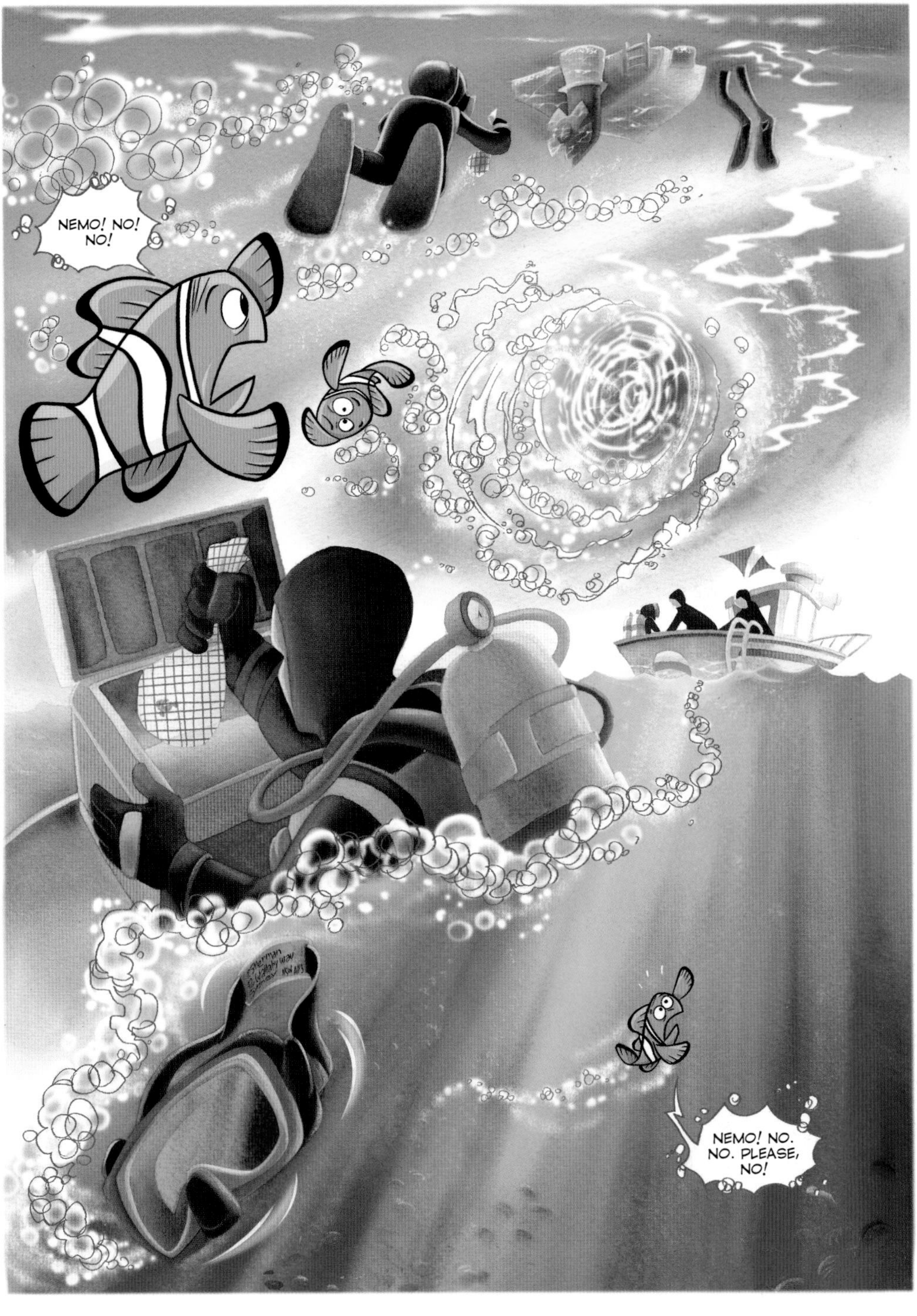
NEMO! NO! NO!
NEMO! NO. NO. PLEASE, NO!

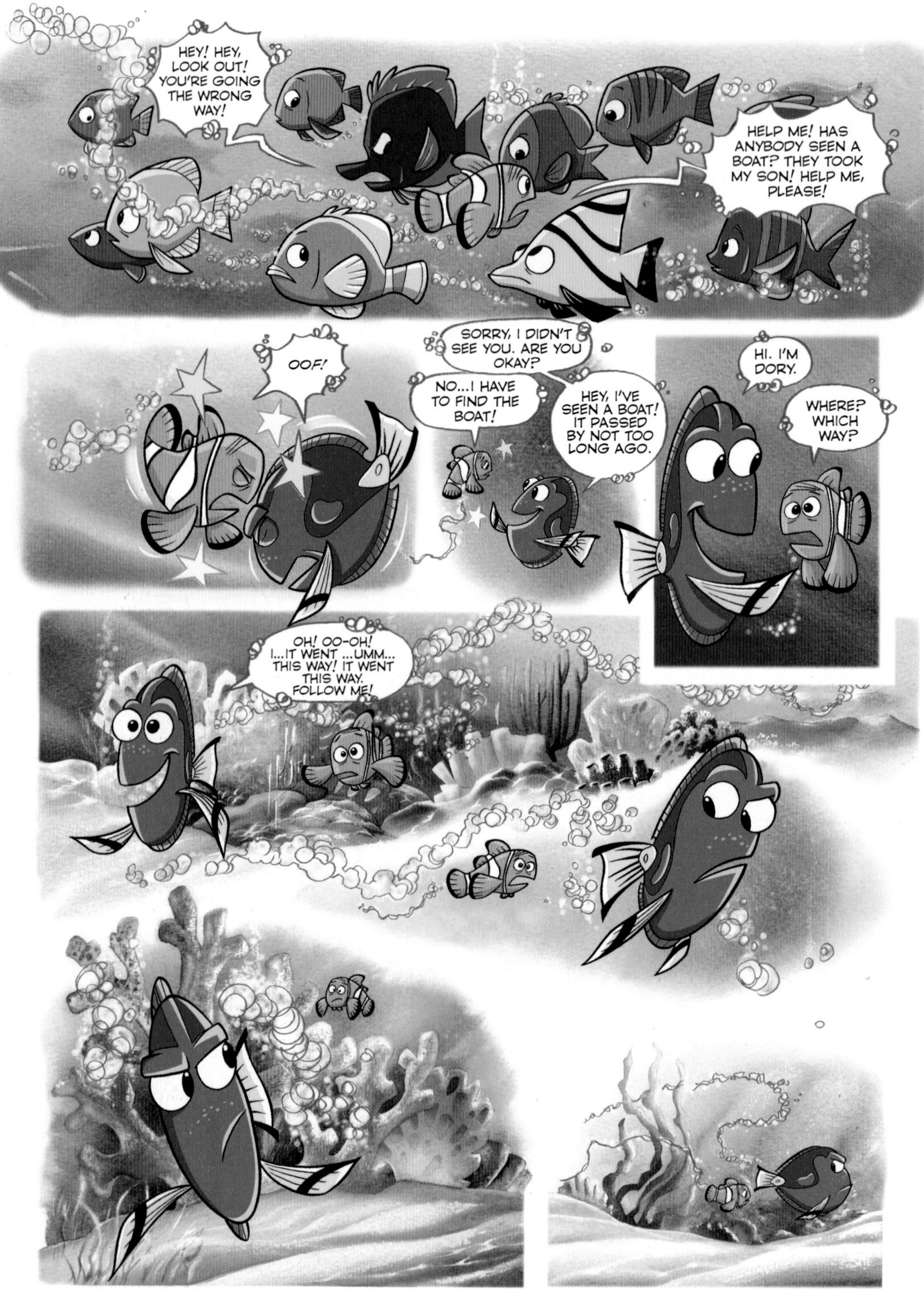
HEY! HEY, LOOK OUT! YOU'RE GOING THE WRONG WAY!
HELP ME! HAS ANYBODY SEEN A BOAT? THEY TOOK MY SON! HELP ME, PLEASE!
OOF!
SORRY, I DIDN'T SEE YOU. ARE YOU OKAY?
NO...I HAVE TO FIND THE BOAT!
HEY, I'VE SEEN A BOAT! IT PASSED BY NOT TOO LONG AGO.
HI. I'M DORY.
WHERE? WHICH WAY?
OH! OO-OH! I...IT WENT ...UMM... THIS WAY! IT WENT THIS WAY. FOLLOW ME!

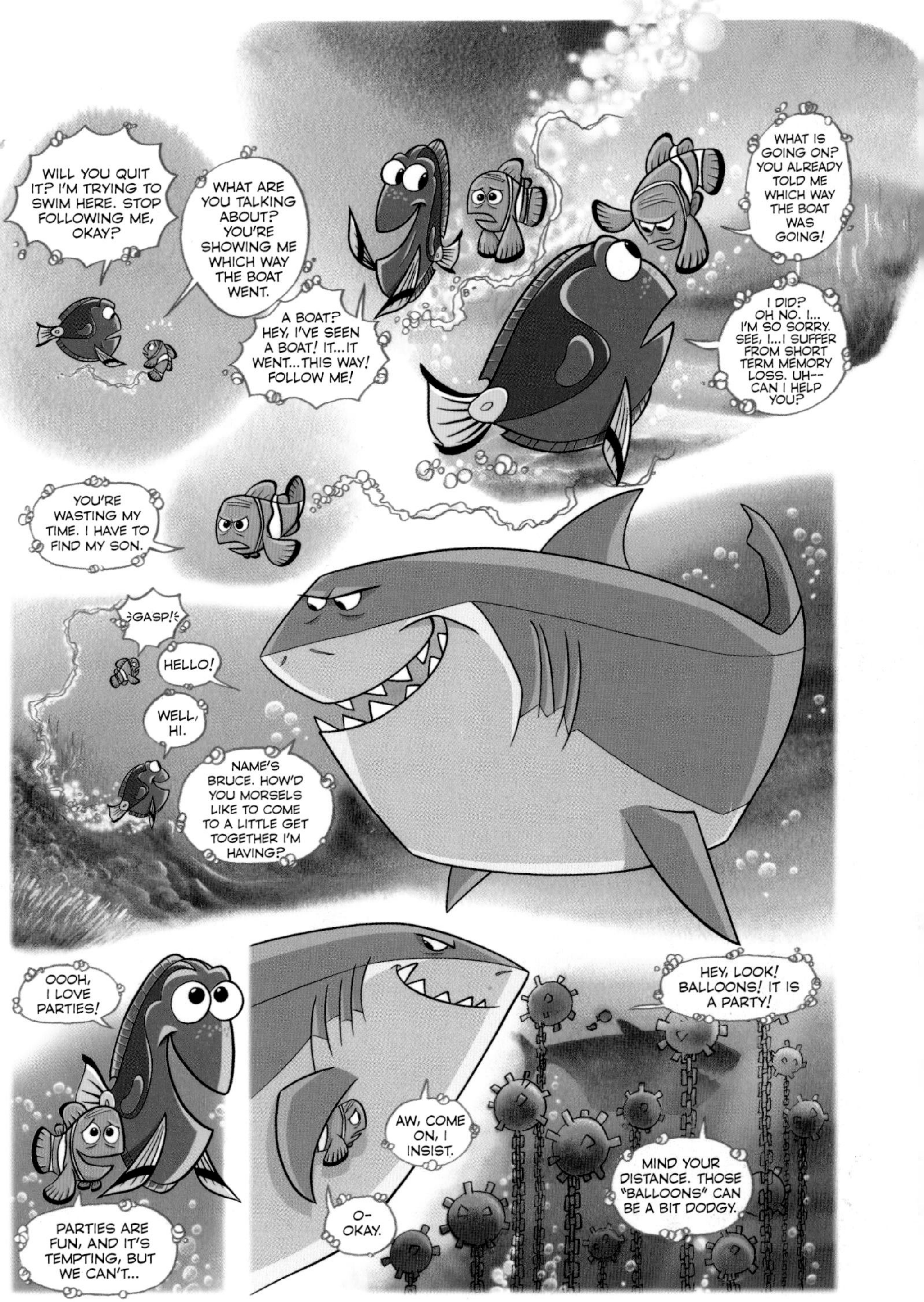
WILL YOU QUIT IT? I'M TRYING TO SWIM HERE. STOP FOLLOWING ME, OKAY?
WHAT ARE YOU TALKING ABOUT? YOU'RE SHOWING ME WHICH WAY THE BOAT WENT.
A BOAT? HEY, I'VE SEEN A BOAT! IT...IT WENT...THIS WAY! FOLLOW ME!
WHAT IS GOING ON? YOU ALREADY TOLD ME WHICH WAY THE BOAT WAS GOING!
I DID? OH NO. I... I'M SO SORRY. SEE, I...I SUFFER FROM SHORT TERM MEMORY LOSS. UH-- CAN I HELP YOU?
YOU'RE WASTING MY TIME. I HAVE TO FIND MY SON.
GASP!
HELLO!
WELL, HI.
NAME'S BRUCE. HOW'D YOU MORSELS LIKE TO COME TO A LITTLE GET TOGETHER I'M HAVING?
OOOH, I LOVE PARTIES!
PARTIES ARE FUN, AND IT'S TEMPTING, BUT WE CAN'T...
AW, COME ON, I INSIST.
O- OKAY.
HEY, LOOK! BALLOONS! IT IS A PARTY!
MIND YOUR DISTANCE. THOSE "BALLOONS" CAN BE A BIT DODGY.

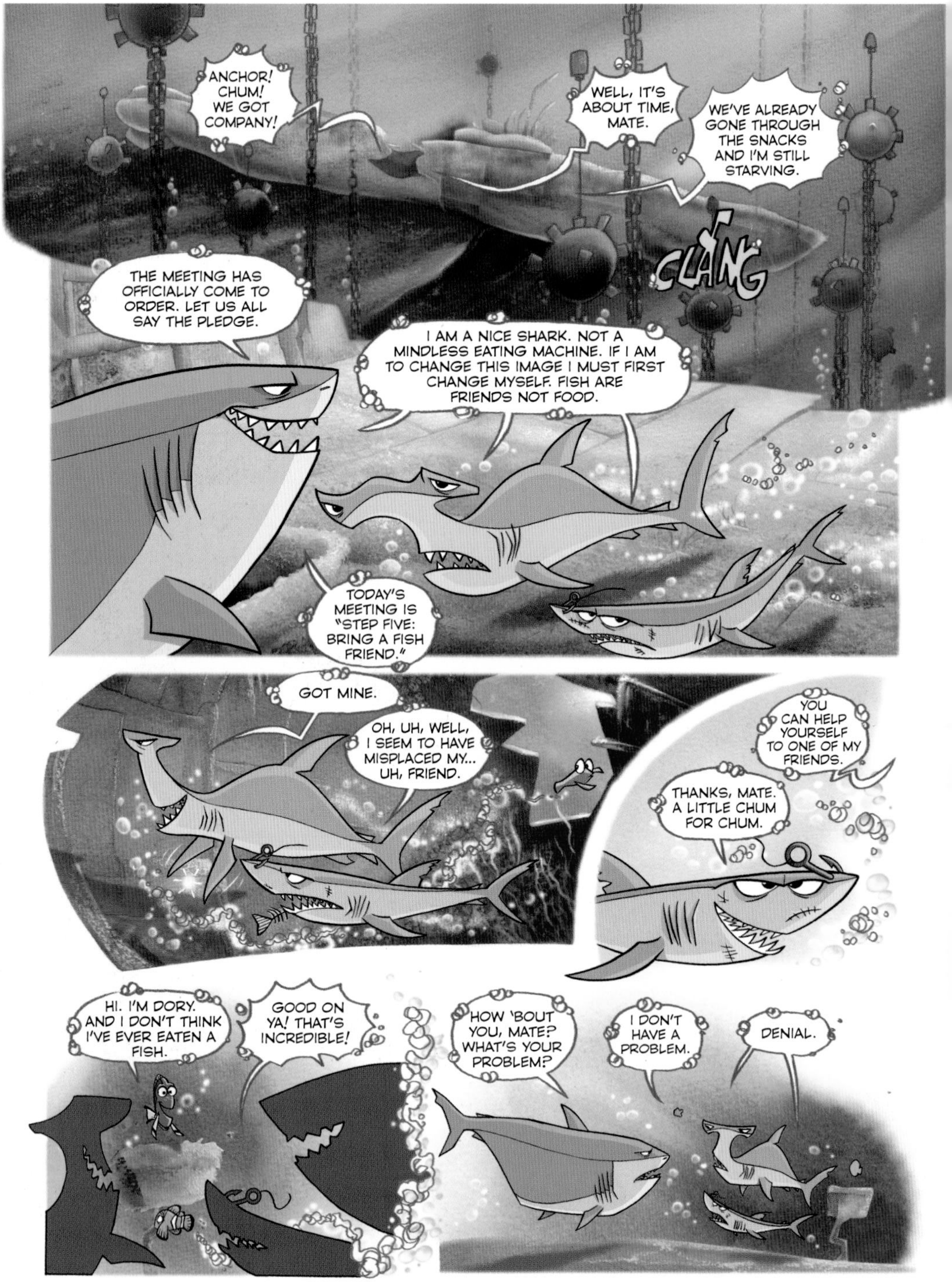

ANCHOR! CHUM! WE GOT COMPANY!
WELL, IT'S ABOUT TIME, MATE.
WE'VE ALREADY GONE THROUGH THE SNACKS AND I'M STILL STARVING.
CLANG
THE MEETING HAS OFFICIALLY COME TO ORDER. LET US ALL SAY THE PLEDGE.
I AM A NICE SHARK. NOT A MINDLESS EATING MACHINE. IF I AM TO CHANGE THIS IMAGE I MUST FIRST CHANGE MYSELF. FISH ARE FRIENDS NOT FOOD.
TODAY'S MEETING IS "STEP FIVE: BRING A FISH FRIEND."
GOT MINE.
OH, UH, WELL, I SEEM TO HAVE MISPLACED MY... UH, FRIEND.
YOU CAN HELP YOURSELF TO ONE OF MY FRIENDS.
THANKS, MATE. A LITTLE CHUM FOR CHUM.
HI. I'M DORY. AND I DON'T THINK I'VE EVER EATEN A FISH.
GOOD ON YA! THAT'S INCREDIBLE!
HOW 'BOUT YOU, MATE? WHAT'S YOUR PROBLEM?
I DON'T HAVE A PROBLEM.
DENIAL.

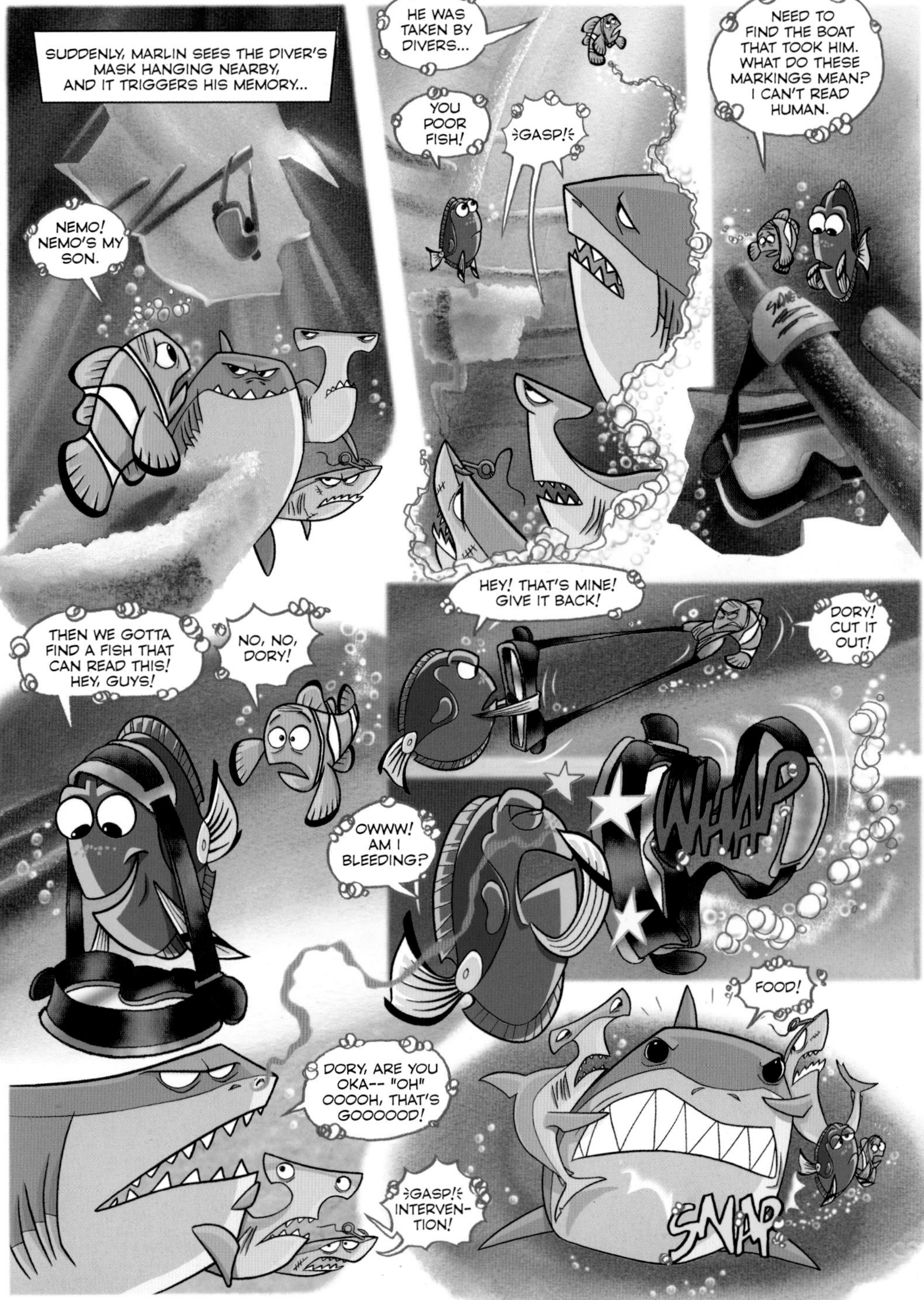
SUDDENLY, MARLIN SEES THE DIVER'S MASK HANGING NEARBY, AND IT TRIGGERS HIS MEMORY...
NEMO! NEMO'S MY SON.
HE WAS TAKEN BY DIVERS...
YOU POOR FISH!
GASP!
NEED TO FIND THE BOAT THAT TOOK HIM. WHAT DO THESE MARKINGS MEAN? I CAN'T READ HUMAN.
THEN WE GOTTA FIND A FISH THAT CAN READ THIS! HEY, GUYS!
NO, NO, DORY!
HEY! THAT'S MINE! GIVE IT BACK!
DORY! CUT IT OUT!
WHAP
OWWW! AM I BLEEDING?
FOOD!
DORY, ARE YOU OKA-- "OH" OOOOH, THAT'S GOOOOOD!
GASP! INTERVEN-TION!
SNAP

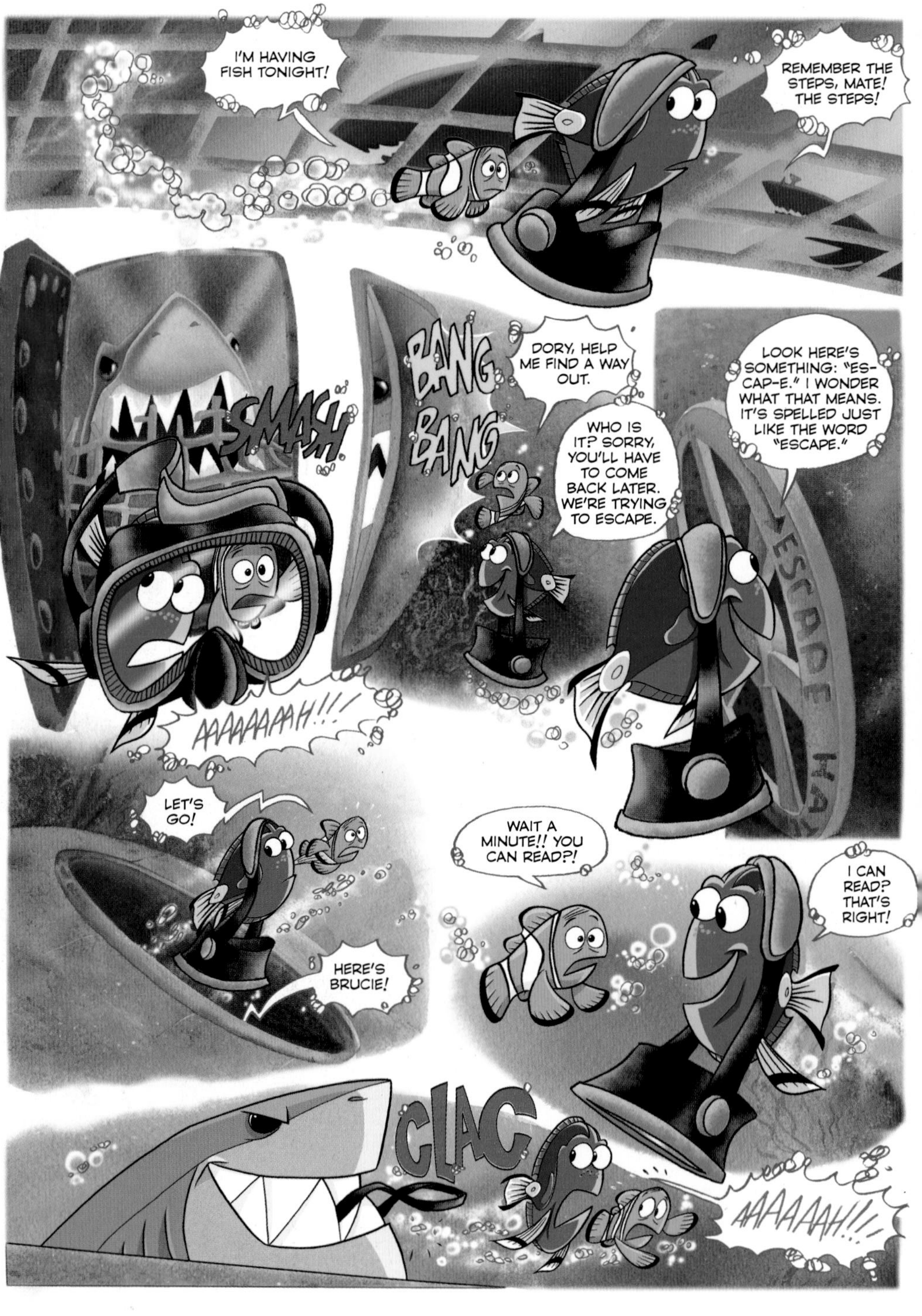
I'M HAVING FISH TONIGHT!
REMEMBER THE STEPS, MATE! THE STEPS!
SMASH
AAAAAAAAH!!!
BANG
BANG
DORY, HELP ME FIND A WAY OUT.
WHO IS IT? SORRY, YOU'LL HAVE TO COME BACK LATER. WE'RE TRYING TO ESCAPE.
LOOK HERE'S SOMETHING: "ES-CAP-E." I WONDER WHAT THAT MEANS. IT'S SPELLED JUST LIKE THE WORD "ESCAPE."
ESCAPE
LET'S GO!
HERE'S BRUCIE!
WAIT A MINUTE!! YOU CAN READ?!
I CAN READ? THAT'S RIGHT!
CLAC
AAAAAAH!!!

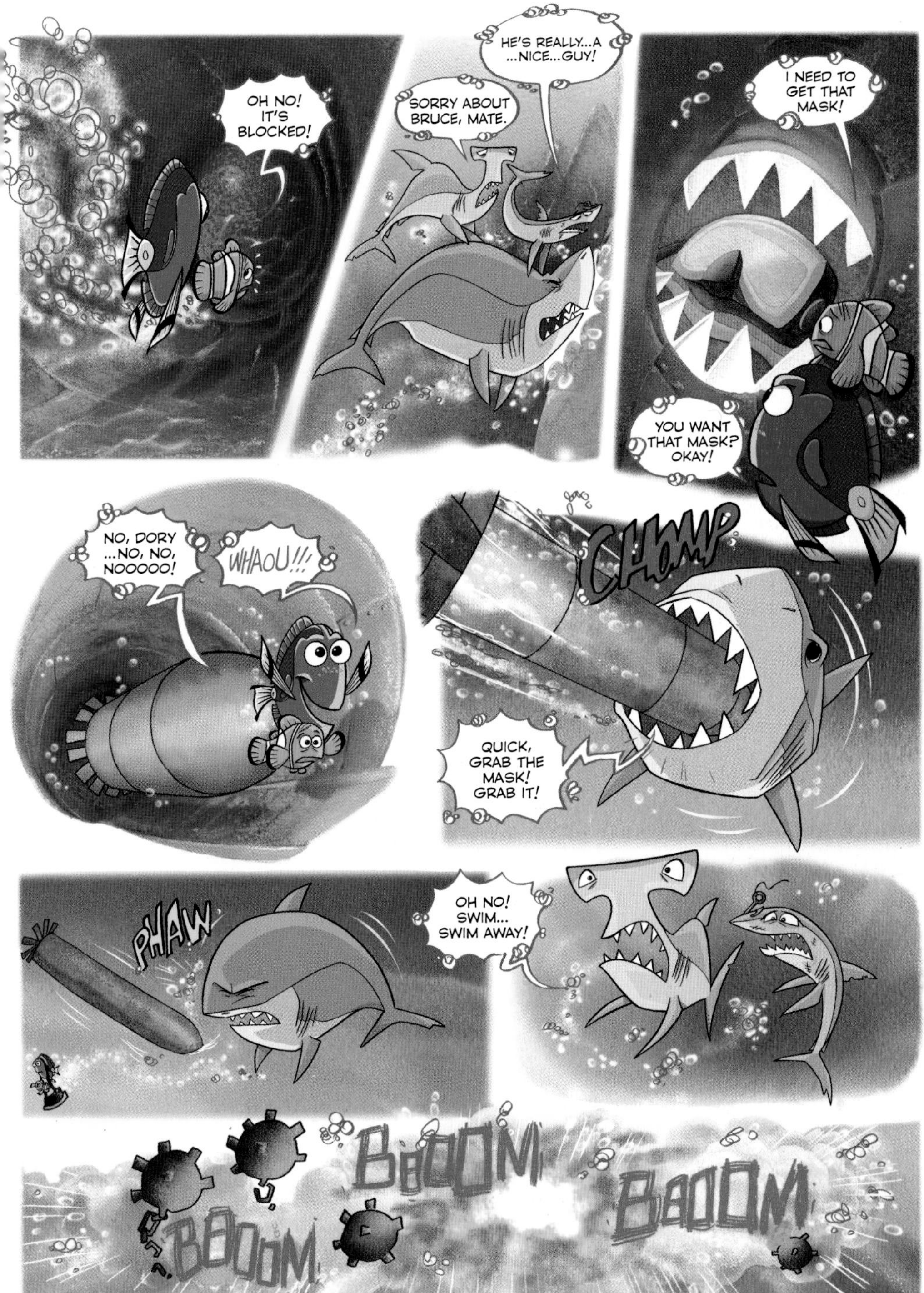
OH NO! IT'S BLOCKED!
HE'S REALLY...A ...NICE...GUY!
SORRY ABOUT BRUCE, MATE.
I NEED TO GET THAT MASK!
YOU WANT THAT MASK? OKAY!
NO, DORY ...NO, NO, NOOOOO!
WHAOU!!!
CHOMP
QUICK, GRAB THE MASK! GRAB IT!
PHAW
OH NO! SWIM... SWIM AWAY!
BOOOM
BOOOM
BOOOM

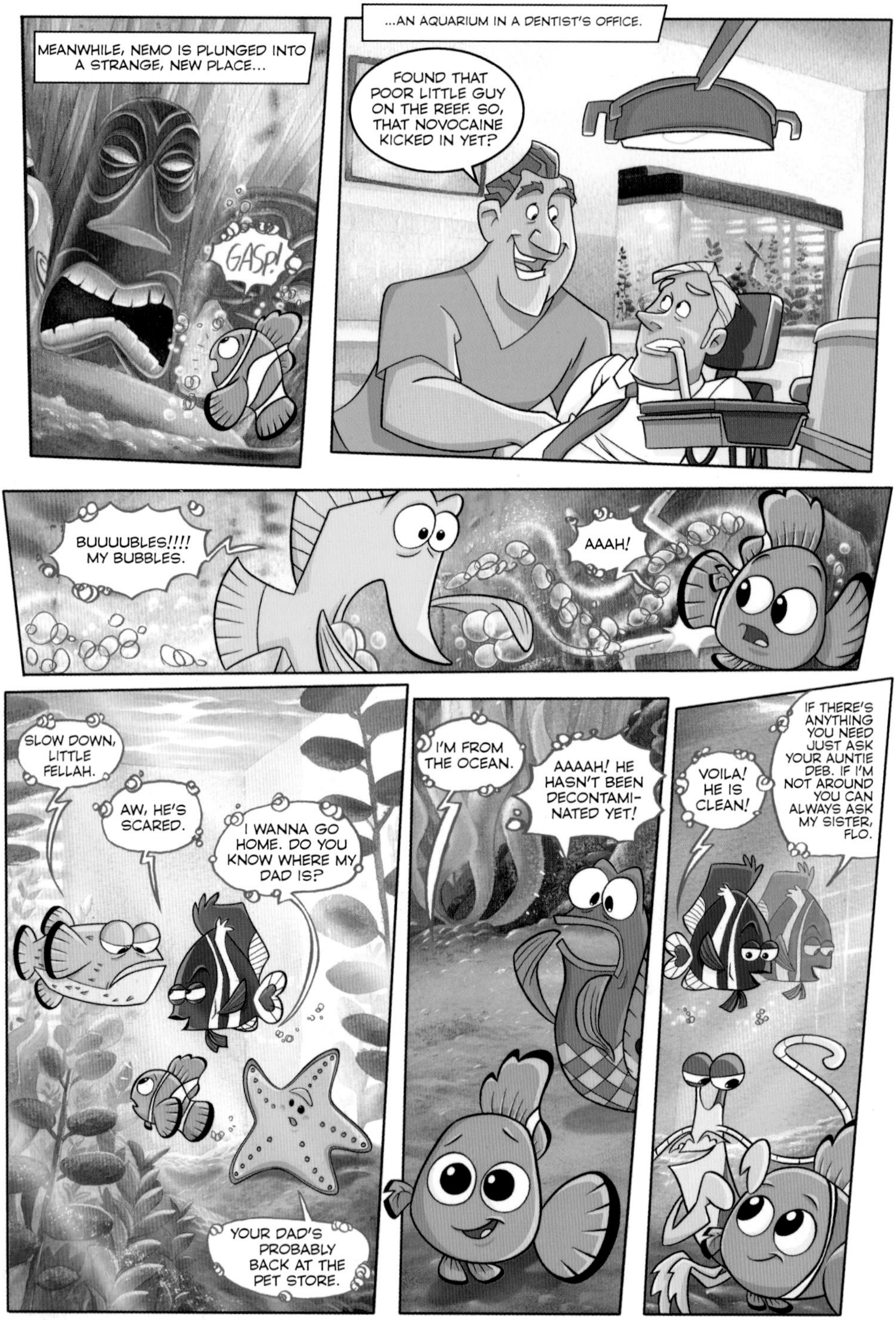
MEANWHILE, NEMO IS PLUNGED INTO A STRANGE, NEW PLACE...
GASP!
...AN AQUARIUM IN A DENTIST'S OFFICE.
FOUND THAT POOR LITTLE GUY ON THE REEF. SO, THAT NOVOCAINE KICKED IN YET?
BUUUUBLES!!!! MY BUBBLES.
AAAH!
SLOW DOWN, LITTLE FELLAH.
AW, HE'S SCARED.
I WANNA GO HOME. DO YOU KNOW WHERE MY DAD IS?
YOUR DAD'S PROBABLY BACK AT THE PET STORE.
I'M FROM THE OCEAN.
AAAAH! HE HASN'T BEEN DECONTAMI-NATED YET!
VOILA! HE IS CLEAN!
IF THERE'S ANYTHING YOU NEED JUST ASK YOUR AUNTIE DEB. IF I'M NOT AROUND YOU CAN ALWAYS ASK MY SISTER, FLO.

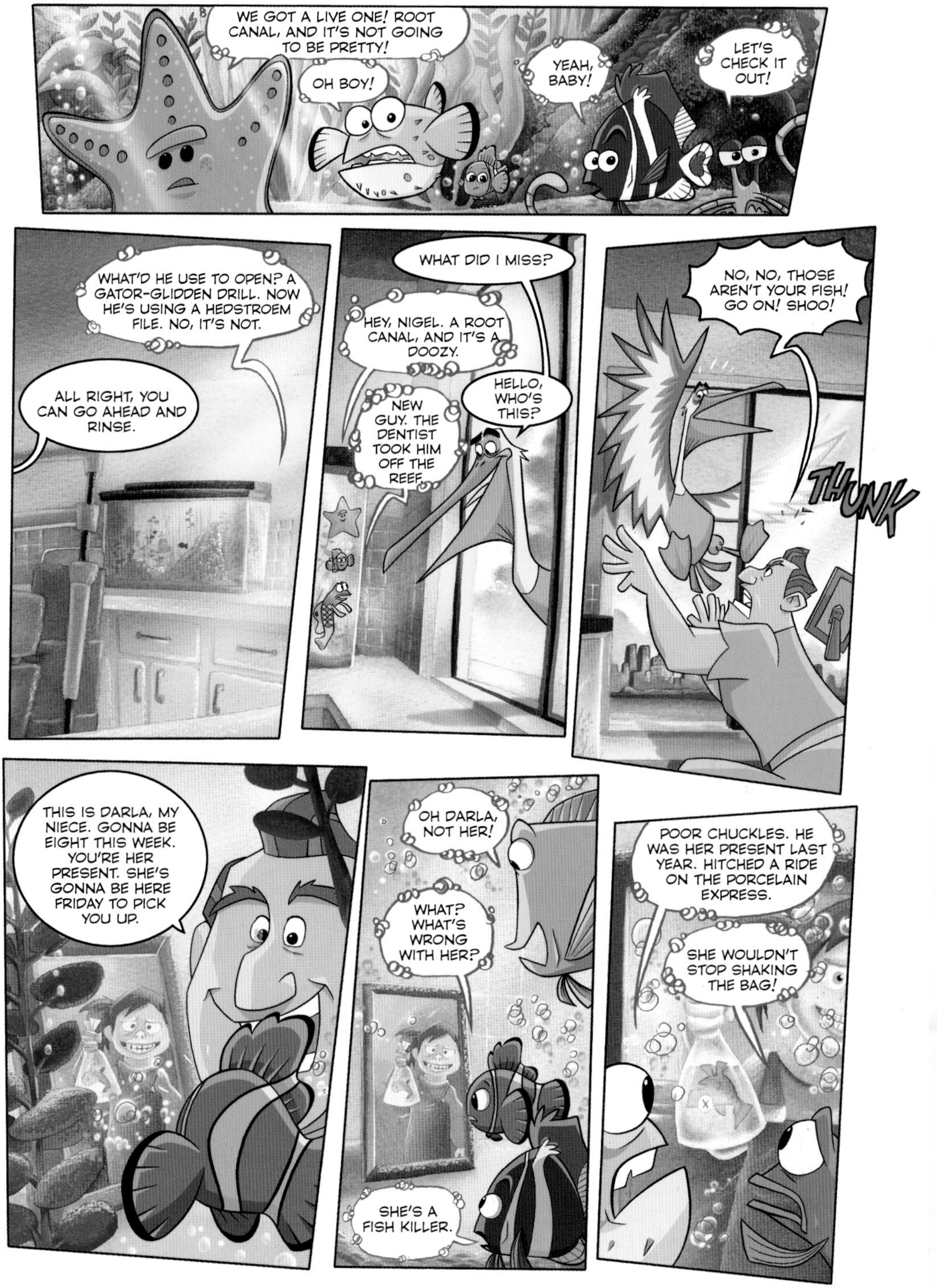
WE GOT A LIVE ONE! ROOT CANAL, AND IT'S NOT GOING TO BE PRETTY!
OH BOY!
YEAH, BABY!
LET'S CHECK IT OUT!
WHAT'D HE USE TO OPEN? A GATOR-GLIDDEN DRILL. NOW HE'S USING A HEDSTROEM FILE. NO, IT'S NOT.
ALL RIGHT, YOU CAN GO AHEAD AND RINSE.
WHAT DID I MISS?
HEY, NIGEL. A ROOT CANAL, AND IT'S A DOOZY.
HELLO, WHO'S THIS?
NEW GUY. THE DENTIST TOOK HIM OFF THE REEF.
NO, NO, THOSE AREN'T YOUR FISH! GO ON! SHOO!
THUNK
THIS IS DARLA, MY NIECE. GONNA BE EIGHT THIS WEEK. YOU'RE HER PRESENT. SHE'S GONNA BE HERE FRIDAY TO PICK YOU UP.
OH DARLA, NOT HER!
WHAT? WHAT'S WRONG WITH HER?
SHE'S A FISH KILLER.
POOR CHUCKLES. HE WAS HER PRESENT LAST YEAR. HITCHED A RIDE ON THE PORCELAIN EXPRESS.
SHE WOULDN'T STOP SHAKING THE BAG!

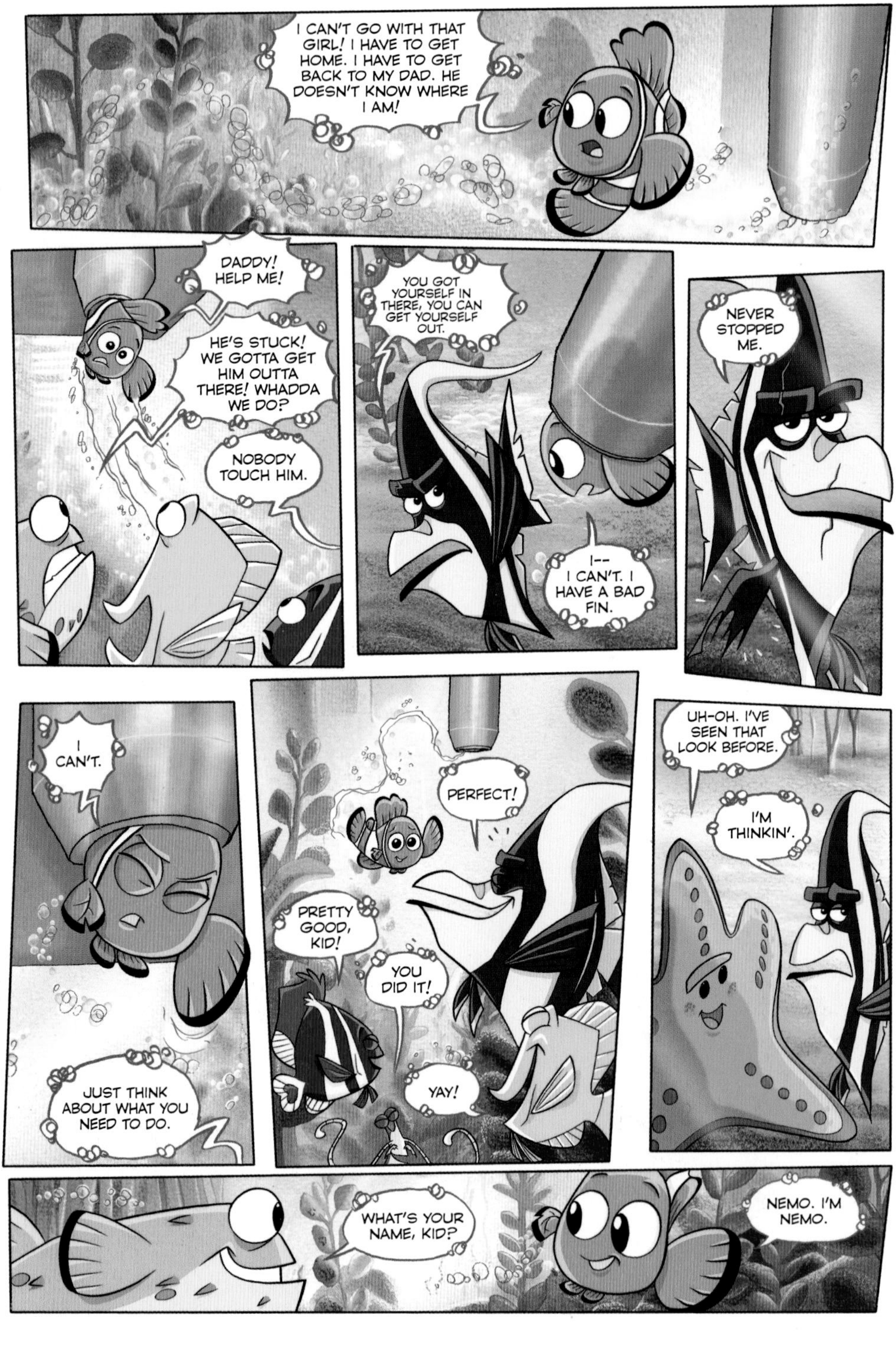
I CAN'T GO WITH THAT GIRL! I HAVE TO GET HOME. I HAVE TO GET BACK TO MY DAD. HE DOESN'T KNOW WHERE I AM!
DADDY! HELP ME!
HE'S STUCK! WE GOTTA GET HIM OUTTA THERE! WHADDA WE DO?
NOBODY TOUCH HIM.
YOU GOT YOURSELF IN THERE, YOU CAN GET YOURSELF OUT.
I-- I CAN'T. I HAVE A BAD FIN.
NEVER STOPPED ME.
I CAN'T.
JUST THINK ABOUT WHAT YOU NEED TO DO.
PERFECT!
PRETTY GOOD, KID!
YOU DID IT!
YAY!
UH-OH. I'VE SEEN THAT LOOK BEFORE.
I'M THINKIN'.
WHAT'S YOUR NAME, KID?
NEMO. I'M NEMO.

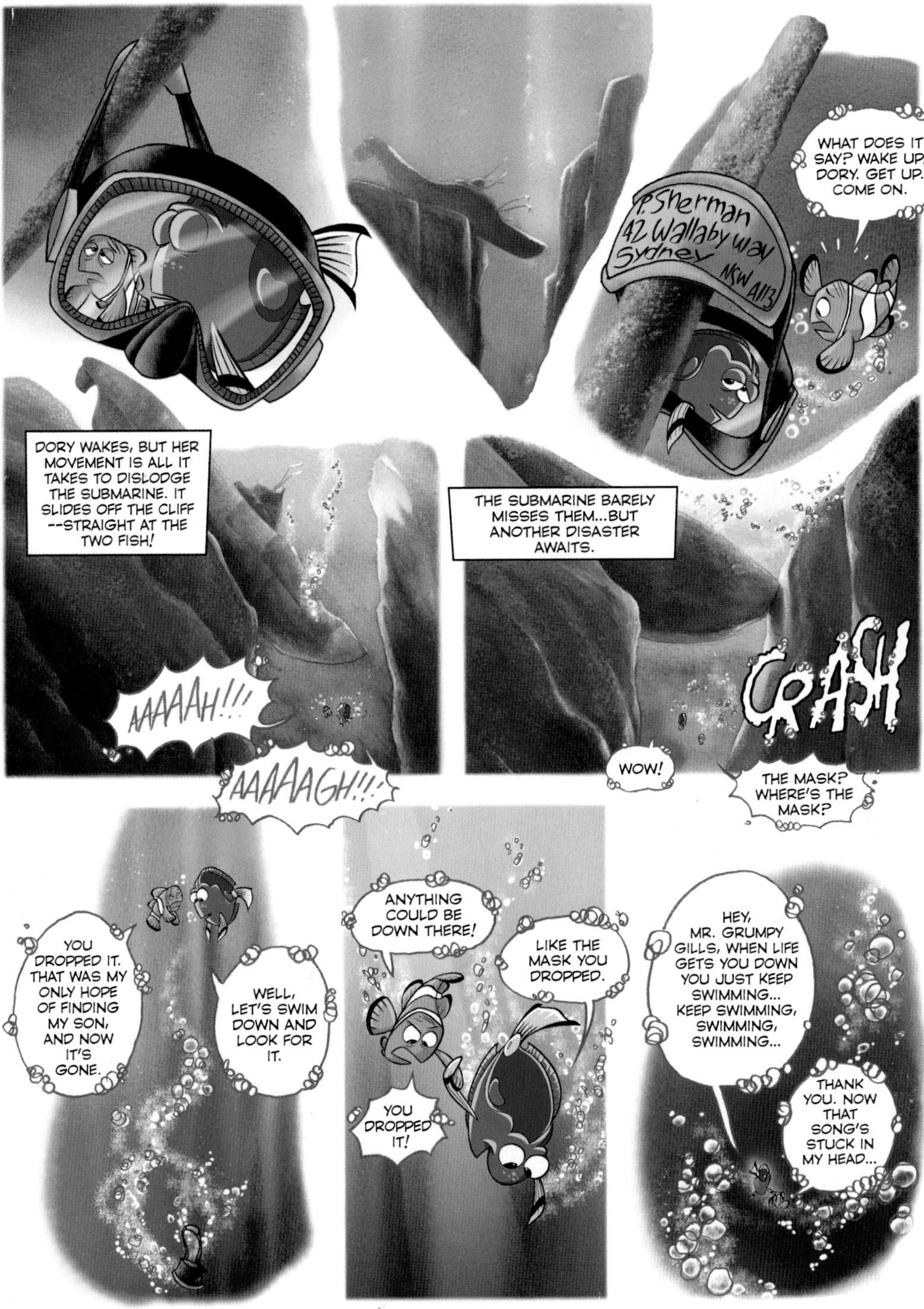

P. Sherman
42 Wallaby way
Sydney NSW A113
WHAT DOES IT SAY? WAKE UP, DORY. GET UP. COME ON.
DORY WAKES, BUT HER MOVEMENT IS ALL IT TAKES TO DISLODGE THE SUBMARINE. IT SLIDES OFF THE CLIFF --STRAIGHT AT THE TWO FISH!
AAAAAH!!!
AAAAAGH!!!
THE SUBMARINE BARELY MISSES THEM...BUT ANOTHER DISASTER AWAITS.
CRASH
WOW!
THE MASK? WHERE'S THE MASK?
YOU DROPPED IT. THAT WAS MY ONLY HOPE OF FINDING MY SON, AND NOW IT'S GONE.
WELL, LET'S SWIM DOWN AND LOOK FOR IT.
ANYTHING COULD BE DOWN THERE!
LIKE THE MASK YOU DROPPED.
YOU DROPPED IT!
HEY, MR. GRUMPY GILLS, WHEN LIFE GETS YOU DOWN YOU JUST KEEP SWIMMING... KEEP SWIMMING, SWIMMING, SWIMMING...
THANK YOU. NOW THAT SONG'S STUCK IN MY HEAD...

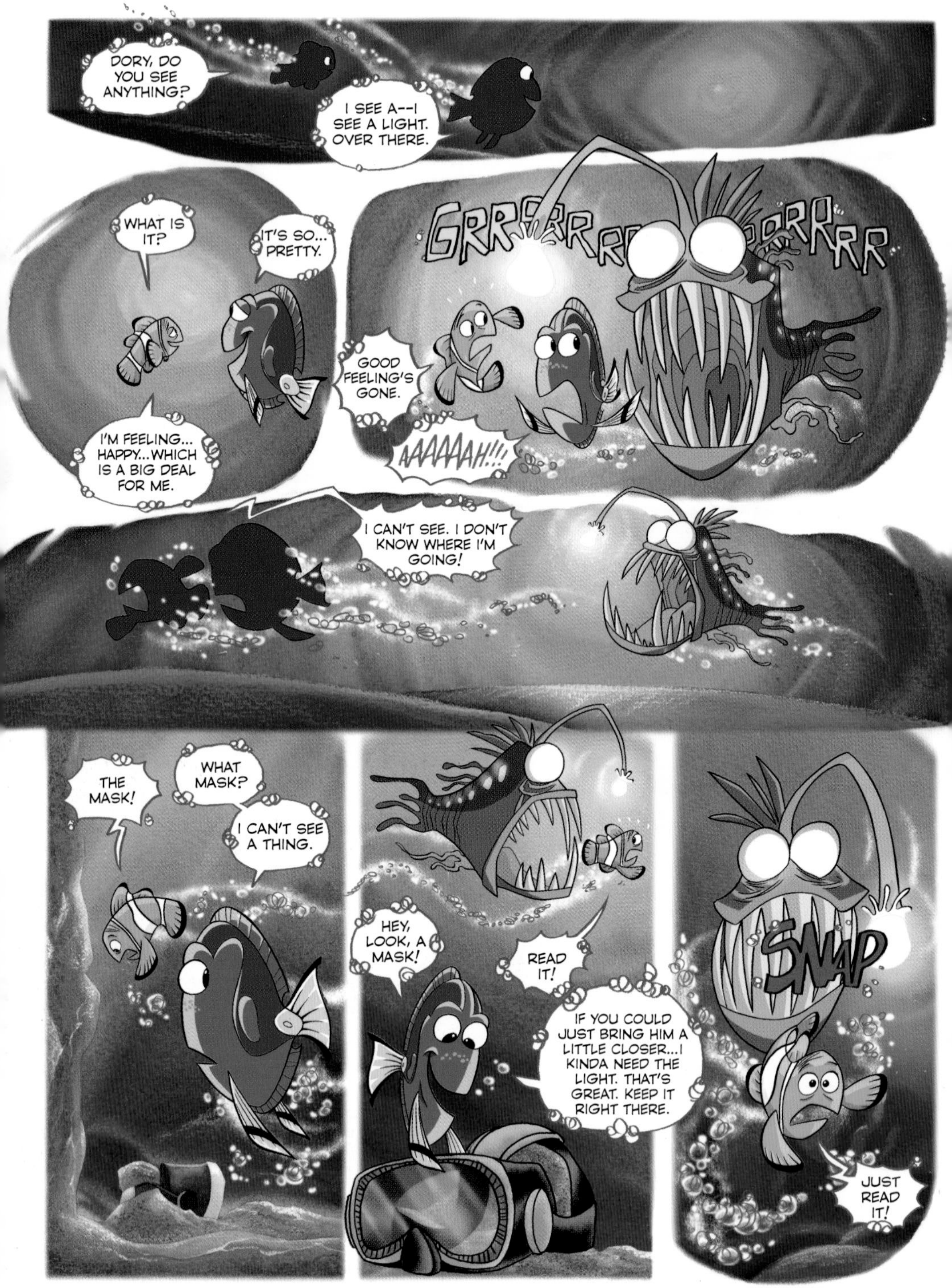
DORY, DO YOU SEE ANYTHING?
I SEE A--I SEE A LIGHT. OVER THERE.
WHAT IS IT?
IT'S SO... PRETTY.
I'M FEELING... HAPPY...WHICH IS A BIG DEAL FOR ME.
GRRRRRRRRRRRRRRR
GOOD FEELING'S GONE.
AAAAAAH!!!
I CAN'T SEE. I DON'T KNOW WHERE I'M GOING!
THE MASK!
WHAT MASK?
I CAN'T SEE A THING.
HEY, LOOK, A MASK!
READ IT!
IF YOU COULD JUST BRING HIM A LITTLE CLOSER...I KINDA NEED THE LIGHT. THAT'S GREAT. KEEP IT RIGHT THERE.
SNAP
JUST READ IT!

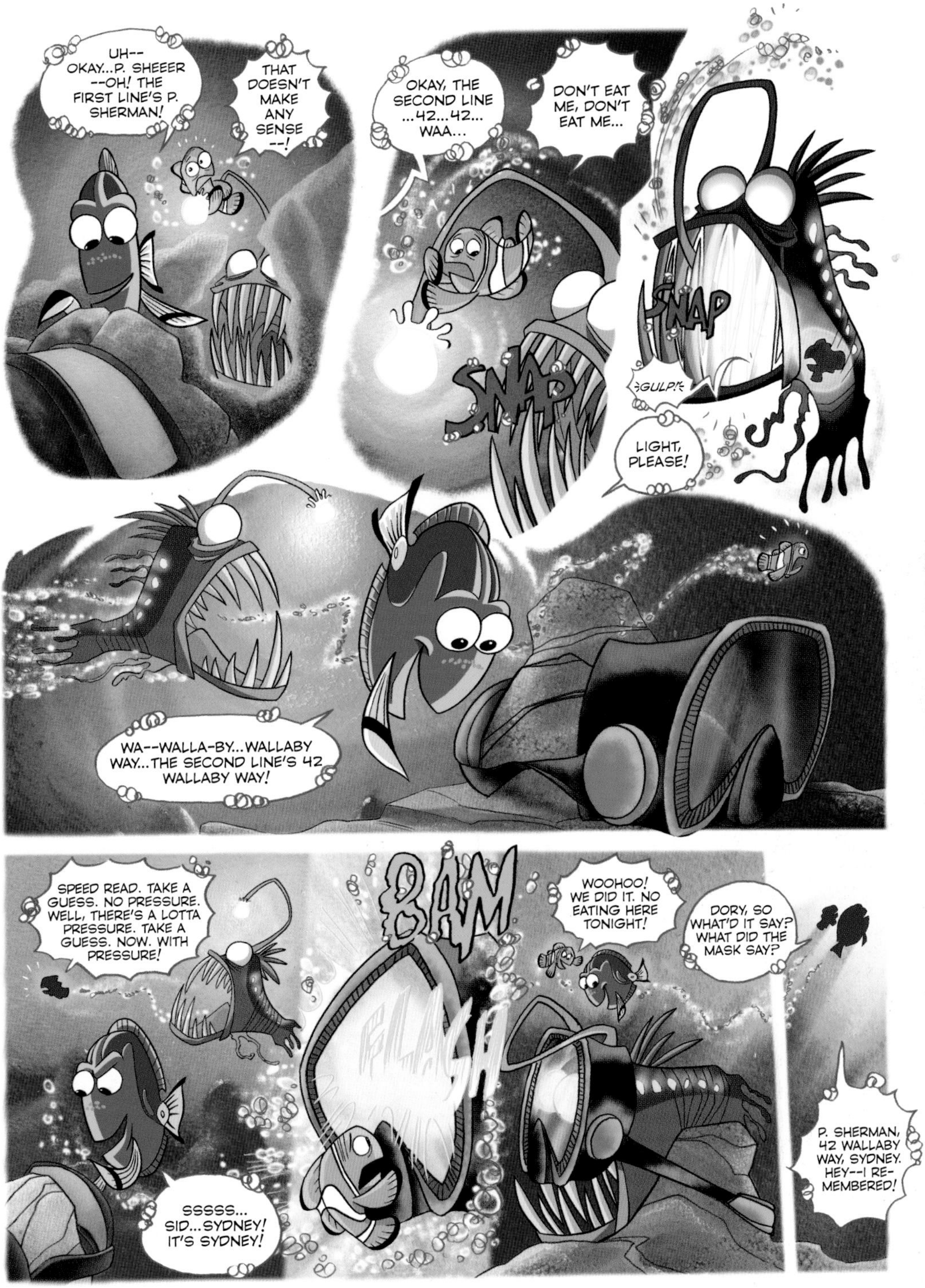
UH-- OKAY...P. SHEEER --OH! THE FIRST LINE'S P. SHERMAN!
THAT DOESN'T MAKE ANY SENSE --!
OKAY, THE SECOND LINE ...42...42... WAA...
DON'T EAT ME, DON'T EAT ME...
SNAP
SNAP
GULP!
LIGHT, PLEASE!
WA--WALLA-BY...WALLABY WAY...THE SECOND LINE'S 42 WALLABY WAY!
SPEED READ. TAKE A GUESS. NO PRESSURE. WELL, THERE'S A LOTTA PRESSURE. TAKE A GUESS. NOW. WITH PRESSURE!
SSSSS... SID...SYDNEY! IT'S SYDNEY!
BAM
FLASH
WOOHOO! WE DID IT. NO EATING HERE TONIGHT!
DORY, SO WHAT'D IT SAY? WHAT DID THE MASK SAY?
P. SHERMAN, 42 WALLABY WAY, SYDNEY. HEY--I RE-MEMBERED!

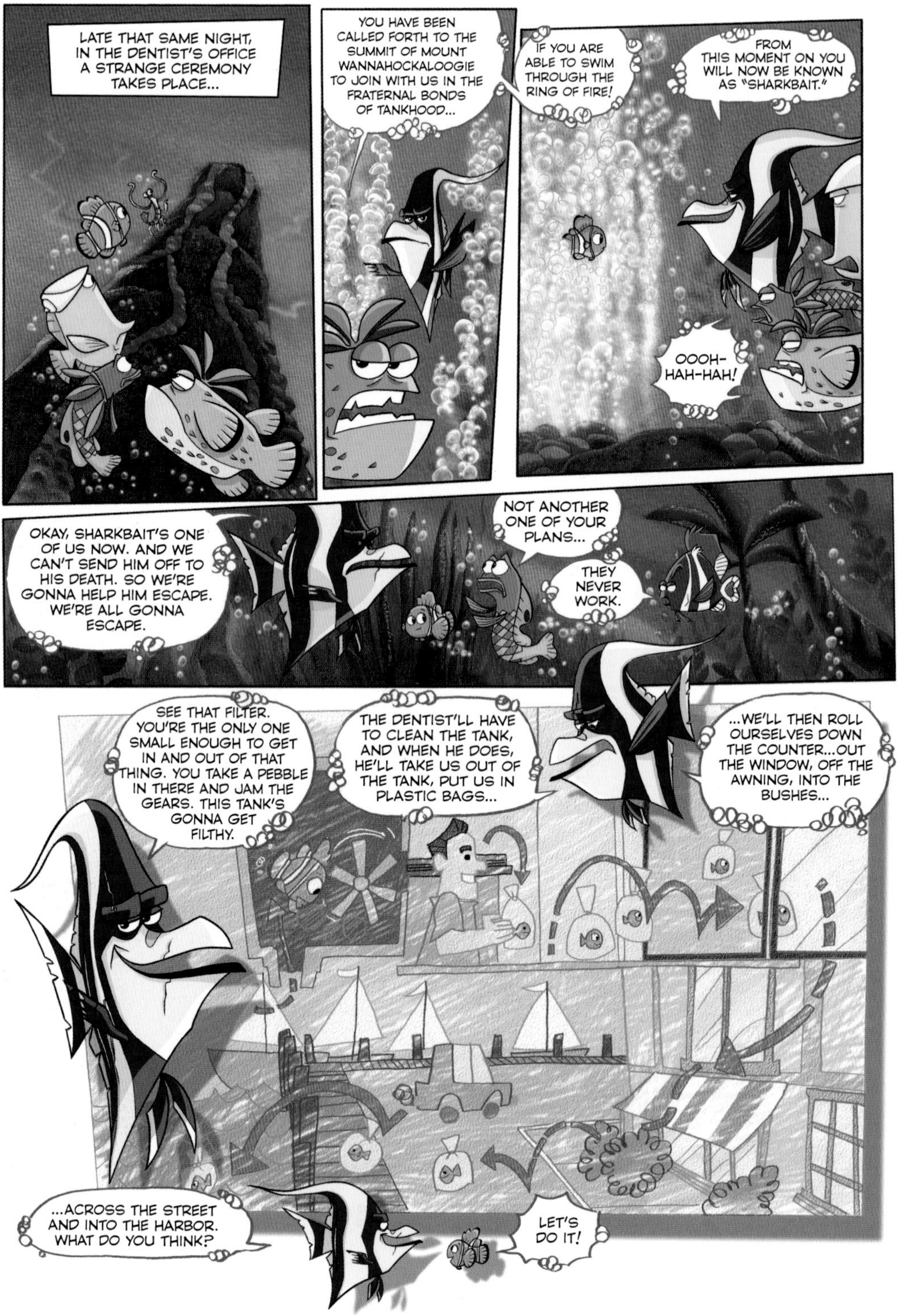
LATE THAT SAME NIGHT, IN THE DENTIST'S OFFICE A STRANGE CEREMONY TAKES PLACE...
YOU HAVE BEEN CALLED FORTH TO THE SUMMIT OF MOUNT WANNAHOCKALOOGIE TO JOIN WITH US IN THE FRATERNAL BONDS OF TANKHOOD...
IF YOU ARE ABLE TO SWIM THROUGH THE RING OF FIRE!
FROM THIS MOMENT ON YOU WILL NOW BE KNOWN AS "SHARKBAIT."
OOOH-HAH-HAH!
OKAY, SHARKBAIT'S ONE OF US NOW. AND WE CAN'T SEND HIM OFF TO HIS DEATH. SO WE'RE GONNA HELP HIM ESCAPE. WE'RE ALL GONNA ESCAPE.
NOT ANOTHER ONE OF YOUR PLANS...
THEY NEVER WORK.
SEE THAT FILTER. YOU'RE THE ONLY ONE SMALL ENOUGH TO GET IN AND OUT OF THAT THING. YOU TAKE A PEBBLE IN THERE AND JAM THE GEARS. THIS TANK'S GONNA GET FILTHY.
THE DENTIST'LL HAVE TO CLEAN THE TANK, AND WHEN HE DOES, HE'LL TAKE US OUT OF THE TANK, PUT US IN PLASTIC BAGS...
...WE'LL THEN ROLL OURSELVES DOWN THE COUNTER...OUT THE WINDOW, OFF THE AWNING, INTO THE BUSHES...
...ACROSS THE STREET AND INTO THE HARBOR. WHAT DO YOU THINK?
LET'S DO IT!

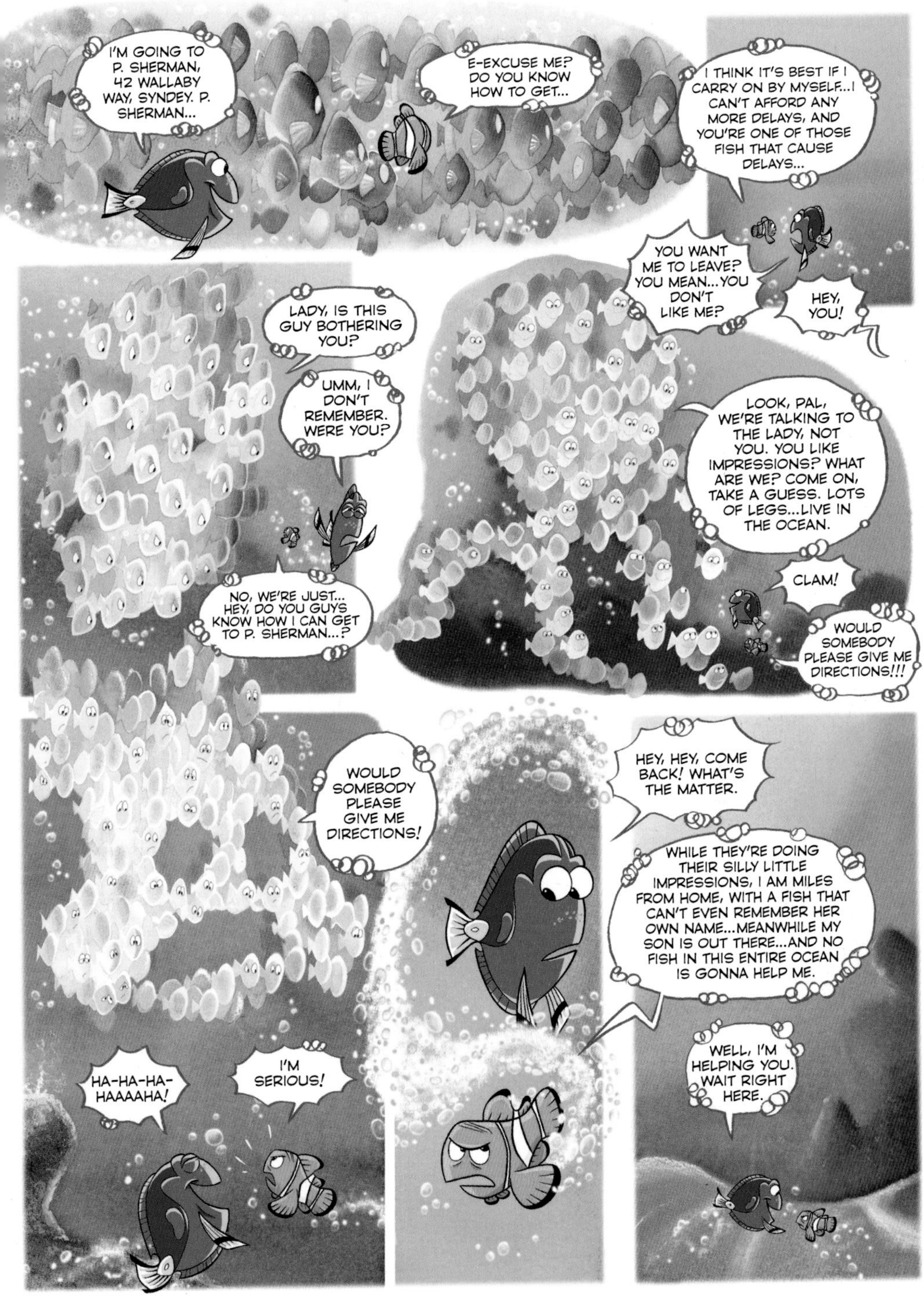
I'M GOING TO P. SHERMAN, 42 WALLABY WAY, SYNDEY. P. SHERMAN...
E-EXCUSE ME? DO YOU KNOW HOW TO GET...
I THINK IT'S BEST IF I CARRY ON BY MYSELF...I CAN'T AFFORD ANY MORE DELAYS, AND YOU'RE ONE OF THOSE FISH THAT CAUSE DELAYS...
YOU WANT ME TO LEAVE? YOU MEAN...YOU DON'T LIKE ME?
HEY, YOU!
LADY, IS THIS GUY BOTHERING YOU?
UMM, I DON'T REMEMBER. WERE YOU?
NO, WE'RE JUST... HEY, DO YOU GUYS KNOW HOW I CAN GET TO P. SHERMAN...?
LOOK, PAL, WE'RE TALKING TO THE LADY, NOT YOU. YOU LIKE IMPRESSIONS? WHAT ARE WE? COME ON, TAKE A GUESS. LOTS OF LEGS...LIVE IN THE OCEAN.
CLAM!
WOULD SOMEBODY PLEASE GIVE ME DIRECTIONS!!!
WOULD SOMEBODY PLEASE GIVE ME DIRECTIONS!
HA-HA-HA-HAAAAHA!
I'M SERIOUS!
HEY, HEY, COME BACK! WHAT'S THE MATTER.
WHILE THEY'RE DOING THEIR SILLY LITTLE IMPRESSIONS, I AM MILES FROM HOME, WITH A FISH THAT CAN'T EVEN REMEMBER HER OWN NAME...MEANWHILE MY SON IS OUT THERE...AND NO FISH IN THIS ENTIRE OCEAN IS GONNA HELP ME.
WELL, I'M HELPING YOU. WAIT RIGHT HERE.

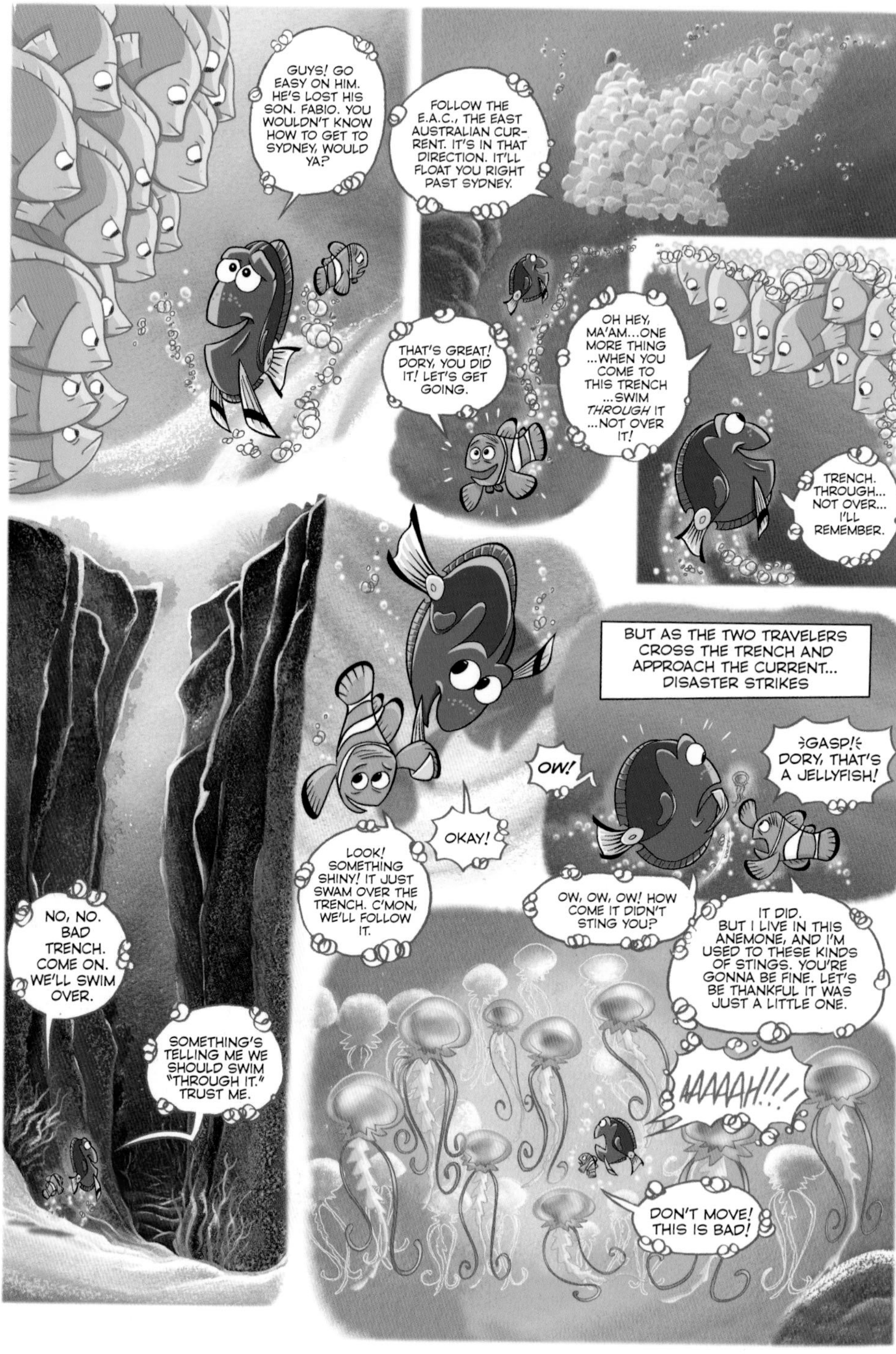
GUYS! GO EASY ON HIM. HE'S LOST HIS SON. FABIO. YOU WOULDN'T KNOW HOW TO GET TO SYDNEY, WOULD YA?
FOLLOW THE E.A.C., THE EAST AUSTRALIAN CURRENT. IT'S IN THAT DIRECTION. IT'LL FLOAT YOU RIGHT PAST SYDNEY.
THAT'S GREAT! DORY, YOU DID IT! LET'S GET GOING.
OH HEY, MA'AM...ONE MORE THING ...WHEN YOU COME TO THIS TRENCH ...SWIM *THROUGH* IT ...NOT OVER IT!
TRENCH. THROUGH... NOT OVER... I'LL REMEMBER.
NO, NO. BAD TRENCH. COME ON. WE'LL SWIM OVER.
SOMETHING'S TELLING ME WE SHOULD SWIM "THROUGH IT." TRUST ME.
LOOK! SOMETHING SHINY! IT JUST SWAM OVER THE TRENCH. C'MON, WE'LL FOLLOW IT.
OKAY!
BUT AS THE TWO TRAVELERS CROSS THE TRENCH AND APPROACH THE CURRENT... DISASTER STRIKES
OW!
GASP! DORY, THAT'S A JELLYFISH!
OW, OW, OW! HOW COME IT DIDN'T STING YOU?
IT DID. BUT I LIVE IN THIS ANEMONE, AND I'M USED TO THESE KINDS OF STINGS. YOU'RE GONNA BE FINE. LET'S BE THANKFUL IT WAS JUST A LITTLE ONE.
AAAAAH!!!
DON'T MOVE! THIS IS BAD!

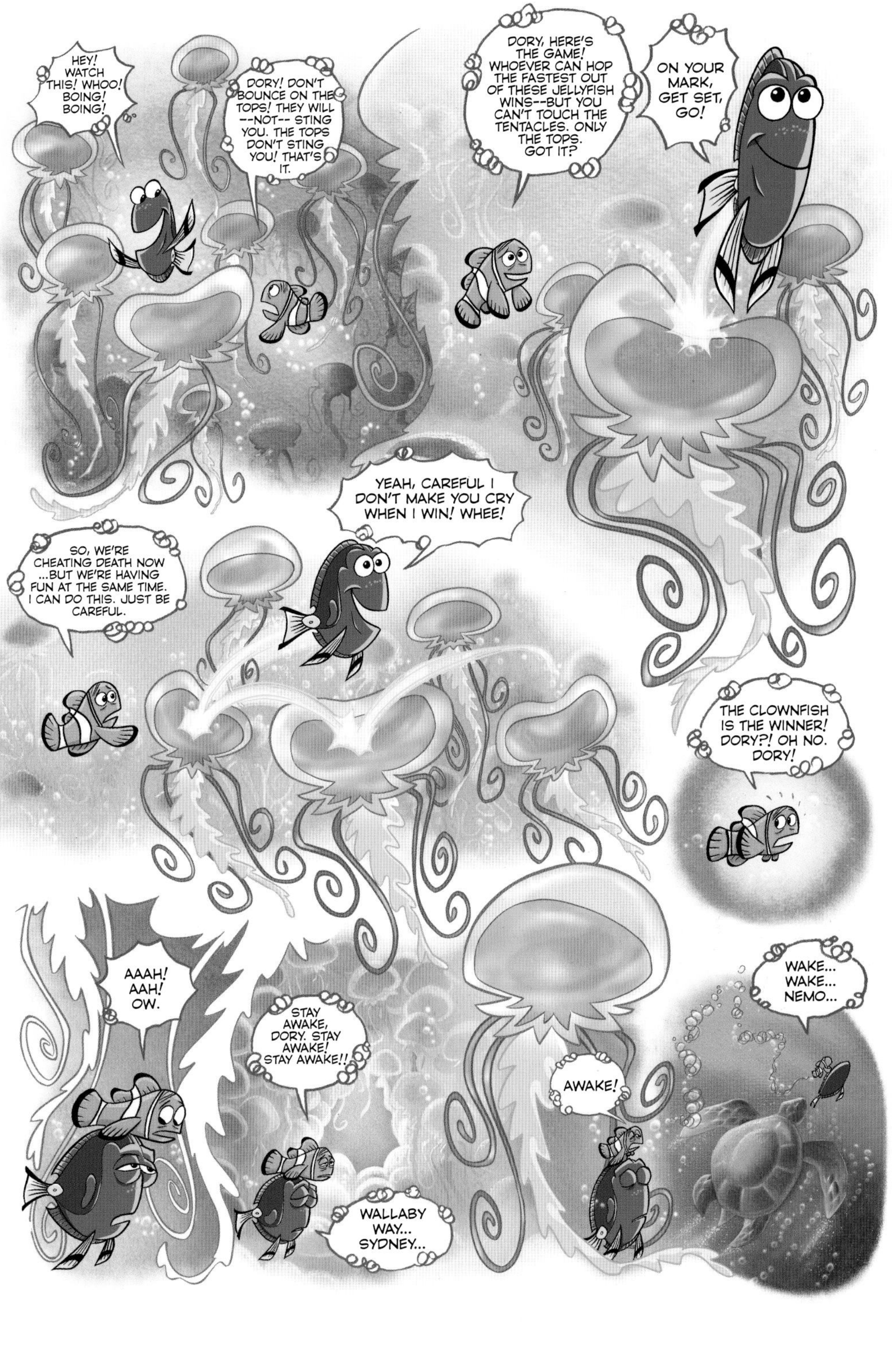
HEY! WATCH THIS! WHOO! BOING! BOING!
DORY! DON'T BOUNCE ON THE TOPS! THEY WILL --NOT-- STING YOU. THE TOPS DON'T STING YOU! THAT'S IT.
DORY, HERE'S THE GAME! WHOEVER CAN HOP THE FASTEST OUT OF THESE JELLYFISH WINS--BUT YOU CAN'T TOUCH THE TENTACLES. ONLY THE TOPS. GOT IT?
ON YOUR MARK, GET SET, GO!
YEAH, CAREFUL I DON'T MAKE YOU CRY WHEN I WIN! WHEE!
SO, WE'RE CHEATING DEATH NOW ...BUT WE'RE HAVING FUN AT THE SAME TIME. I CAN DO THIS. JUST BE CAREFUL.
THE CLOWNFISH IS THE WINNER! DORY?! OH NO. DORY!
AAAH! AAH! OW.
STAY AWAKE, DORY. STAY AWAKE! STAY AWAKE!!
WALLABY WAY... SYDNEY...
AWAKE!
WAKE... WAKE... NEMO...

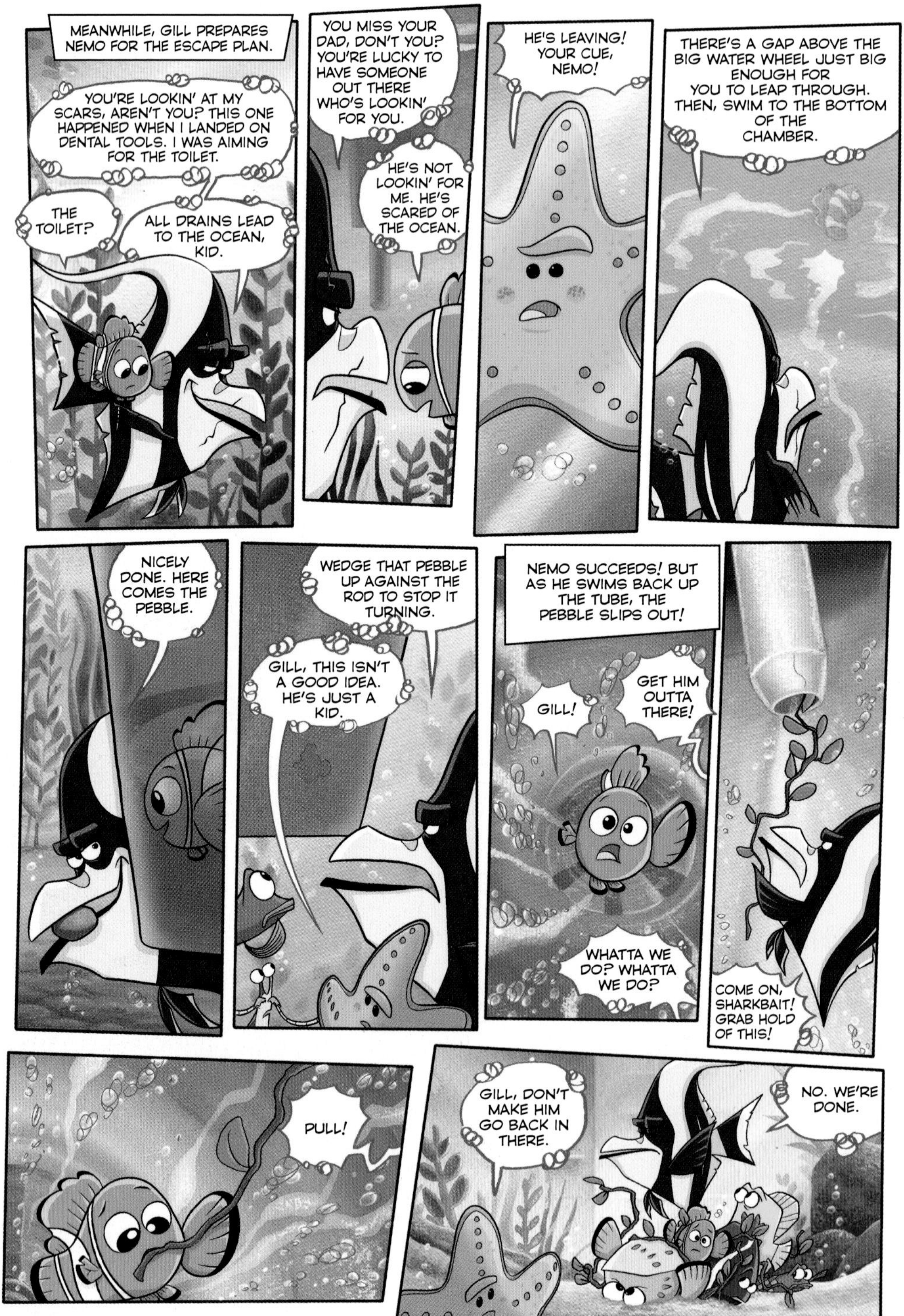
MEANWHILE, GILL PREPARES NEMO FOR THE ESCAPE PLAN.
YOU'RE LOOKIN' AT MY SCARS, AREN'T YOU? THIS ONE HAPPENED WHEN I LANDED ON DENTAL TOOLS. I WAS AIMING FOR THE TOILET.
THE TOILET?
ALL DRAINS LEAD TO THE OCEAN, KID.
YOU MISS YOUR DAD, DON'T YOU? YOU'RE LUCKY TO HAVE SOMEONE OUT THERE WHO'S LOOKIN' FOR YOU.
HE'S NOT LOOKIN' FOR ME. HE'S SCARED OF THE OCEAN.
HE'S LEAVING! YOUR CUE, NEMO!
THERE'S A GAP ABOVE THE BIG WATER WHEEL JUST BIG ENOUGH FOR YOU TO LEAP THROUGH. THEN, SWIM TO THE BOTTOM OF THE CHAMBER.
NICELY DONE. HERE COMES THE PEBBLE.
WEDGE THAT PEBBLE UP AGAINST THE ROD TO STOP IT TURNING.
GILL, THIS ISN'T A GOOD IDEA. HE'S JUST A KID.
NEMO SUCCEEDS! BUT AS HE SWIMS BACK UP THE TUBE, THE PEBBLE SLIPS OUT!
GILL!
GET HIM OUTTA THERE!
WHATTA WE DO? WHATTA WE DO?
COME ON, SHARKBAIT! GRAB HOLD OF THIS!
PULL!
GILL, DON'T MAKE HIM GO BACK IN THERE.
NO. WE'RE DONE.

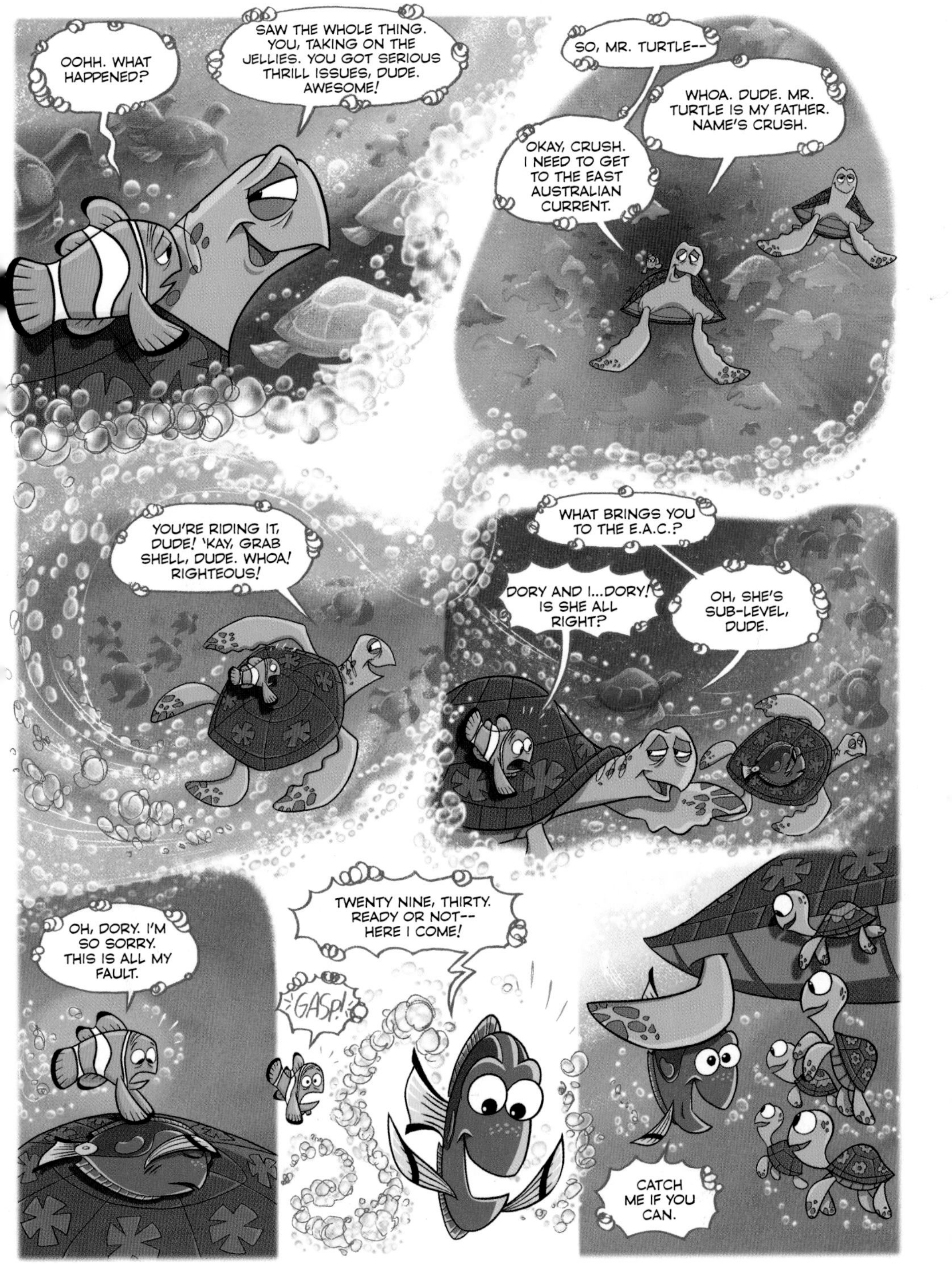
OOHH. WHAT HAPPENED?
SAW THE WHOLE THING. YOU, TAKING ON THE JELLIES. YOU GOT SERIOUS THRILL ISSUES, DUDE. AWESOME!
SO, MR. TURTLE--
WHOA. DUDE. MR. TURTLE IS MY FATHER. NAME'S CRUSH.
OKAY, CRUSH. I NEED TO GET TO THE EAST AUSTRALIAN CURRENT.
YOU'RE RIDING IT, DUDE! 'KAY, GRAB SHELL, DUDE. WHOA! RIGHTEOUS!
WHAT BRINGS YOU TO THE E.A.C.?
DORY AND I...DORY! IS SHE ALL RIGHT?
OH, SHE'S SUB-LEVEL, DUDE.
OH, DORY. I'M SO SORRY. THIS IS ALL MY FAULT.
GASP!
TWENTY NINE, THIRTY. READY OR NOT-- HERE I COME!
CATCH ME IF YOU CAN.

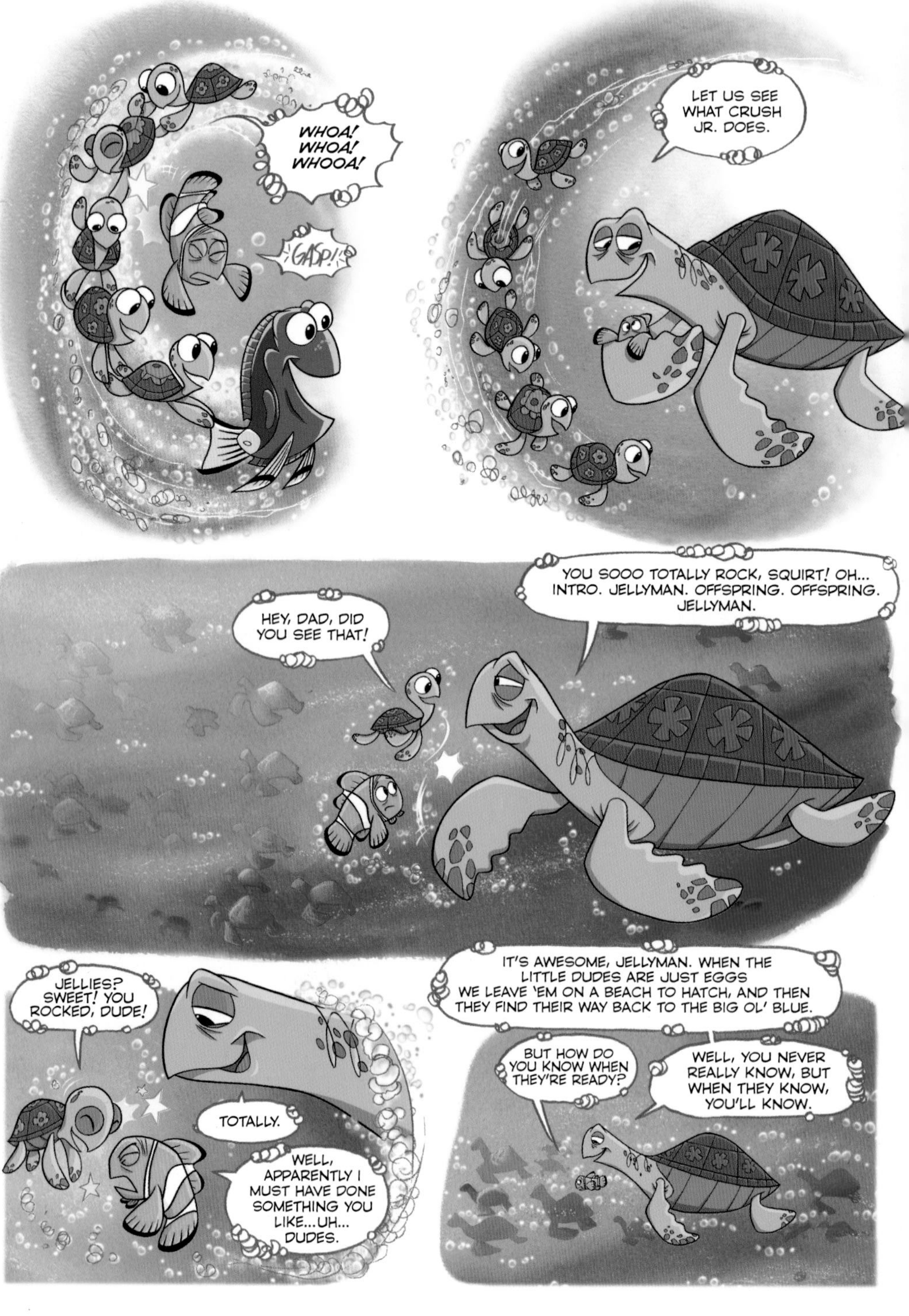
WHOA! WHOA! WHOOA!
GASP!
LET US SEE WHAT CRUSH JR. DOES.
HEY, DAD, DID YOU SEE THAT!
YOU SOOO TOTALLY ROCK, SQUIRT! OH... INTRO. JELLYMAN. OFFSPRING. OFFSPRING. JELLYMAN.
JELLIES? SWEET! YOU ROCKED, DUDE!
TOTALLY.
WELL, APPARENTLY I MUST HAVE DONE SOMETHING YOU LIKE...UH... DUDES.
IT'S AWESOME, JELLYMAN. WHEN THE LITTLE DUDES ARE JUST EGGS WE LEAVE 'EM ON A BEACH TO HATCH, AND THEN THEY FIND THEIR WAY BACK TO THE BIG OL' BLUE.
BUT HOW DO YOU KNOW WHEN THEY'RE READY?
WELL, YOU NEVER REALLY KNOW, BUT WHEN THEY KNOW, YOU'LL KNOW.

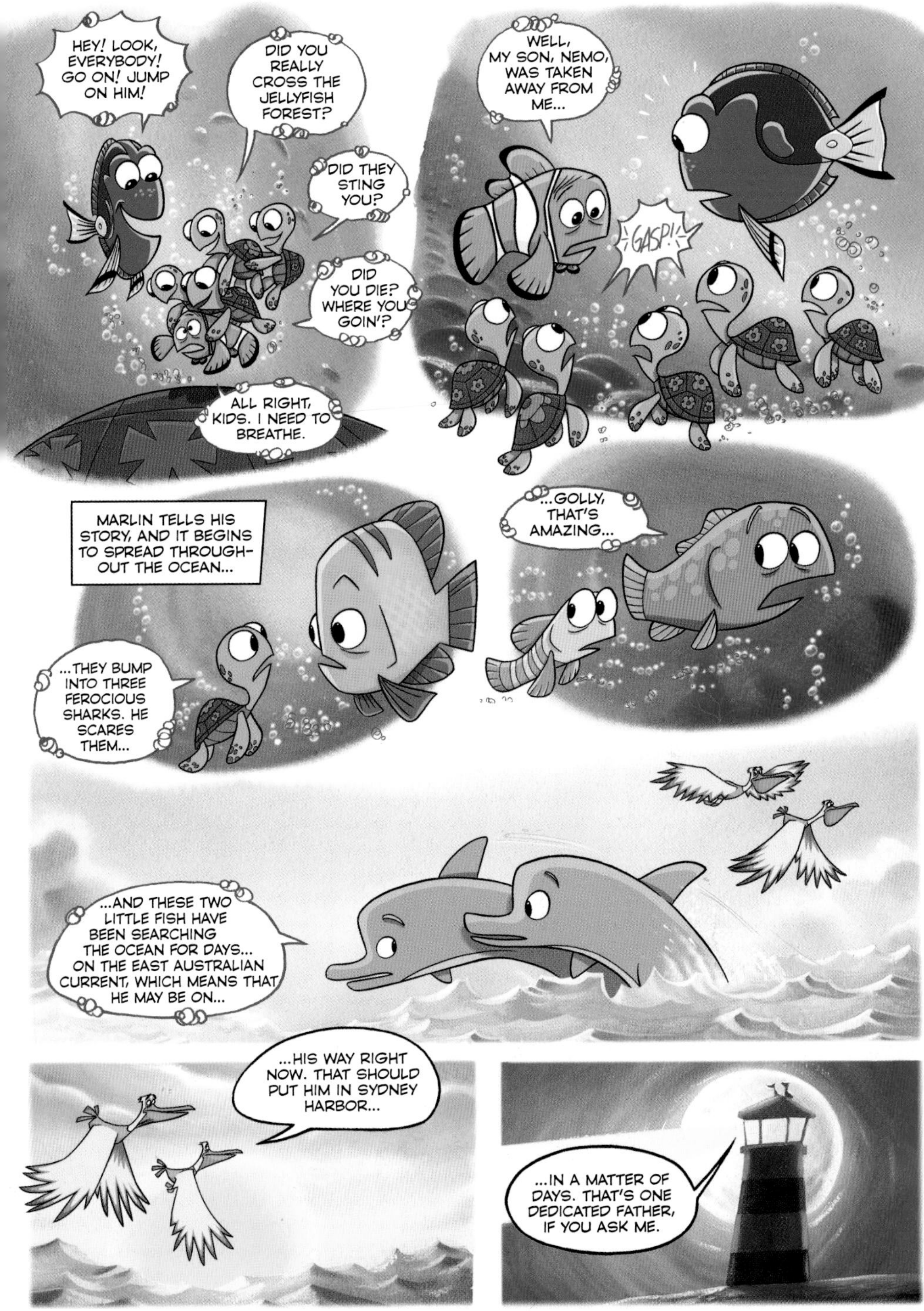
HEY! LOOK, EVERYBODY! GO ON! JUMP ON HIM!
DID YOU REALLY CROSS THE JELLYFISH FOREST?
DID THEY STING YOU?
DID YOU DIE? WHERE YOU GOIN'?
ALL RIGHT, KIDS. I NEED TO BREATHE.
WELL, MY SON, NEMO, WAS TAKEN AWAY FROM ME...
GASP!
MARLIN TELLS HIS STORY, AND IT BEGINS TO SPREAD THROUGH-OUT THE OCEAN...
...THEY BUMP INTO THREE FEROCIOUS SHARKS. HE SCARES THEM...
...GOLLY, THAT'S AMAZING...
...AND THESE TWO LITTLE FISH HAVE BEEN SEARCHING THE OCEAN FOR DAYS... ON THE EAST AUSTRALIAN CURRENT, WHICH MEANS THAT HE MAY BE ON...
...HIS WAY RIGHT NOW. THAT SHOULD PUT HIM IN SYDNEY HARBOR...
...IN A MATTER OF DAYS. THAT'S ONE DEDICATED FATHER, IF YOU ASK ME.

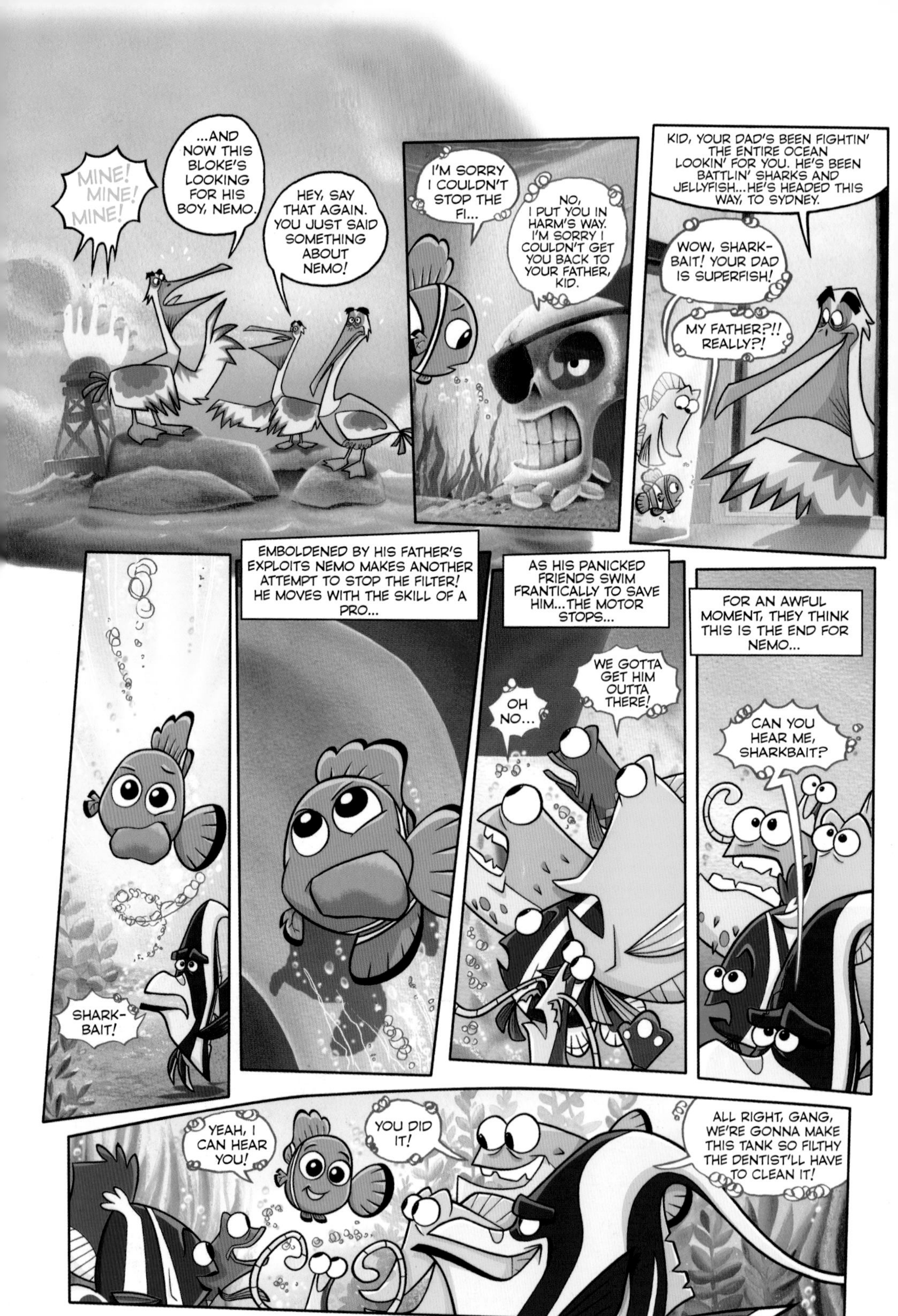
MINE! MINE! MINE!
...AND NOW THIS BLOKE'S LOOKING FOR HIS BOY, NEMO.
HEY, SAY THAT AGAIN. YOU JUST SAID SOMETHING ABOUT NEMO!
I'M SORRY I COULDN'T STOP THE FI...
NO, I PUT YOU IN HARM'S WAY. I'M SORRY I COULDN'T GET YOU BACK TO YOUR FATHER, KID.
KID, YOUR DAD'S BEEN FIGHTIN' THE ENTIRE OCEAN LOOKIN' FOR YOU. HE'S BEEN BATTLIN' SHARKS AND JELLYFISH...HE'S HEADED THIS WAY, TO SYDNEY.
WOW, SHARK-BAIT! YOUR DAD IS SUPERFISH!
MY FATHER?!! REALLY?!
SHARK-BAIT!
EMBOLDENED BY HIS FATHER'S EXPLOITS NEMO MAKES ANOTHER ATTEMPT TO STOP THE FILTER! HE MOVES WITH THE SKILL OF A PRO...
AS HIS PANICKED FRIENDS SWIM FRANTICALLY TO SAVE HIM...THE MOTOR STOPS...
OH NO...
WE GOTTA GET HIM OUTTA THERE!
FOR AN AWFUL MOMENT, THEY THINK THIS IS THE END FOR NEMO...
CAN YOU HEAR ME, SHARKBAIT?
YEAH, I CAN HEAR YOU!
YOU DID IT!
ALL RIGHT, GANG, WE'RE GONNA MAKE THIS TANK SO FILTHY THE DENTIST'LL HAVE TO CLEAN IT!

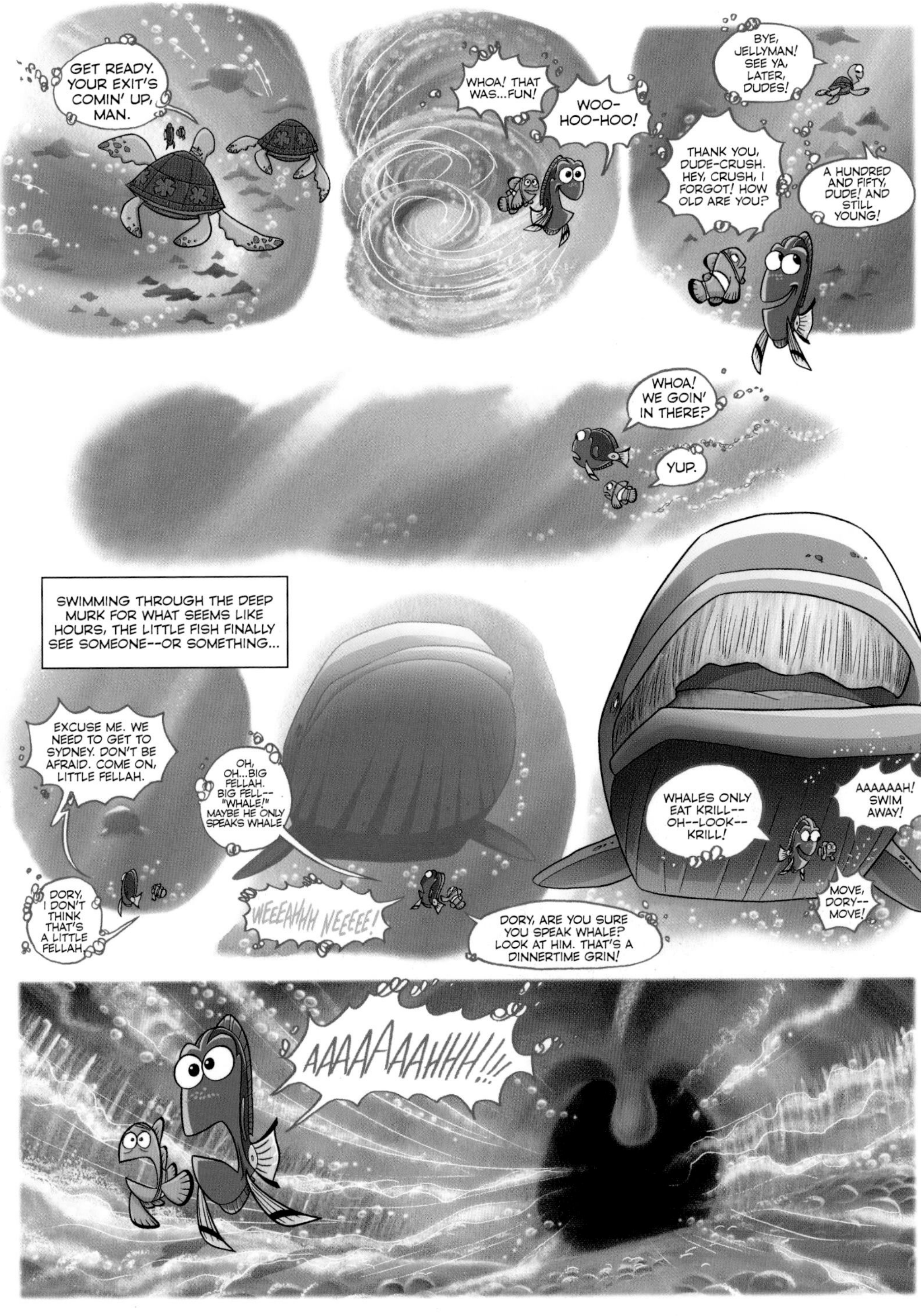
GET READY. YOUR EXIT'S COMIN' UP, MAN.
WHOA! THAT WAS...FUN!
WOO-HOO-HOO!
BYE, JELLYMAN! SEE YA, LATER, DUDES!
THANK YOU, DUDE-CRUSH. HEY, CRUSH, I FORGOT! HOW OLD ARE YOU?
A HUNDRED AND FIFTY, DUDE! AND STILL YOUNG!
WHOA! WE GOIN' IN THERE?
YUP.
SWIMMING THROUGH THE DEEP MURK FOR WHAT SEEMS LIKE HOURS, THE LITTLE FISH FINALLY SEE SOMEONE--OR SOMETHING...
EXCUSE ME. WE NEED TO GET TO SYDNEY. DON'T BE AFRAID. COME ON, LITTLE FELLAH.
DORY, I DON'T THINK THAT'S A LITTLE FELLAH.
OH, OH...BIG FELLAH. BIG FELL-- "WHALE!" MAYBE HE ONLY SPEAKS WHALE.
WEEEAHHH NEEEEE!
DORY, ARE YOU SURE YOU SPEAK WHALE? LOOK AT HIM. THAT'S A DINNERTIME GRIN!
WHALES ONLY EAT KRILL-- OH--LOOK-- KRILL!
AAAAAAH! SWIM AWAY!
MOVE, DORY-- MOVE!
AAAAAAAHHH!!!

HAVE YOU EVER SEEN SUCH BEAUTIFUL FILTH? AND IT'S ALL THANKS TO YOU, LAD.
ME? WOW!
WHAT A STATE! I BETTER CLEAN THE FISH TANK BEFORE DARLA GETS HERE TOMORROW.
HE'S GONNA CLEAN THE TANK! WE DID IT!
AND YOUR DAD'S PROBABLY WAITING FOR YOU IN THE HARBOR.
MEANWHILE, IN THE BELLY OF THE WHALE...
WILL YOU STOP IT?! WE'RE IN A WHALE! DON'T YOU GET IT?
WHEEE! A WHALE? WOW! YOU KNOW, I SPEAK WHALE!
...I HAVE TO GET OUT. I HAVE TO FIND MY SON. I HAVE TO TELL HIM HOW OLD SEA TURTLES ARE. I PROMISED HIM I'D NEVER LET ANYTHING HAPPEN TO HIM.
THAT'S A FUNNY THING TO PROMISE. YOU CAN'T NEVER LET ANYTHING HAPPEN TO HIM. THEN NOTHING WOULD EVER HAPPEN TO HIM. NOT MUCH FUN FOR LITTLE HARPO.
BOOOM BOOOM BOOOM
HMMM. HE SAID WE SHOULD GO TO THE BACK OF THE THROAT...
OF COURSE HE WANTS US TO GO THERE! THAT'S EATING US!
BOOOM BOOOM
HE SAYS IT'S TIME TO LET GO! EVERYTHING'S GONNA BE ALL RIGHT. JUST HAVE A LITTLE FAITH AND LET GO!
NEMO!
AAAAAH!

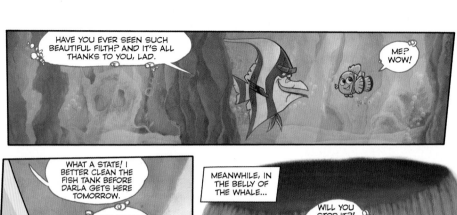

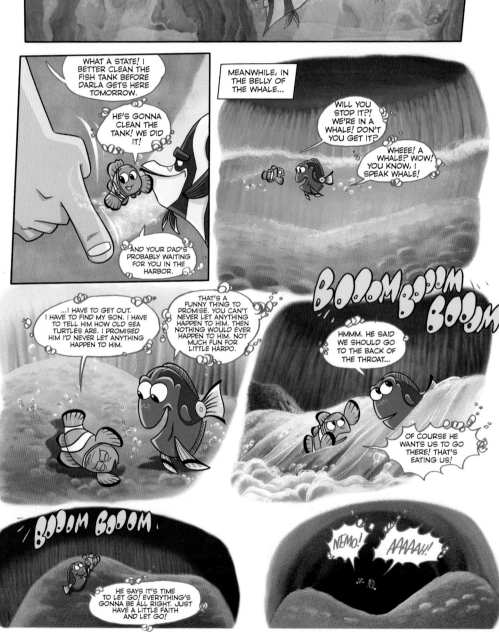

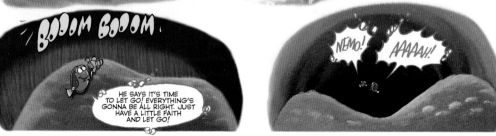

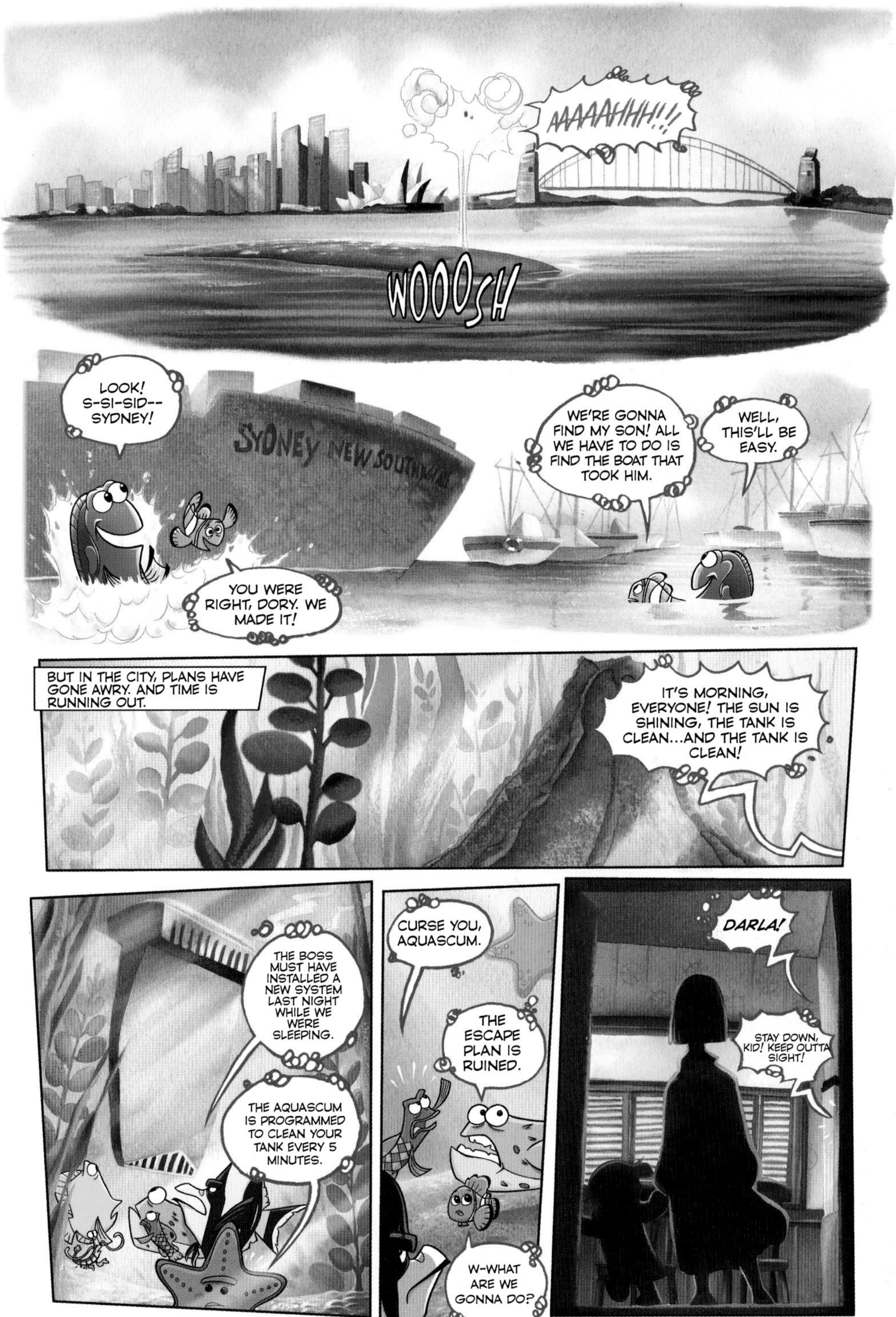
AAAAAHHH!!!
WOOOSH
LOOK! S-SI-SID-- SYDNEY!
SYDNEY NEW SOUTH WALES
YOU WERE RIGHT, DORY. WE MADE IT!
WE'RE GONNA FIND MY SON! ALL WE HAVE TO DO IS FIND THE BOAT THAT TOOK HIM.
WELL, THIS'LL BE EASY.
BUT IN THE CITY, PLANS HAVE GONE AWRY. AND TIME IS RUNNING OUT.
IT'S MORNING, EVERYONE! THE SUN IS SHINING, THE TANK IS CLEAN...AND THE TANK IS CLEAN!
THE BOSS MUST HAVE INSTALLED A NEW SYSTEM LAST NIGHT WHILE WE WERE SLEEPING.
THE AQUASCUM IS PROGRAMMED TO CLEAN YOUR TANK EVERY 5 MINUTES.
CURSE YOU, AQUASCUM.
THE ESCAPE PLAN IS RUINED.
W-WHAT ARE WE GONNA DO?
DARLA!
STAY DOWN, KID! KEEP OUTTA SIGHT!

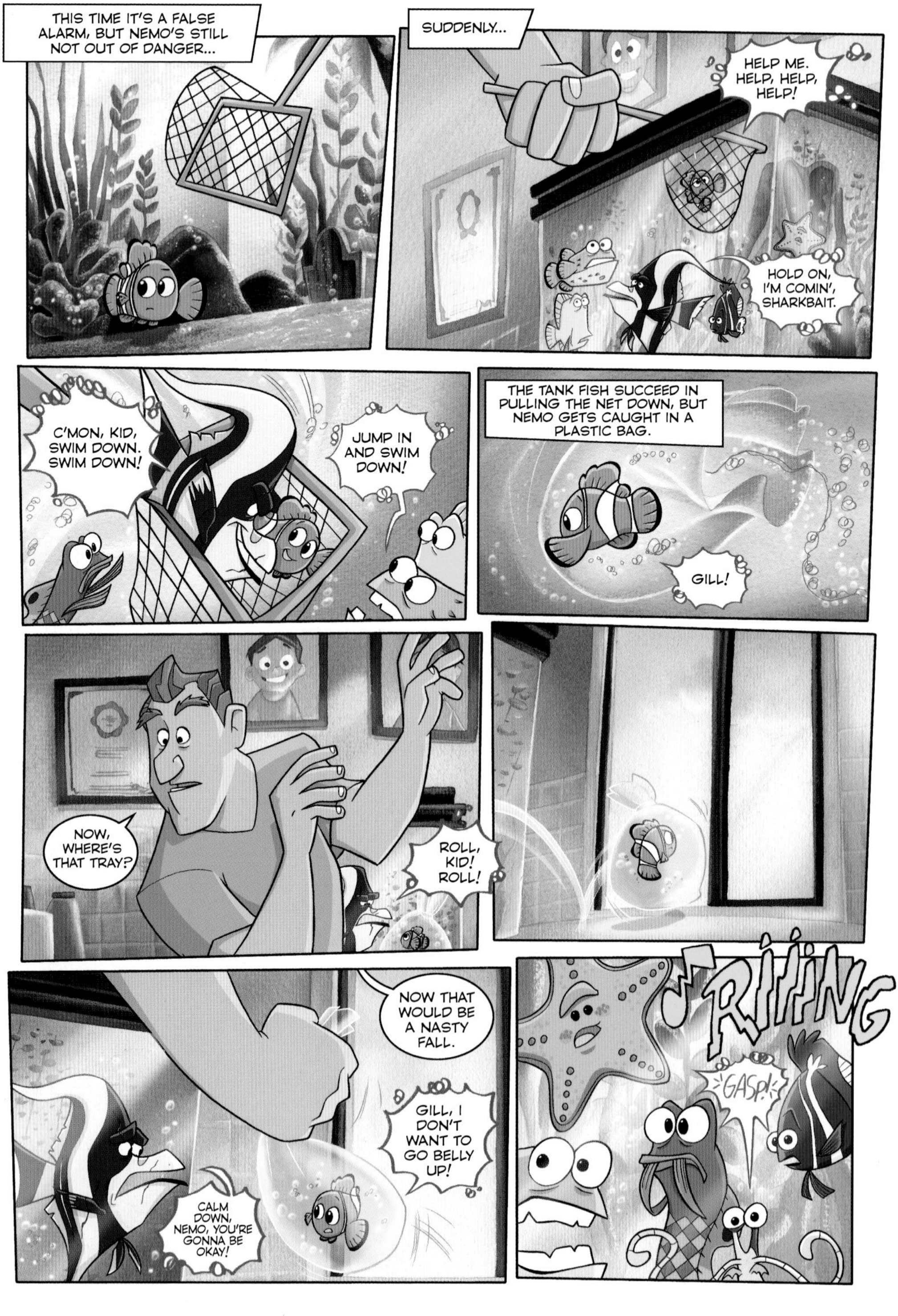
THIS TIME IT'S A FALSE ALARM, BUT NEMO'S STILL NOT OUT OF DANGER...
SUDDENLY...
HELP ME. HELP, HELP, HELP!
HOLD ON, I'M COMIN', SHARKBAIT.
C'MON, KID, SWIM DOWN. SWIM DOWN!
JUMP IN AND SWIM DOWN!
THE TANK FISH SUCCEED IN PULLING THE NET DOWN, BUT NEMO GETS CAUGHT IN A PLASTIC BAG.
GILL!
NOW, WHERE'S THAT TRAY?
ROLL, KID! ROLL!
NOW THAT WOULD BE A NASTY FALL.
GILL, I DON'T WANT TO GO BELLY UP!
CALM DOWN, NEMO, YOU'RE GONNA BE OKAY!
RIIING
GASP!

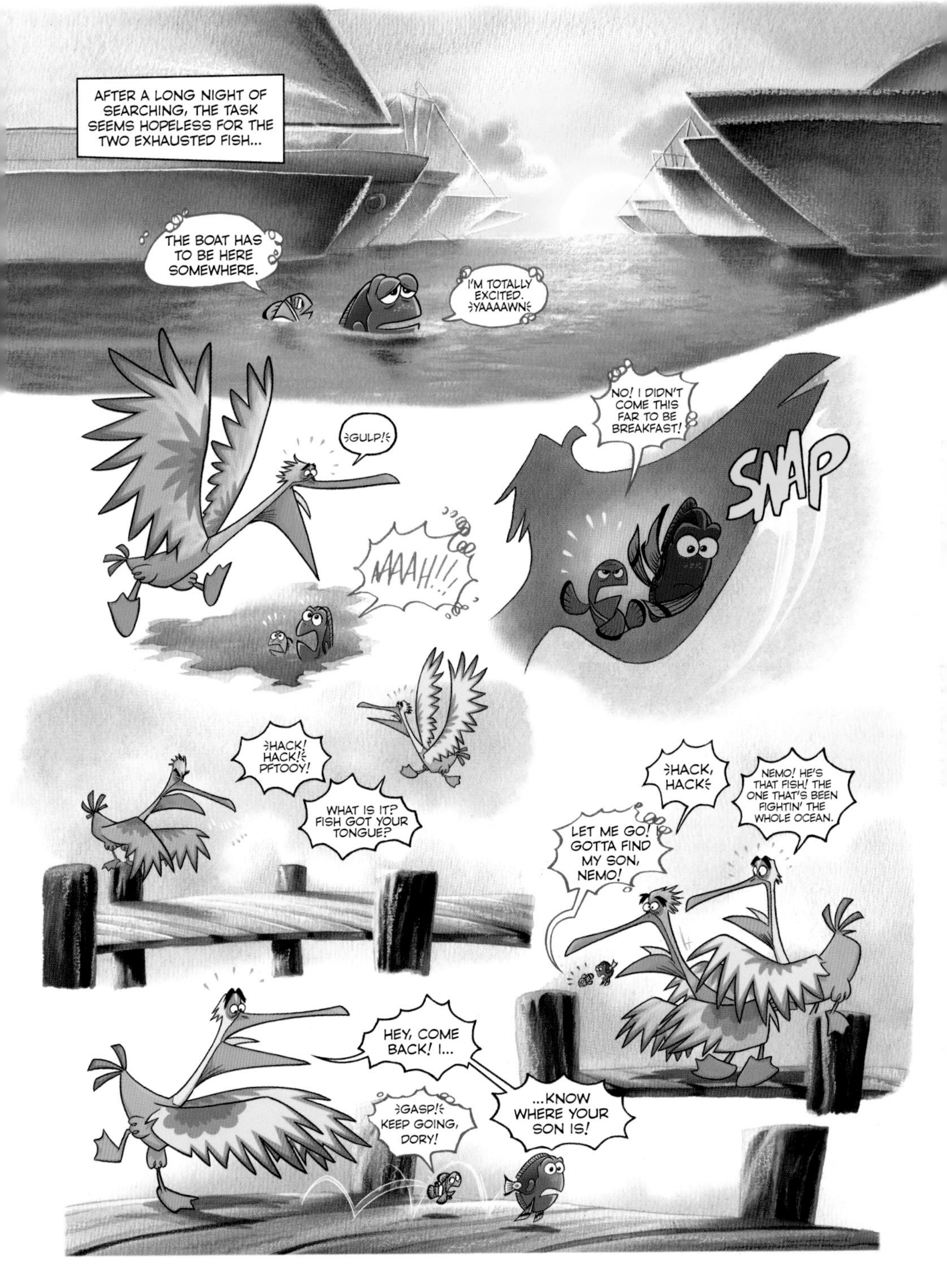
AFTER A LONG NIGHT OF SEARCHING, THE TASK SEEMS HOPELESS FOR THE TWO EXHAUSTED FISH...
THE BOAT HAS TO BE HERE SOMEWHERE.
I'M TOTALLY EXCITED. *YAAAAWN*
GULP!
AAAAH!!!
NO! I DIDN'T COME THIS FAR TO BE BREAKFAST!
SNAP
HACK! HACK! PFTOOY!
WHAT IS IT? FISH GOT YOUR TONGUE?
HACK, HACK
NEMO! HE'S THAT FISH! THE ONE THAT'S BEEN FIGHTIN' THE WHOLE OCEAN.
LET ME GO! GOTTA FIND MY SON, NEMO!
HEY, COME BACK! I...
...KNOW WHERE YOUR SON IS!
GASP! KEEP GOING, DORY!

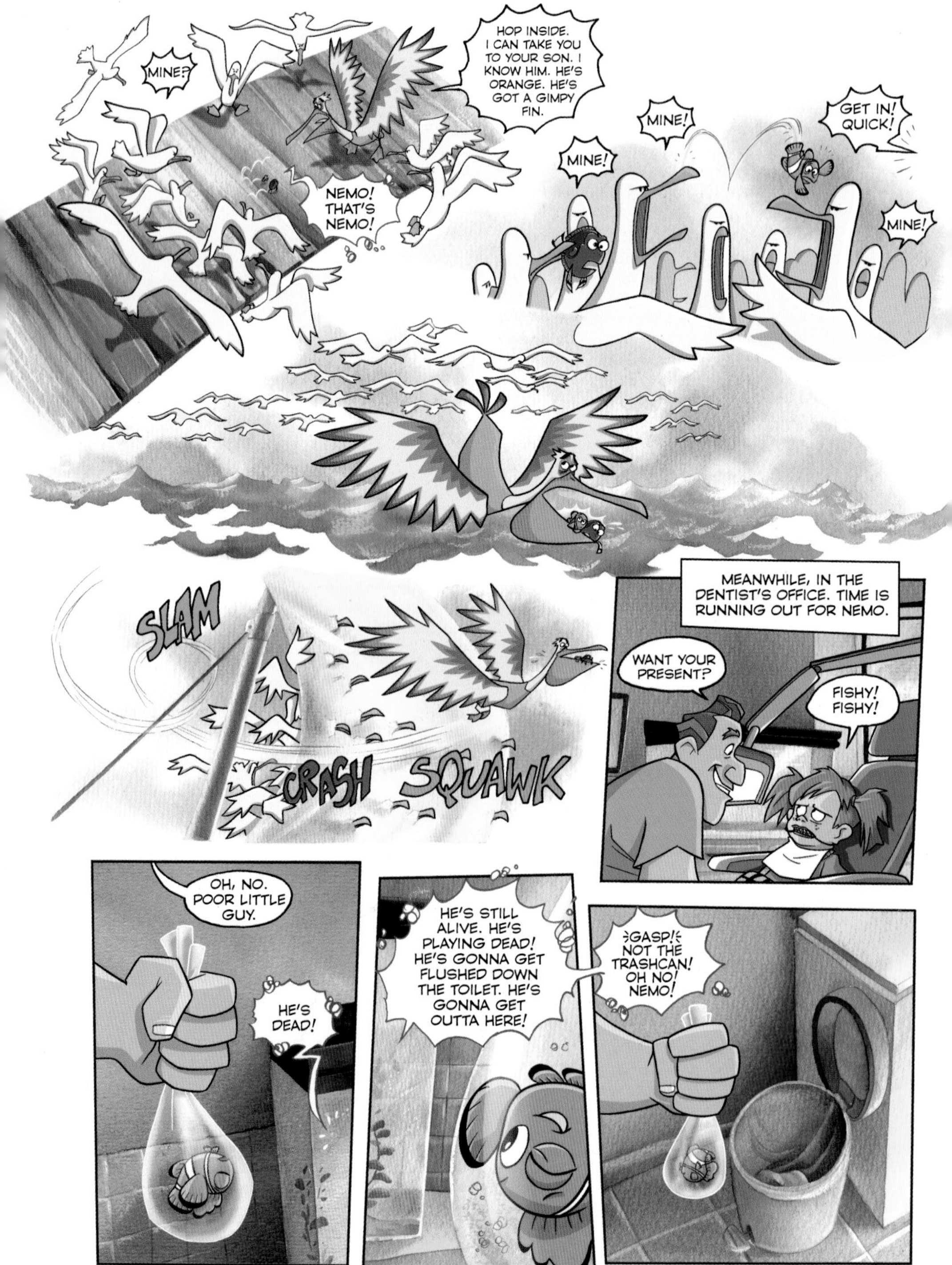
MINE?
HOP INSIDE. I CAN TAKE YOU TO YOUR SON. I KNOW HIM. HE'S ORANGE. HE'S GOT A GIMPY FIN.
NEMO! THAT'S NEMO!
MINE!
MINE!
GET IN! QUICK!
MINE!
SLAM
CRASH
SQUAWK
MEANWHILE, IN THE DENTIST'S OFFICE. TIME IS RUNNING OUT FOR NEMO.
WANT YOUR PRESENT?
FISHY! FISHY!
OH, NO. POOR LITTLE GUY.
HE'S DEAD!
HE'S STILL ALIVE. HE'S PLAYING DEAD! HE'S GONNA GET FLUSHED DOWN THE TOILET. HE'S GONNA GET OUTTA HERE!
GASP! NOT THE TRASHCAN! OH NO! NEMO!

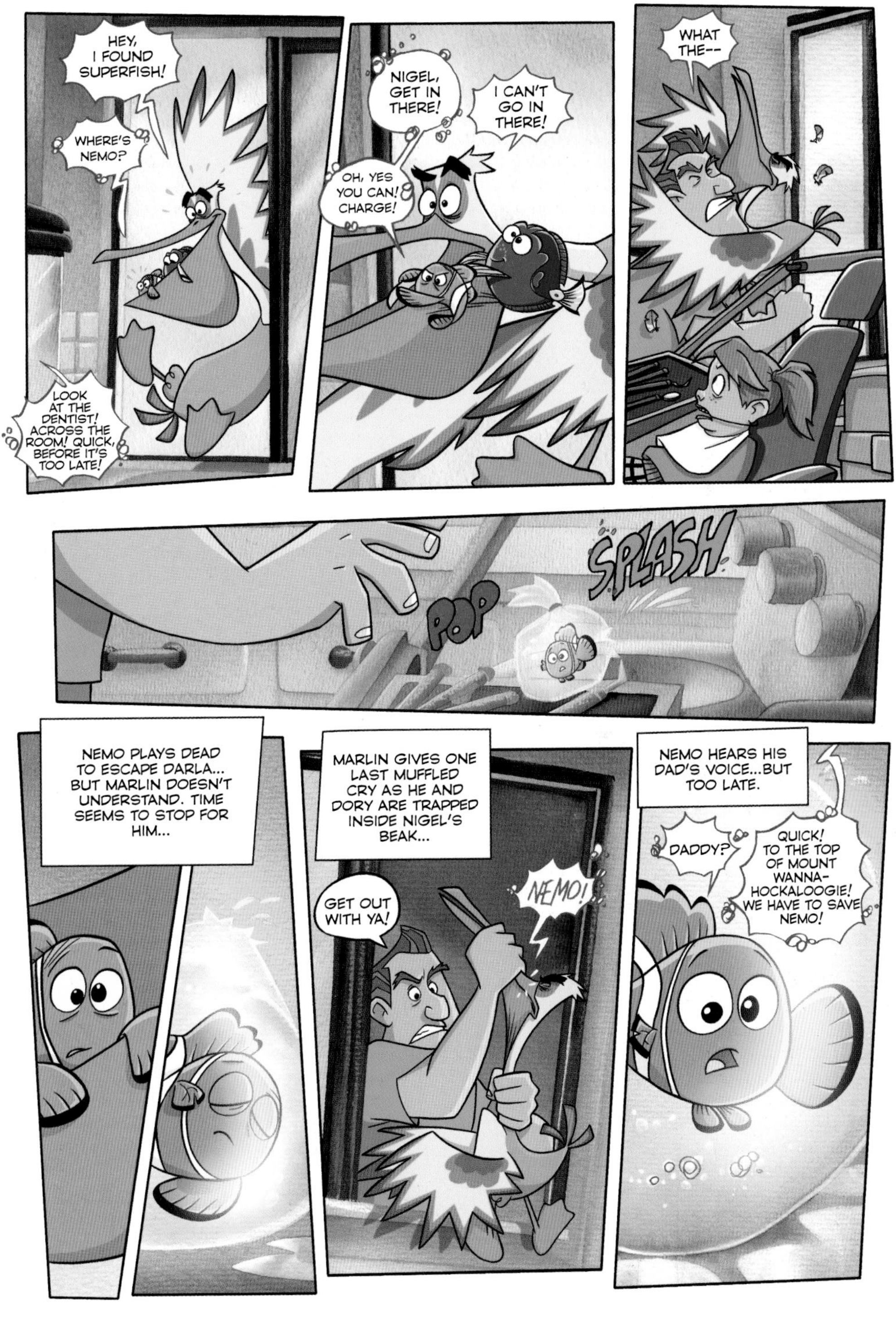
HEY, I FOUND SUPERFISH!
WHERE'S NEMO?
LOOK AT THE DENTIST! ACROSS THE ROOM! QUICK, BEFORE IT'S TOO LATE!
NIGEL, GET IN THERE!
I CAN'T GO IN THERE!
OH, YES YOU CAN! CHARGE!
WHAT THE--
POP
SPLASH
NEMO PLAYS DEAD TO ESCAPE DARLA... BUT MARLIN DOESN'T UNDERSTAND. TIME SEEMS TO STOP FOR HIM...
MARLIN GIVES ONE LAST MUFFLED CRY AS HE AND DORY ARE TRAPPED INSIDE NIGEL'S BEAK...
GET OUT WITH YA!
NEMO!
NEMO HEARS HIS DAD'S VOICE...BUT TOO LATE.
DADDY?
QUICK! TO THE TOP OF MOUNT WANNA-HOCKALOOGIE! WE HAVE TO SAVE NEMO!

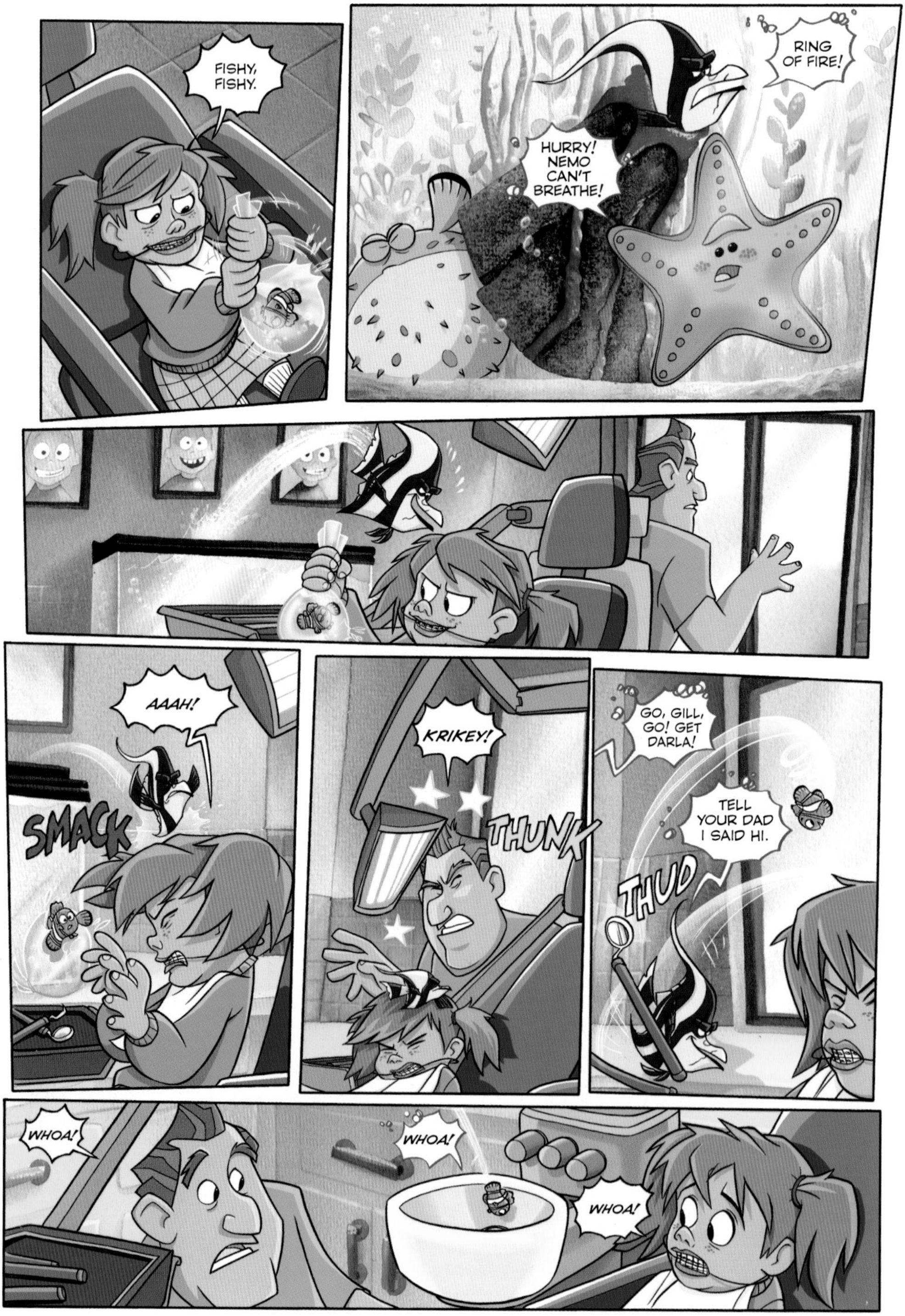
FISHY, FISHY.
RING OF FIRE!
HURRY! NEMO CAN'T BREATHE!
AAAH!
SMACK
KRIKEY!
THUNK
GO, GILL, GO! GET DARLA!
TELL YOUR DAD I SAID HI.
THUD
WHOA!
WHOA!
WHOA!

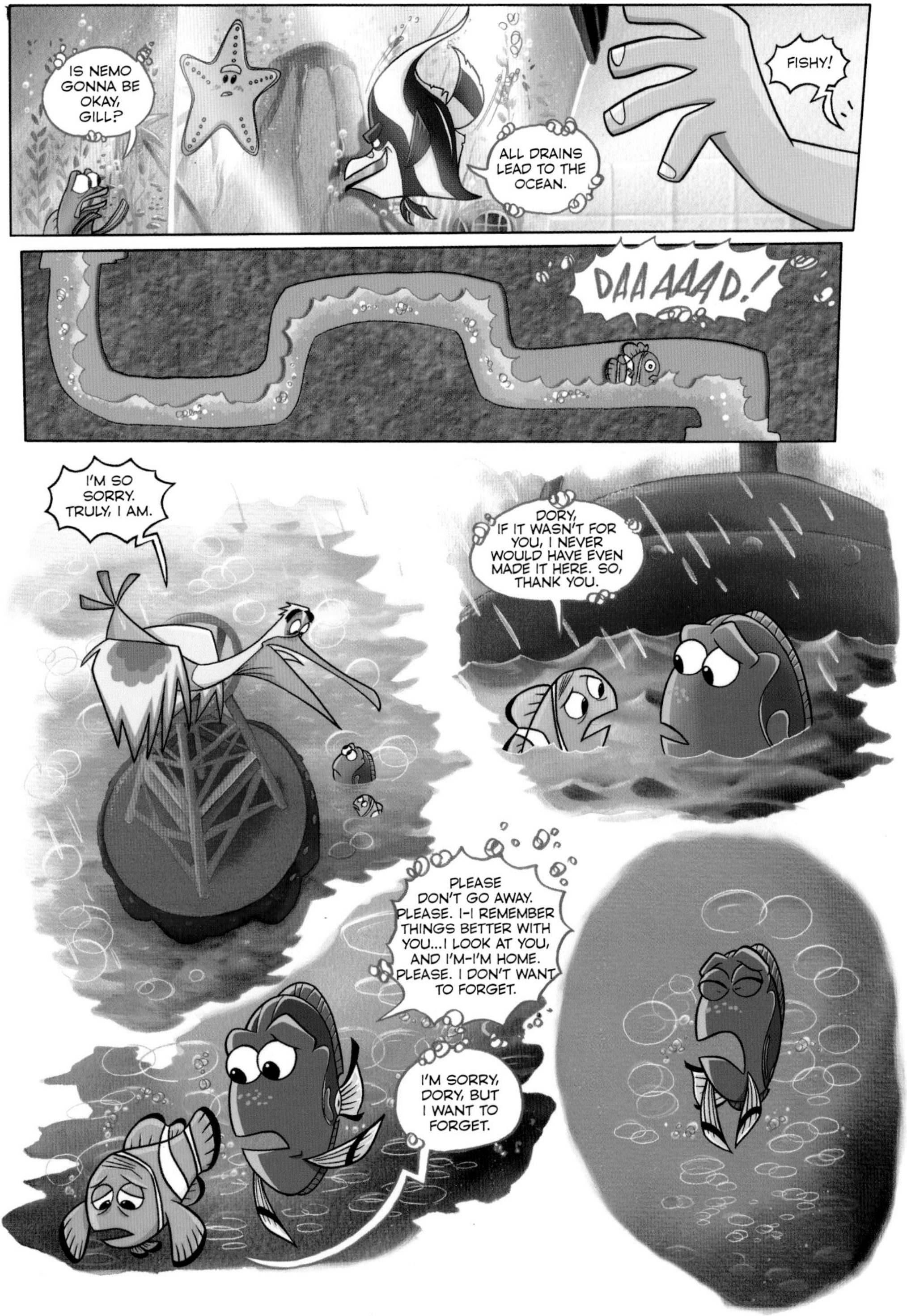
IS NEMO GONNA BE OKAY, GILL?
ALL DRAINS LEAD TO THE OCEAN.
FISHY!
DAAAAAD!
I'M SO SORRY. TRULY, I AM.
DORY, IF IT WASN'T FOR YOU, I NEVER WOULD HAVE EVEN MADE IT HERE. SO, THANK YOU.
PLEASE DON'T GO AWAY. PLEASE. I-I REMEMBER THINGS BETTER WITH YOU...I LOOK AT YOU, AND I'M-I'M HOME. PLEASE. I DON'T WANT TO FORGET.
I'M SORRY, DORY, BUT I WANT TO FORGET.

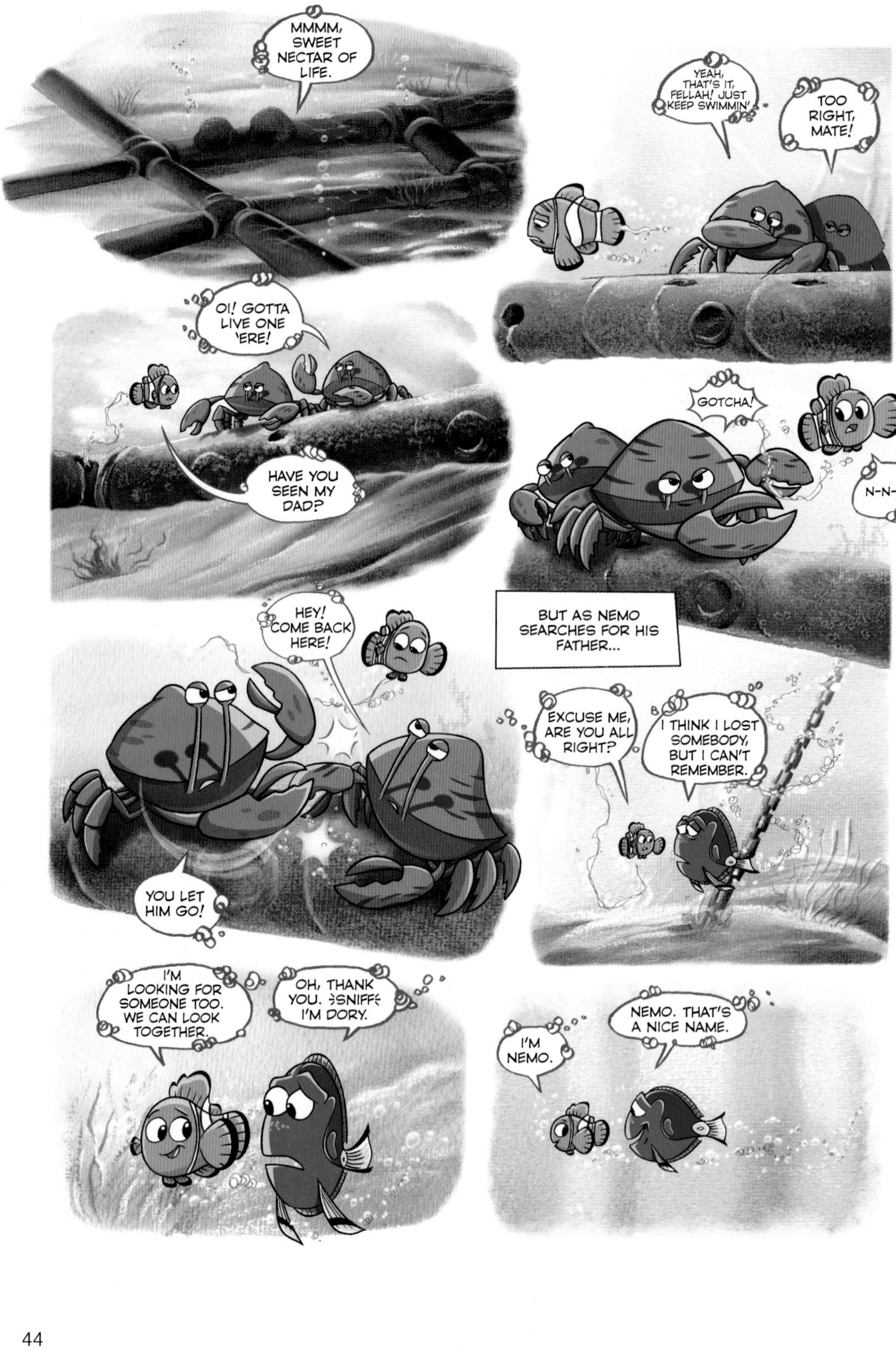
MMMM, SWEET NECTAR OF LIFE.
YEAH, THAT'S IT, FELLAH! JUST KEEP SWIMMIN'
TOO RIGHT, MATE!
OI! GOTTA LIVE ONE 'ERE!
HAVE YOU SEEN MY DAD?
GOTCHA!
N-N-N
HEY! COME BACK HERE!
YOU LET HIM GO!
BUT AS NEMO SEARCHES FOR HIS FATHER...
EXCUSE ME, ARE YOU ALL RIGHT?
I THINK I LOST SOMEBODY, BUT I CAN'T REMEMBER.
I'M LOOKING FOR SOMEONE TOO. WE CAN LOOK TOGETHER.
OH, THANK YOU. ⋺SNIFF⋲ I'M DORY.
I'M NEMO.
NEMO. THAT'S A NICE NAME.

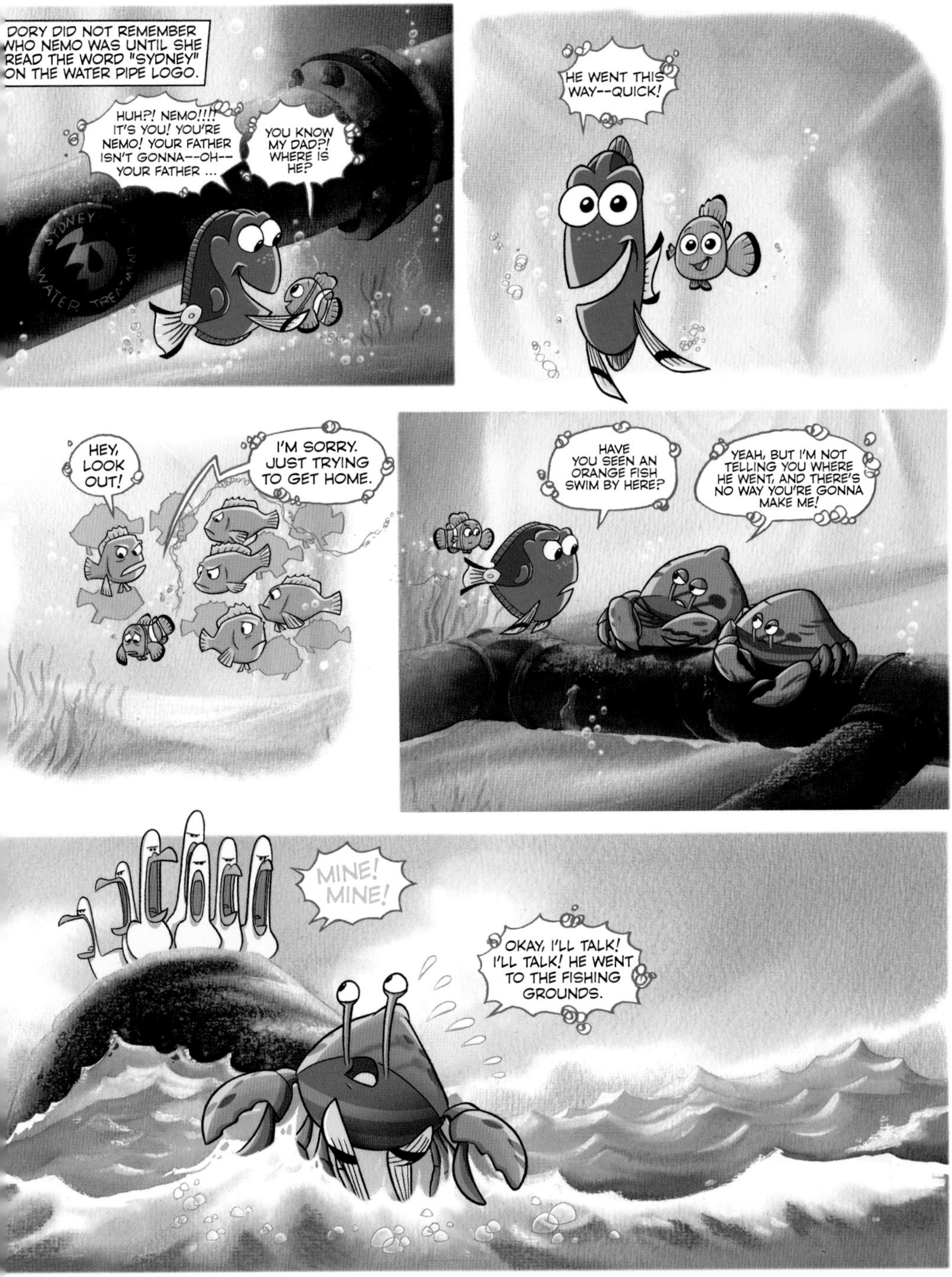
DORY DID NOT REMEMBER WHO NEMO WAS UNTIL SHE READ THE WORD "SYDNEY" ON THE WATER PIPE LOGO.
HUH?! NEMO!!!! IT'S YOU! YOU'RE NEMO! YOUR FATHER ISN'T GONNA--OH-- YOUR FATHER ...
YOU KNOW MY DAD?! WHERE IS HE?
SYDNEY WATER TREATMENT
HE WENT THIS WAY--QUICK!
HEY, LOOK OUT!
I'M SORRY. JUST TRYING TO GET HOME.
HAVE YOU SEEN AN ORANGE FISH SWIM BY HERE?
YEAH, BUT I'M NOT TELLING YOU WHERE HE WENT, AND THERE'S NO WAY YOU'RE GONNA MAKE ME!
MINE! MINE!
OKAY, I'LL TALK! I'LL TALK! HE WENT TO THE FISHING GROUNDS.

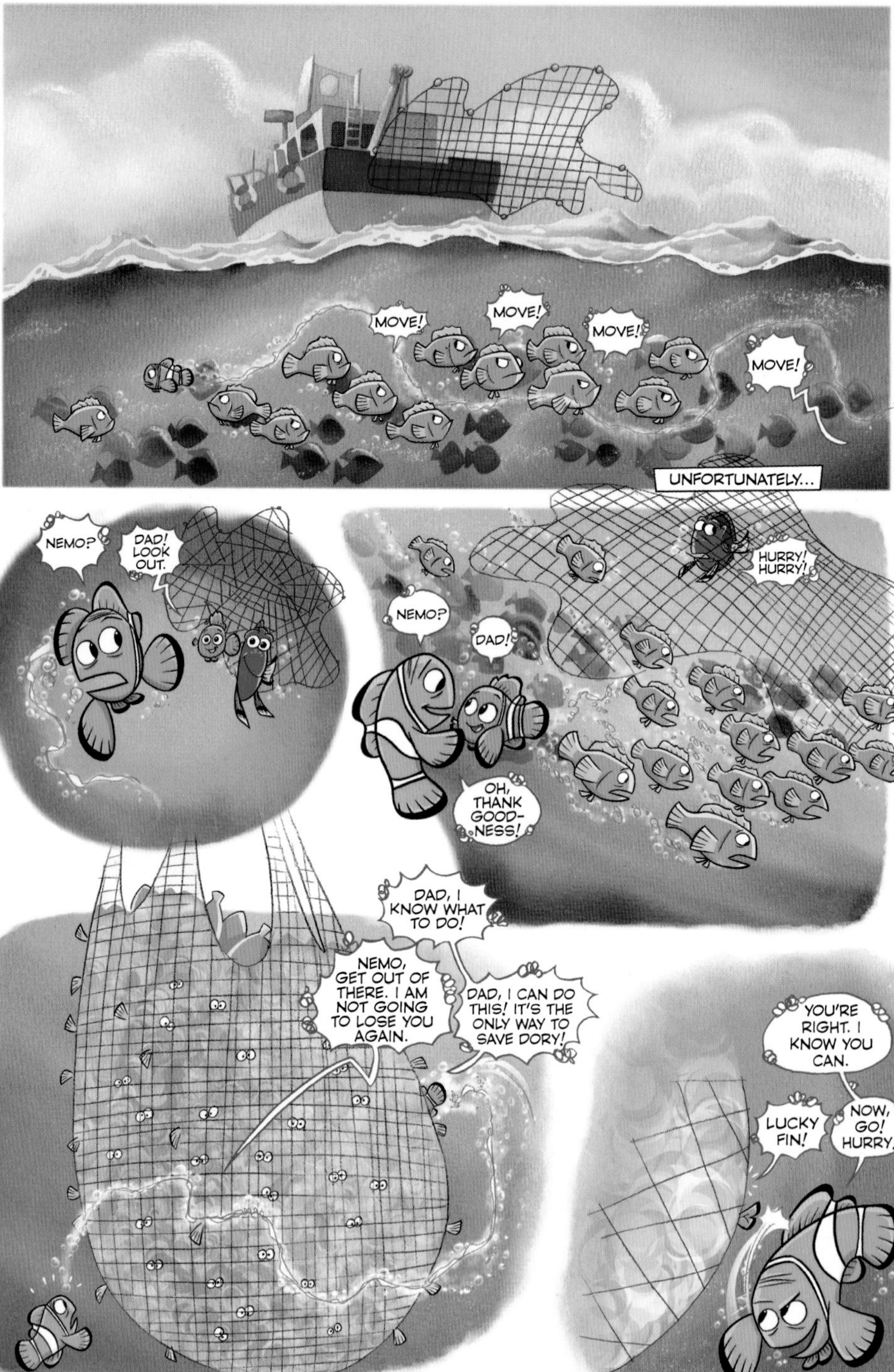
MOVE!
MOVE!
MOVE!
MOVE!
UNFORTUNATELY...
NEMO?
DAD! LOOK OUT.
HURRY! HURRY!
NEMO?
DAD!
OH, THANK GOOD-NESS!
DAD, I KNOW WHAT TO DO!
NEMO, GET OUT OF THERE. I AM NOT GOING TO LOSE YOU AGAIN.
DAD, I CAN DO THIS! IT'S THE ONLY WAY TO SAVE DORY!
YOU'RE RIGHT. I KNOW YOU CAN.
LUCKY FIN!
NOW, GO! HURRY!

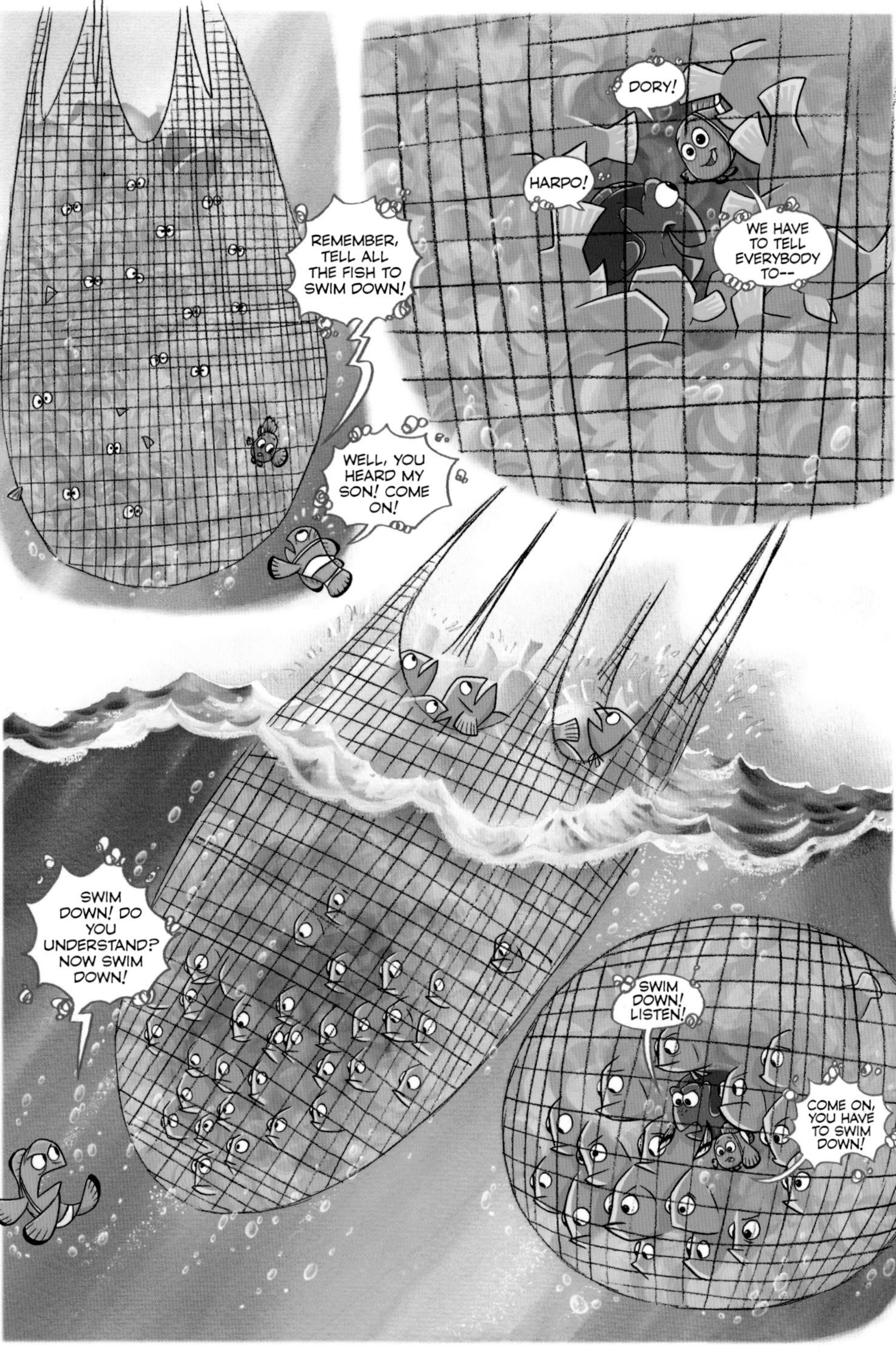
DORY!
HARPO!
WE HAVE TO TELL EVERYBODY TO--
REMEMBER, TELL ALL THE FISH TO SWIM DOWN!
WELL, YOU HEARD MY SON! COME ON!
SWIM DOWN! DO YOU UNDERSTAND? NOW SWIM DOWN!
SWIM DOWN! LISTEN!
COME ON, YOU HAVE TO SWIM DOWN!

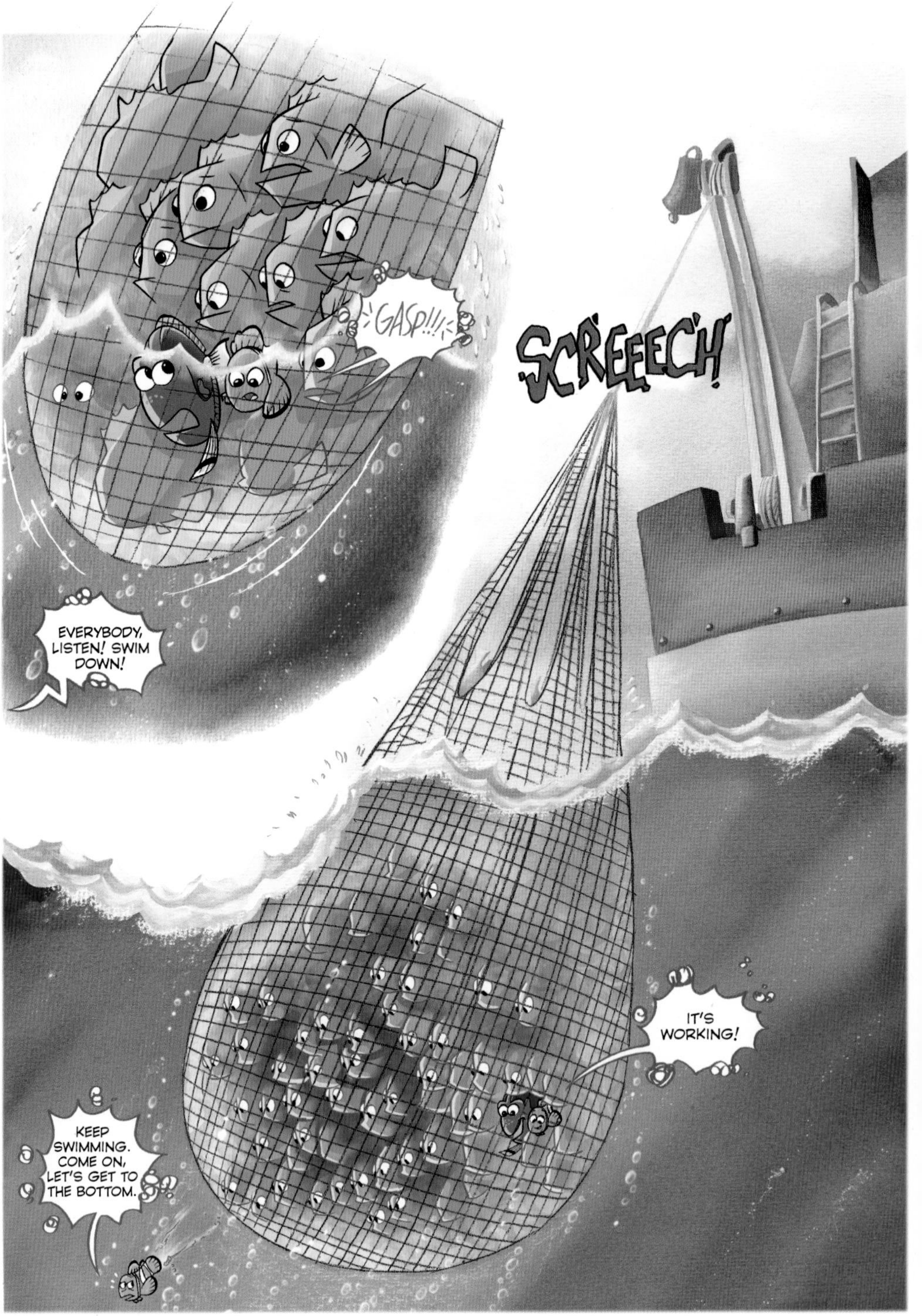
GASP!!!
SCREEECH!
EVERYBODY, LISTEN! SWIM DOWN!
IT'S WORKING!
KEEP SWIMMING. COME ON, LET'S GET TO THE BOTTOM.

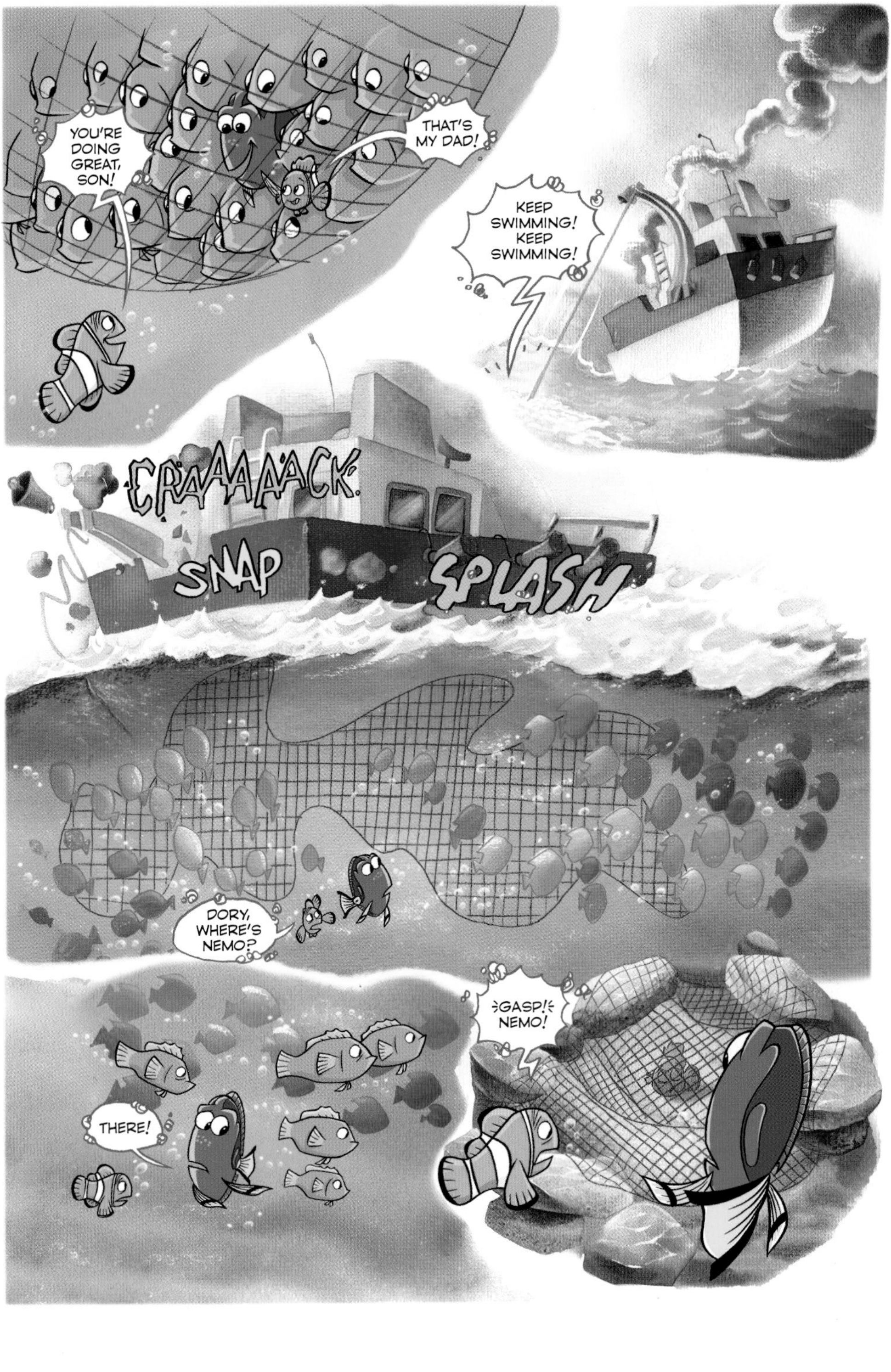
YOU'RE DOING GREAT, SON!
THAT'S MY DAD!
KEEP SWIMMING! KEEP SWIMMING!
CRAAAAACK
SNAP
SPLASH
DORY, WHERE'S NEMO?
GASP! NEMO!
THERE!

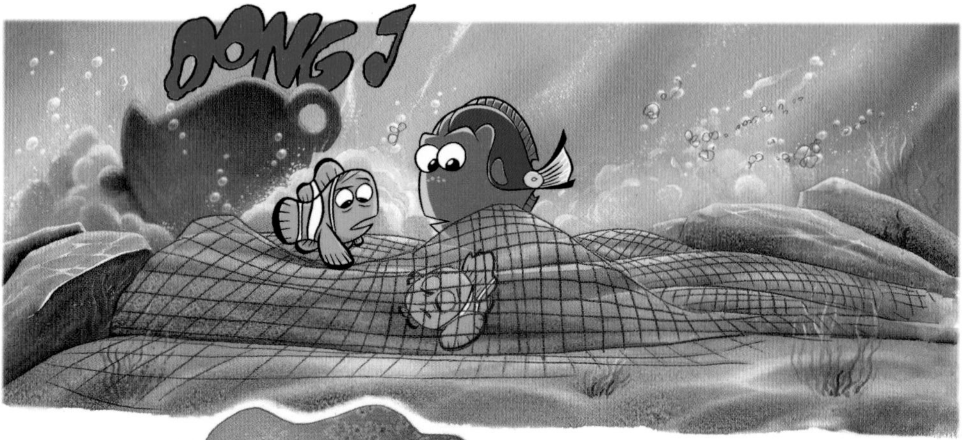
DONG

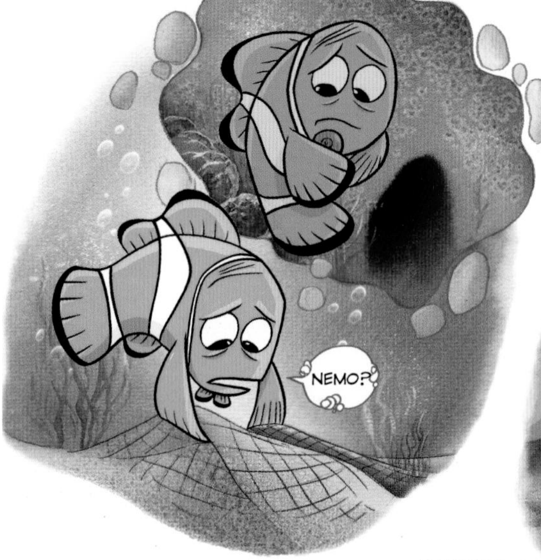
NEMO?

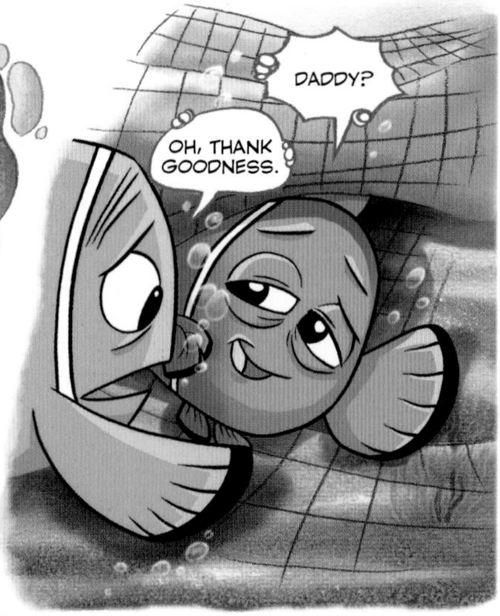
DADDY?
OH, THANK GOODNESS.

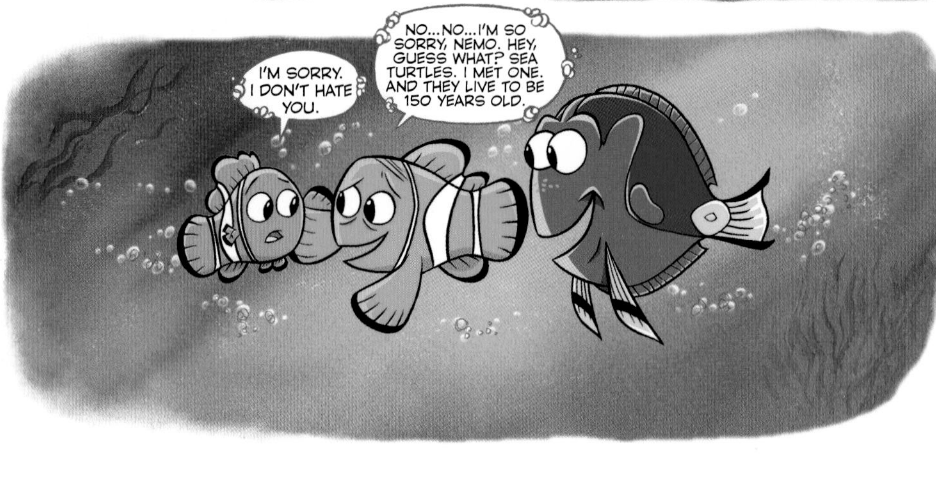
I'M SORRY. I DON'T HATE YOU.
NO...NO...I'M SO SORRY, NEMO. HEY, GUESS WHAT? SEA TURTLES. I MET ONE. AND THEY LIVE TO BE 150 YEARS OLD.

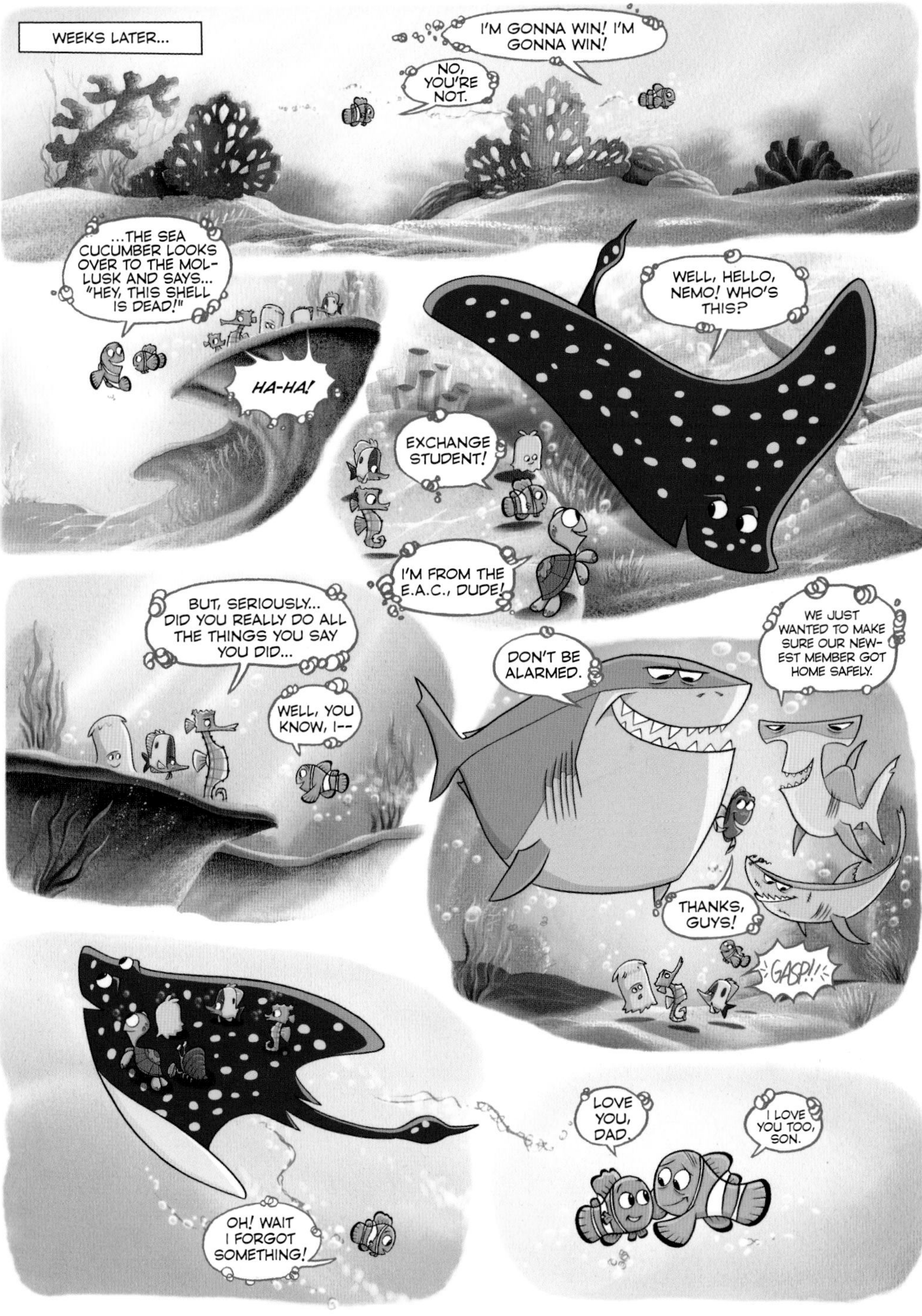
WEEKS LATER...
I'M GONNA WIN! I'M GONNA WIN!
NO, YOU'RE NOT.
...THE SEA CUCUMBER LOOKS OVER TO THE MOL-LUSK AND SAYS... "HEY, THIS SHELL IS DEAD!"
HA-HA!
WELL, HELLO, NEMO! WHO'S THIS?
EXCHANGE STUDENT!
I'M FROM THE E.A.C., DUDE!
BUT, SERIOUSLY... DID YOU REALLY DO ALL THE THINGS YOU SAY YOU DID...
WELL, YOU KNOW, I--
DON'T BE ALARMED.
WE JUST WANTED TO MAKE SURE OUR NEW-EST MEMBER GOT HOME SAFELY.
THANKS, GUYS!
GASP!!
OH! WAIT I FORGOT SOMETHING!
LOVE YOU, DAD.
I LOVE YOU TOO, SON.

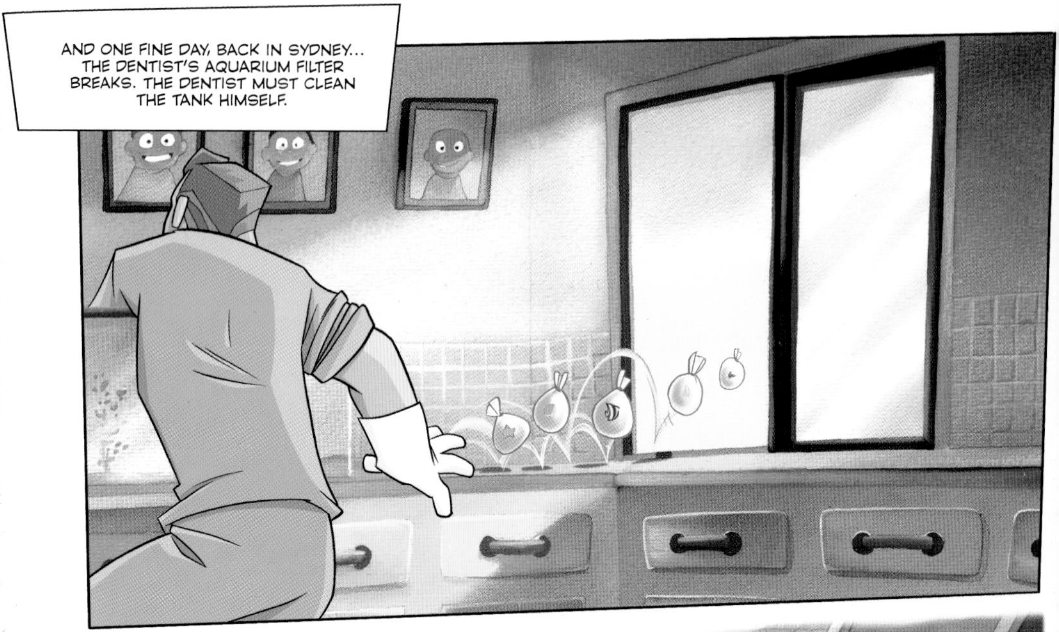
AND ONE FINE DAY, BACK IN SYDNEY...
THE DENTIST'S AQUARIUM FILTER BREAKS. THE DENTIST MUST CLEAN THE TANK HIMSELF.

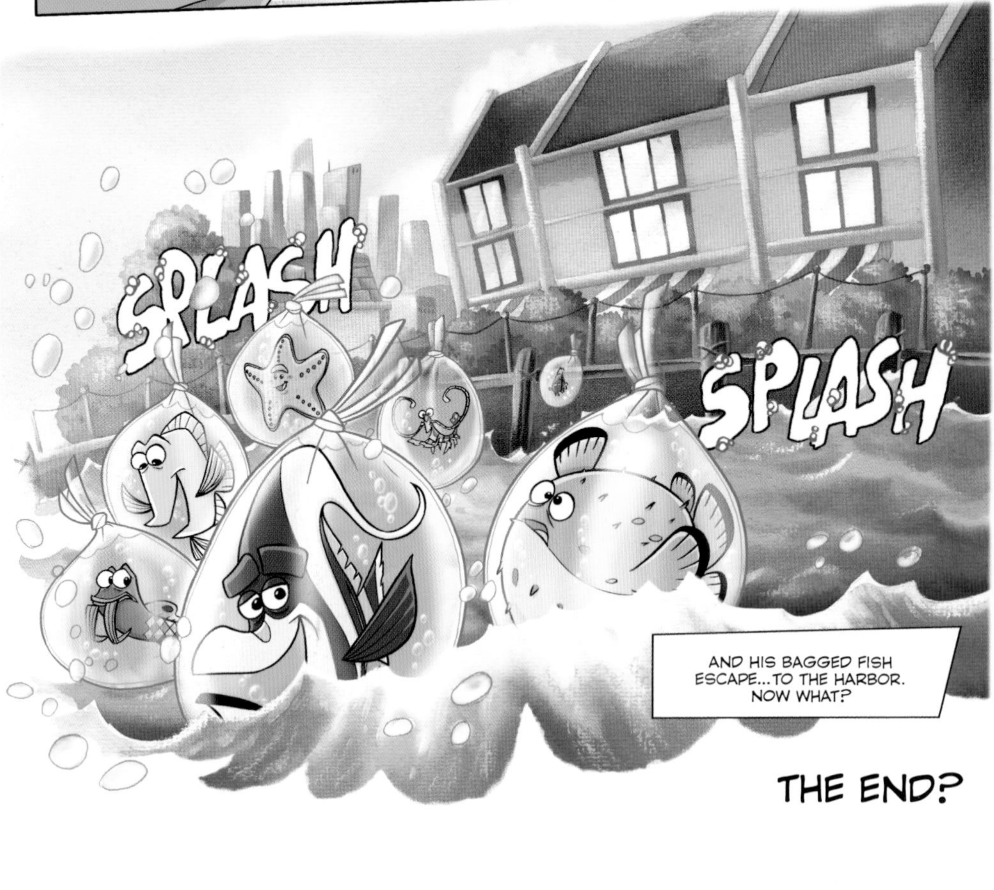
SPLASH
SPLASH
AND HIS BAGGED FISH ESCAPE...TO THE HARBOR. NOW WHAT?

THE END?

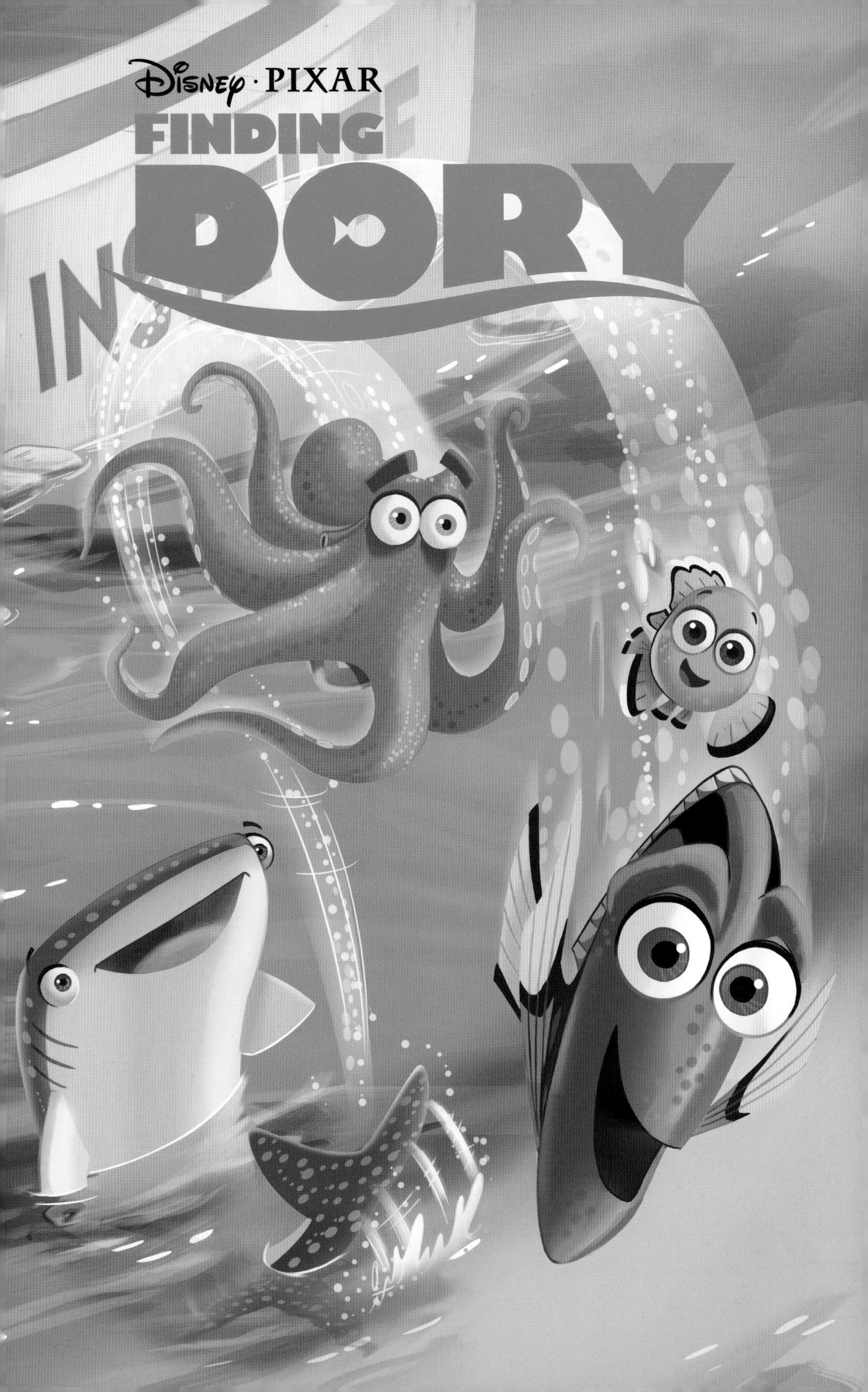
Disney · PIXAR
FINDING
DORY

Script adaptation
ALESSANDRO FERRARI

Layouts
NICOLA SAMMARCO

Pencils
ANDREA GREPPI

Color
DARIO CALABRIA
MARA DAMIANI

Letters
CHRIS DICKEY

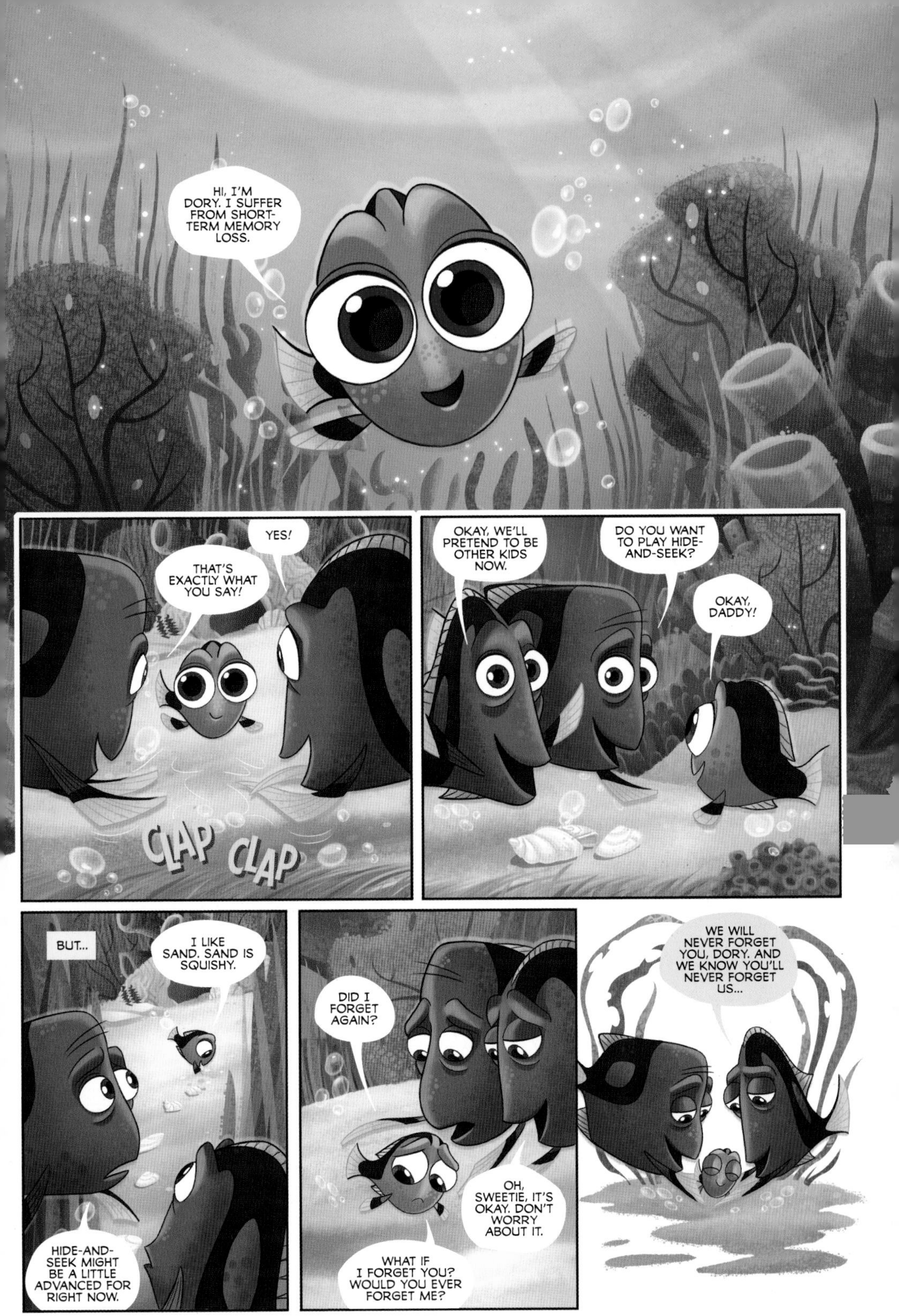
HI, I'M DORY. I SUFFER FROM SHORT-TERM MEMORY LOSS.
THAT'S EXACTLY WHAT YOU SAY!
YES!
CLAP CLAP
OKAY, WE'LL PRETEND TO BE OTHER KIDS NOW.
DO YOU WANT TO PLAY HIDE-AND-SEEK?
OKAY, DADDY!
BUT...
I LIKE SAND. SAND IS SQUISHY.
HIDE-AND-SEEK MIGHT BE A LITTLE ADVANCED FOR RIGHT NOW.
DID I FORGET AGAIN?
OH, SWEETIE, IT'S OKAY. DON'T WORRY ABOUT IT.
WHAT IF I FORGET YOU? WOULD YOU EVER FORGET ME?
WE WILL NEVER FORGET YOU, DORY. AND WE KNOW YOU'LL NEVER FORGET US...

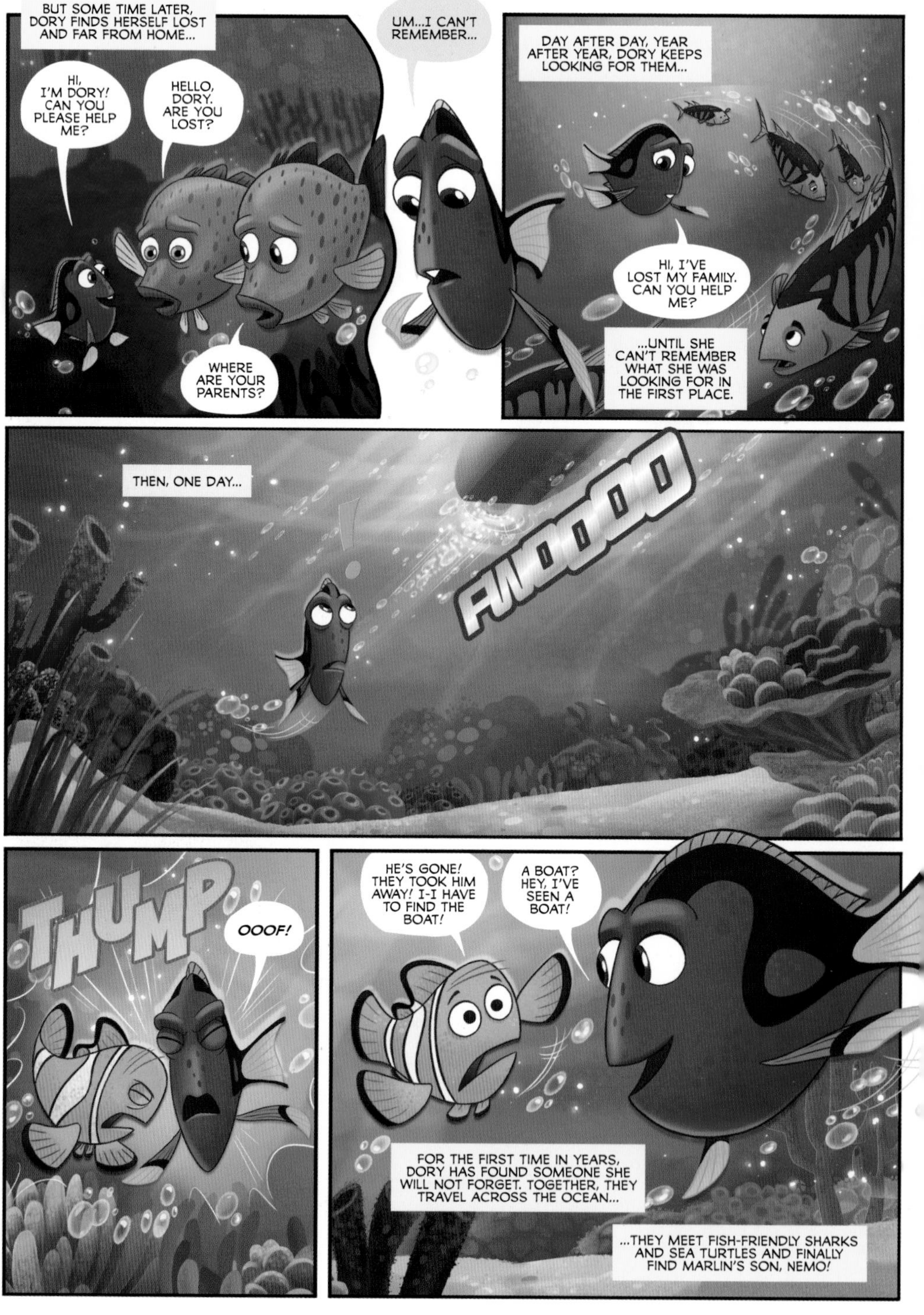
BUT SOME TIME LATER, DORY FINDS HERSELF LOST AND FAR FROM HOME...
HI, I'M DORY! CAN YOU PLEASE HELP ME?
HELLO, DORY. ARE YOU LOST?
WHERE ARE YOUR PARENTS?
UM...I CAN'T REMEMBER...
DAY AFTER DAY, YEAR AFTER YEAR, DORY KEEPS LOOKING FOR THEM...
HI, I'VE LOST MY FAMILY. CAN YOU HELP ME?
...UNTIL SHE CAN'T REMEMBER WHAT SHE WAS LOOKING FOR IN THE FIRST PLACE.
THEN, ONE DAY...
AWOOOO
THUMP
OOOF!
HE'S GONE! THEY TOOK HIM AWAY! I-I HAVE TO FIND THE BOAT!
A BOAT? HEY, I'VE SEEN A BOAT!
FOR THE FIRST TIME IN YEARS, DORY HAS FOUND SOMEONE SHE WILL NOT FORGET. TOGETHER, THEY TRAVEL ACROSS THE OCEAN...
...THEY MEET FISH-FRIENDLY SHARKS AND SEA TURTLES AND FINALLY FIND MARLIN'S SON, NEMO!

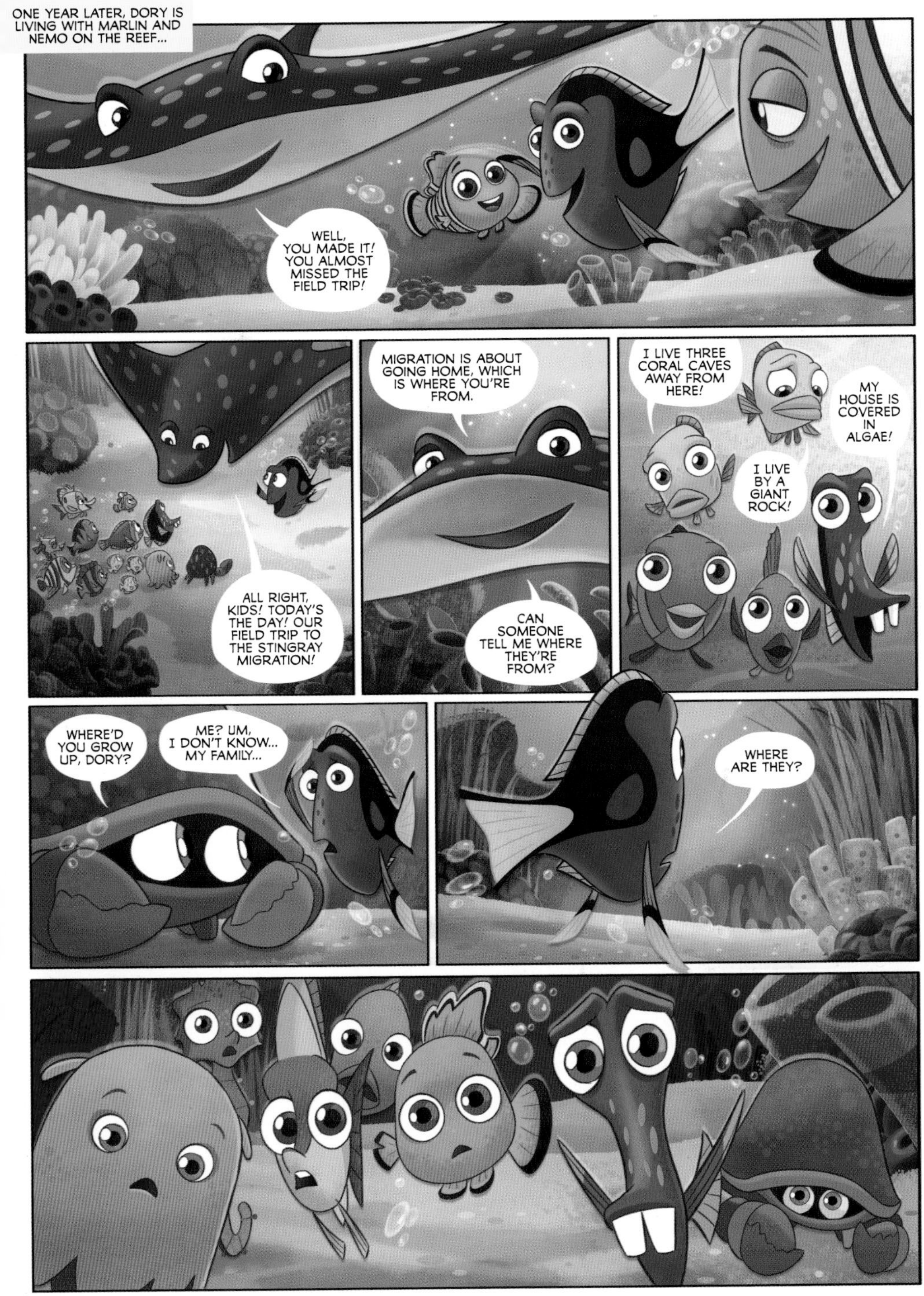

ONE YEAR LATER, DORY IS LIVING WITH MARLIN AND NEMO ON THE REEF...
WELL, YOU MADE IT! YOU ALMOST MISSED THE FIELD TRIP!
ALL RIGHT, KIDS! TODAY'S THE DAY! OUR FIELD TRIP TO THE STINGRAY MIGRATION!
MIGRATION IS ABOUT GOING HOME, WHICH IS WHERE YOU'RE FROM.
CAN SOMEONE TELL ME WHERE THEY'RE FROM?
I LIVE THREE CORAL CAVES AWAY FROM HERE!
MY HOUSE IS COVERED IN ALGAE!
I LIVE BY A GIANT ROCK!
WHERE'D YOU GROW UP, DORY?
ME? UM, I DON'T KNOW... MY FAMILY...
WHERE ARE THEY?

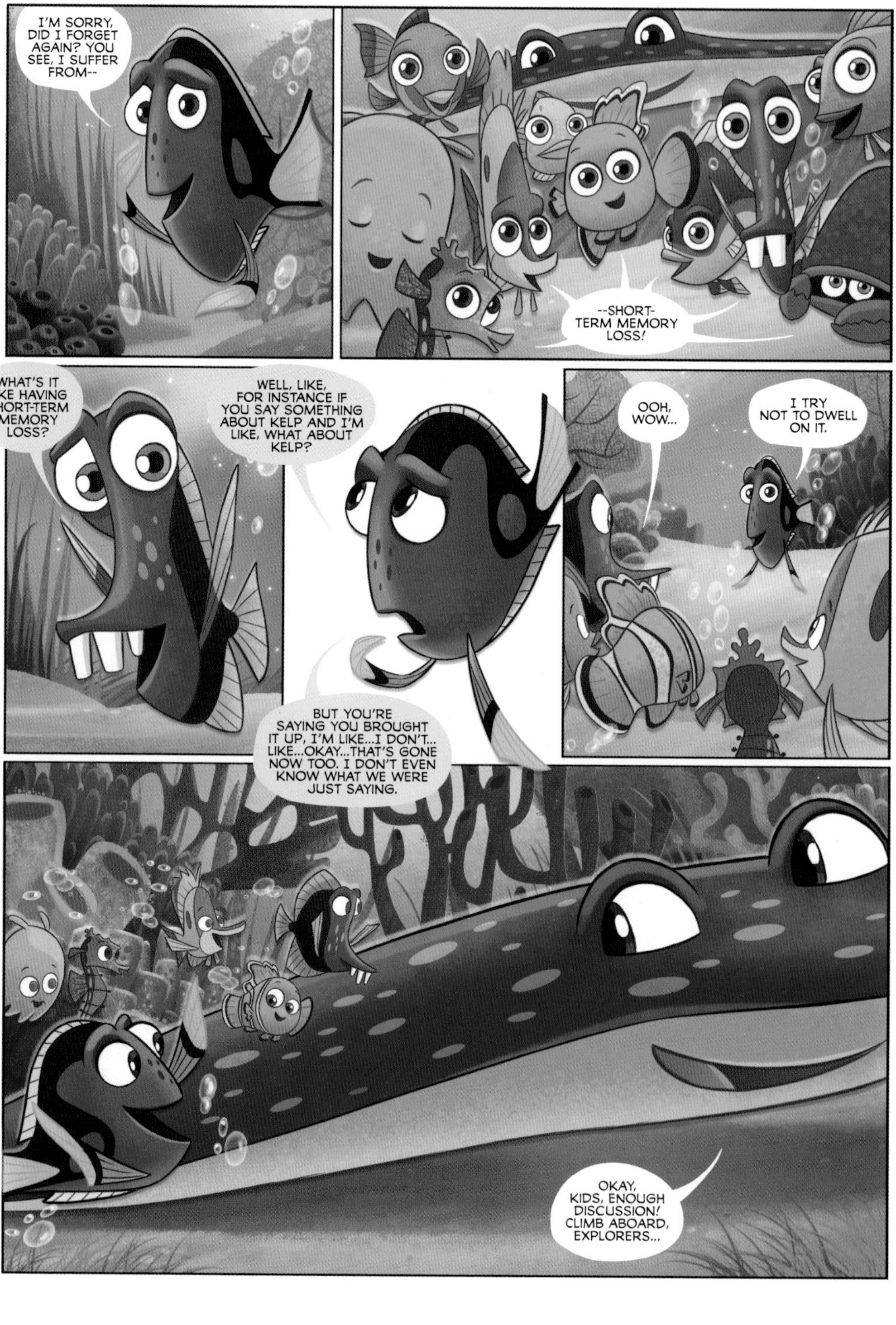
I'M SORRY, DID I FORGET AGAIN? YOU SEE, I SUFFER FROM--
--SHORT-TERM MEMORY LOSS!
WHAT'S IT LIKE HAVING SHORT-TERM MEMORY LOSS?
WELL, LIKE, FOR INSTANCE IF YOU SAY SOMETHING ABOUT KELP AND I'M LIKE, WHAT ABOUT KELP?
BUT YOU'RE SAYING YOU BROUGHT IT UP, I'M LIKE...I DON'T... LIKE...OKAY...THAT'S GONE NOW TOO. I DON'T EVEN KNOW WHAT WE WERE JUST SAYING.
OOH, WOW...
I TRY NOT TO DWELL ON IT.
OKAY, KIDS, ENOUGH DISCUSSION! CLIMB ABOARD, EXPLORERS...

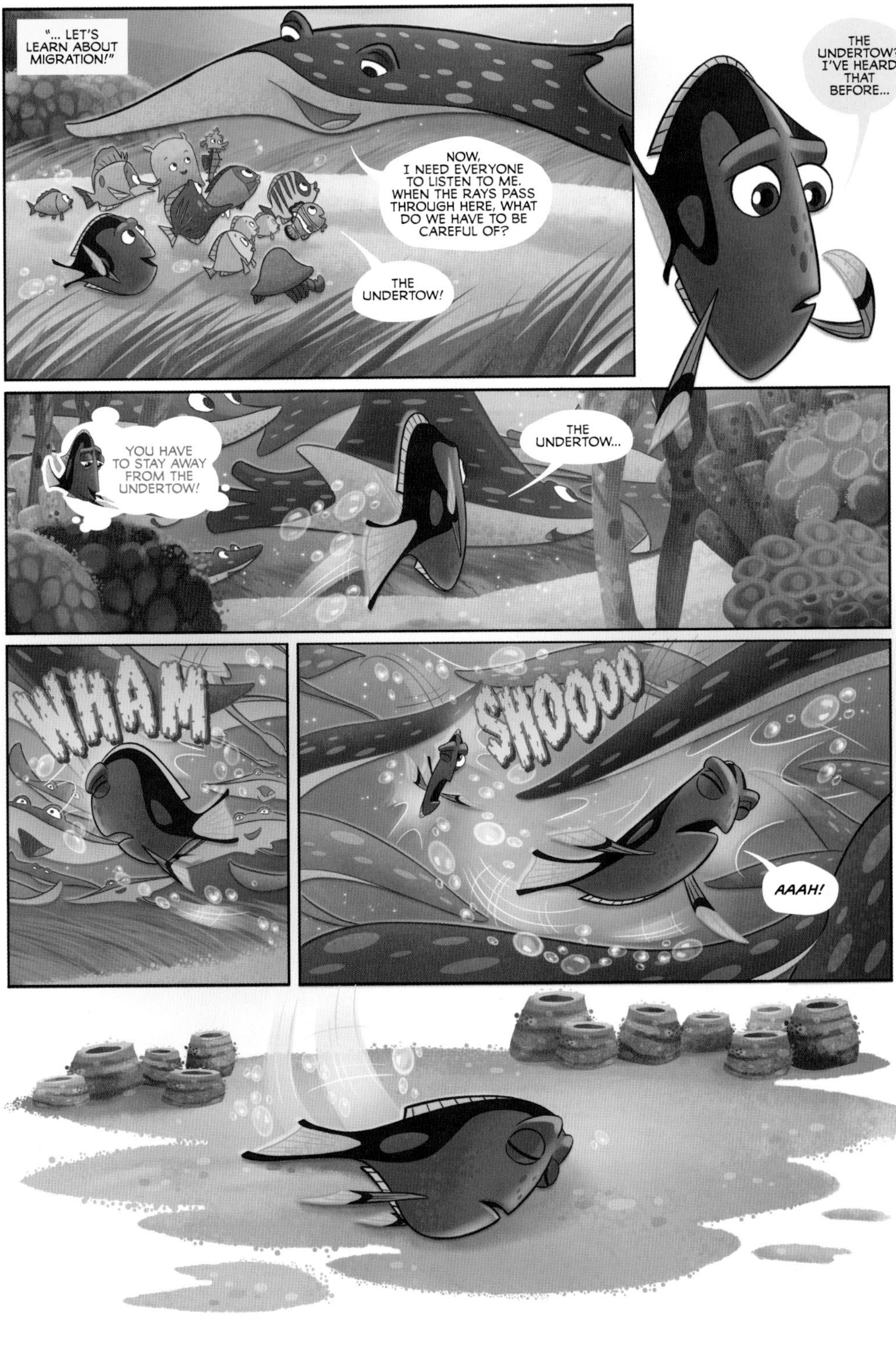
"... LET'S LEARN ABOUT MIGRATION!"
NOW, I NEED EVERYONE TO LISTEN TO ME. WHEN THE RAYS PASS THROUGH HERE, WHAT DO WE HAVE TO BE CAREFUL OF?
THE UNDERTOW!
THE UNDERTOW? I'VE HEARD THAT BEFORE...
YOU HAVE TO STAY AWAY FROM THE UNDERTOW!
THE UNDERTOW...
WHAM
SHOOOO
AAAH!

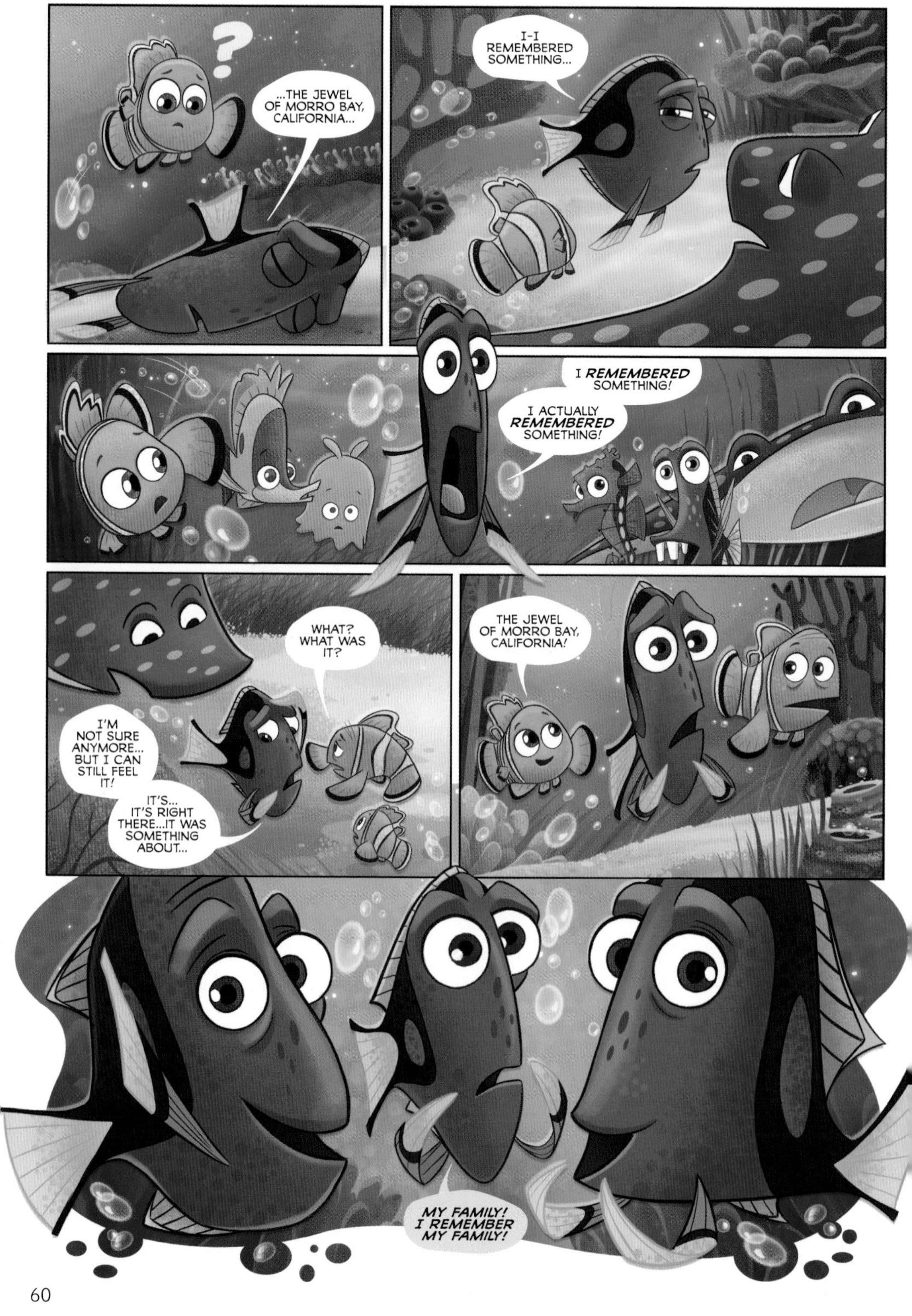
...THE JEWEL OF MORRO BAY, CALIFORNIA...
I-I REMEMBERED SOMETHING...
I **REMEMBERED** SOMETHING!
I ACTUALLY **REMEMBERED** SOMETHING!
WHAT? WHAT WAS IT?
I'M NOT SURE ANYMORE... BUT I CAN STILL FEEL IT!
IT'S... IT'S RIGHT THERE...IT WAS SOMETHING ABOUT...
THE JEWEL OF MORRO BAY, CALIFORNIA!
MY FAMILY! I REMEMBER MY FAMILY!

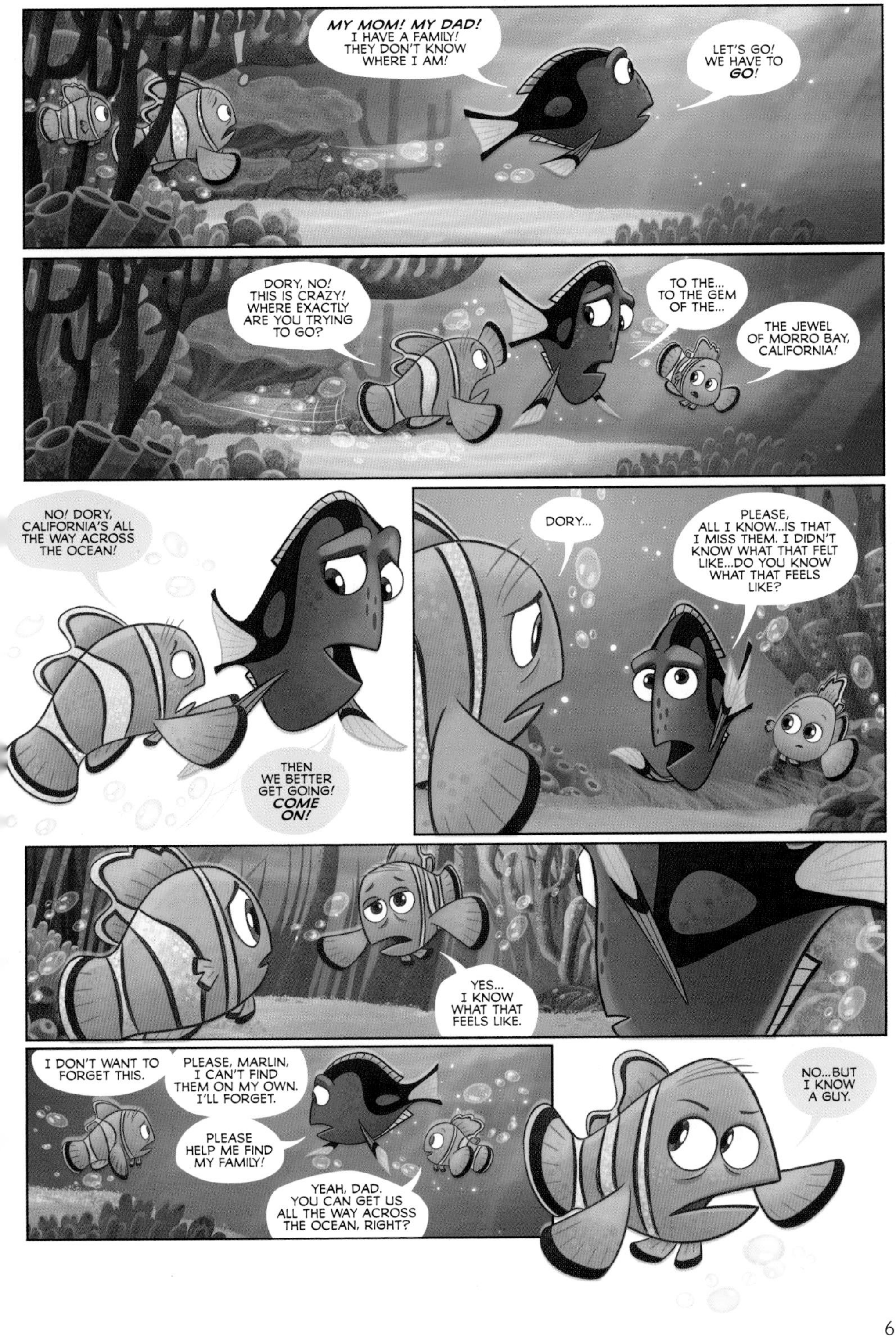
MY MOM! MY DAD! I HAVE A FAMILY! THEY DON'T KNOW WHERE I AM!
LET'S GO! WE HAVE TO GO!
DORY, NO! THIS IS CRAZY! WHERE EXACTLY ARE YOU TRYING TO GO?
TO THE... TO THE GEM OF THE...
THE JEWEL OF MORRO BAY, CALIFORNIA!
NO! DORY, CALIFORNIA'S ALL THE WAY ACROSS THE OCEAN!
THEN WE BETTER GET GOING! COME ON!
DORY...
PLEASE, ALL I KNOW...IS THAT I MISS THEM. I DIDN'T KNOW WHAT THAT FELT LIKE...DO YOU KNOW WHAT THAT FEELS LIKE?
YES... I KNOW WHAT THAT FEELS LIKE.
I DON'T WANT TO FORGET THIS.
PLEASE, MARLIN, I CAN'T FIND THEM ON MY OWN. I'LL FORGET.
PLEASE HELP ME FIND MY FAMILY!
YEAH, DAD. YOU CAN GET US ALL THE WAY ACROSS THE OCEAN, RIGHT?
NO...BUT I KNOW A GUY.

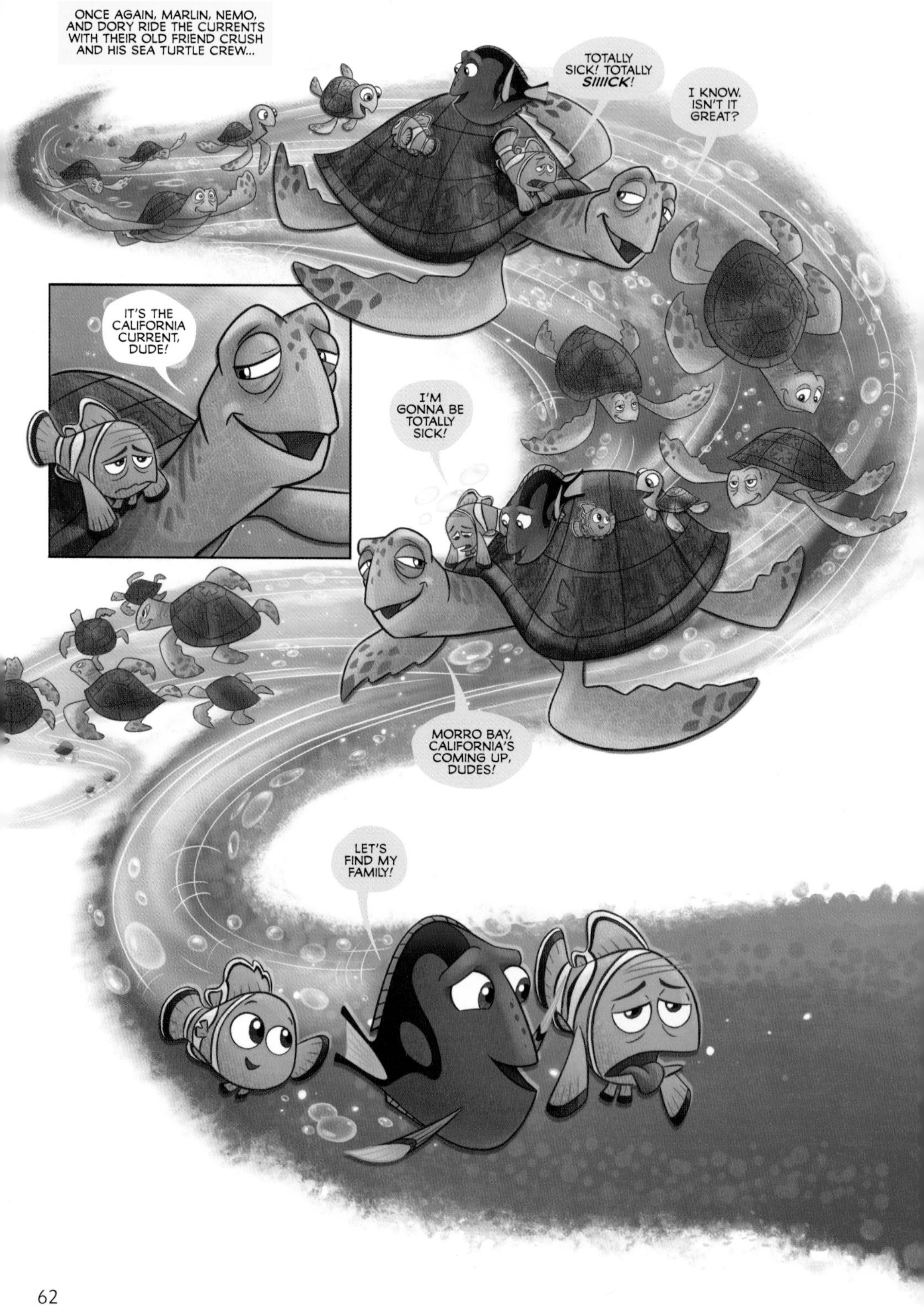
ONCE AGAIN, MARLIN, NEMO, AND DORY RIDE THE CURRENTS WITH THEIR OLD FRIEND CRUSH AND HIS SEA TURTLE CREW...
TOTALLY SICK! TOTALLY SIIIICK!
I KNOW. ISN'T IT GREAT?
IT'S THE CALIFORNIA CURRENT, DUDE!
I'M GONNA BE TOTALLY SICK!
MORRO BAY, CALIFORNIA'S COMING UP, DUDES!
LET'S FIND MY FAMILY!

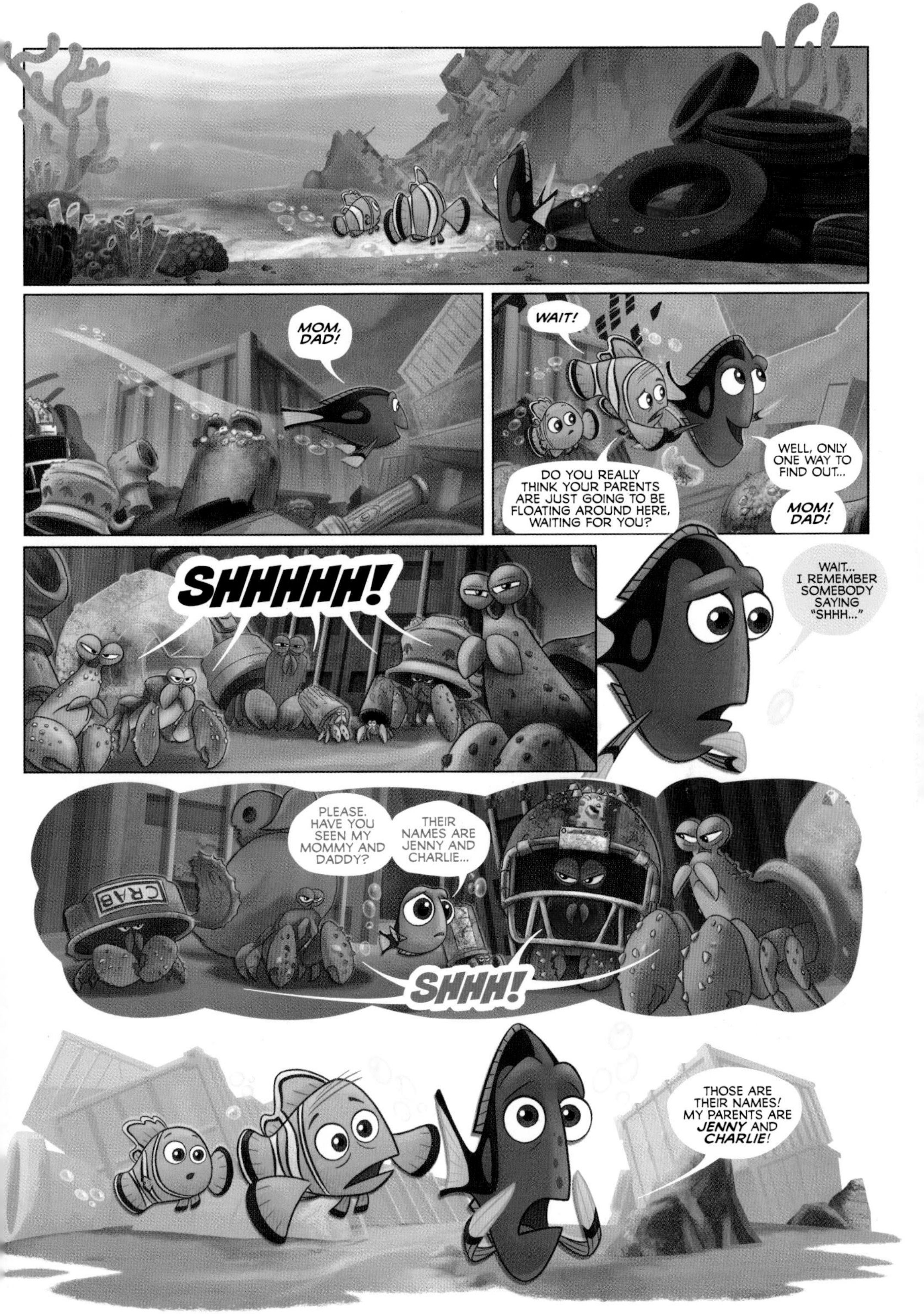

MOM, DAD!
WAIT!
DO YOU REALLY THINK YOUR PARENTS ARE JUST GOING TO BE FLOATING AROUND HERE, WAITING FOR YOU?
WELL, ONLY ONE WAY TO FIND OUT...
MOM! DAD!
SHHHHH!
WAIT... I REMEMBER SOMEBODY SAYING "SHHH..."
PLEASE. HAVE YOU SEEN MY MOMMY AND DADDY?
THEIR NAMES ARE JENNY AND CHARLIE...
CRAB
SHHH!
THOSE ARE THEIR NAMES! MY PARENTS ARE *JENNY* AND *CHARLIE*!

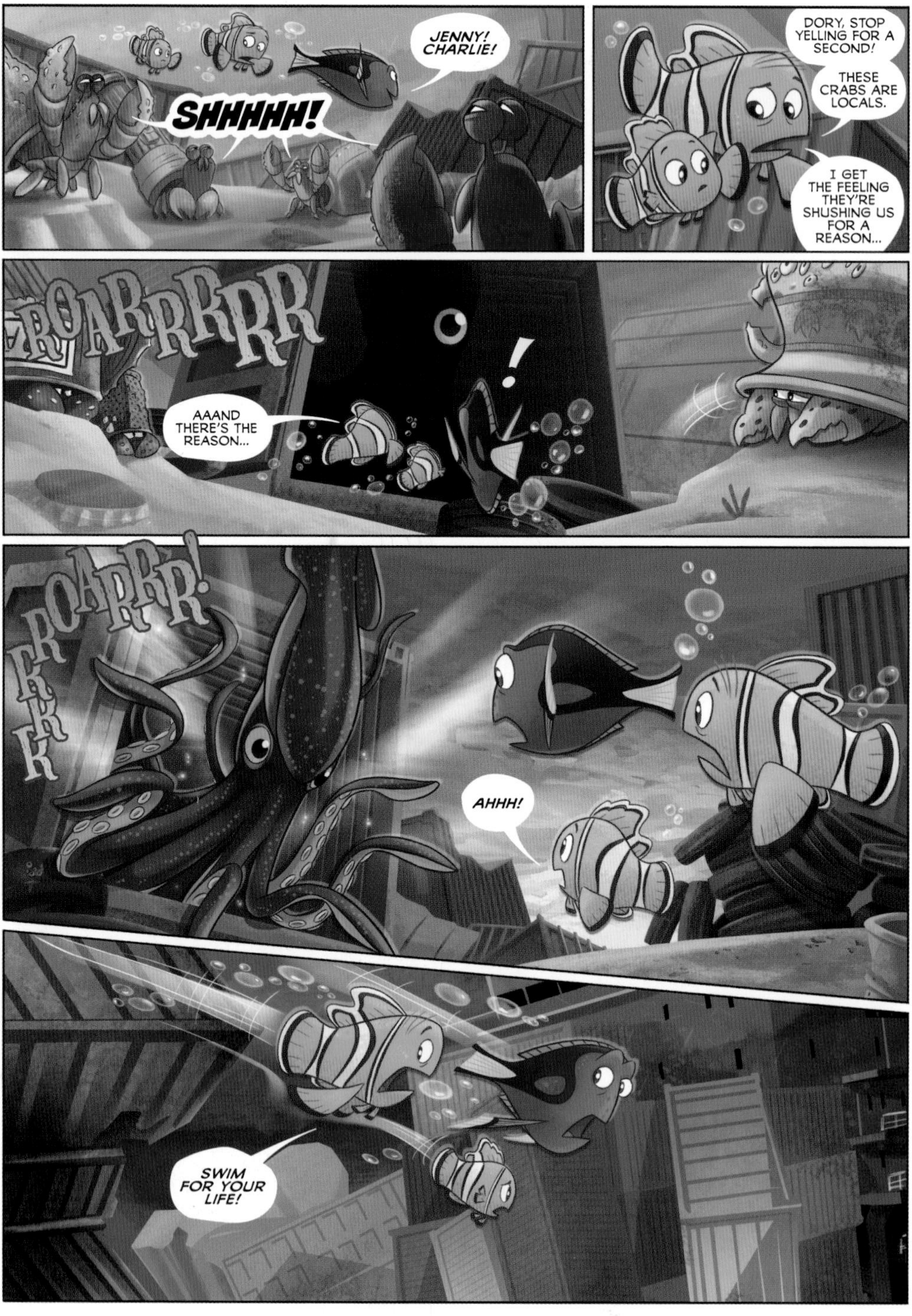
JENNY! CHARLIE!
SHHHHH!
DORY, STOP YELLING FOR A SECOND!
THESE CRABS ARE LOCALS.
I GET THE FEELING THEY'RE SHUSHING US FOR A REASON...
ROARRRRR
!
AAAND THERE'S THE REASON...
ROARRR!
RRRR
AHHH!
SWIM FOR YOUR LIFE!

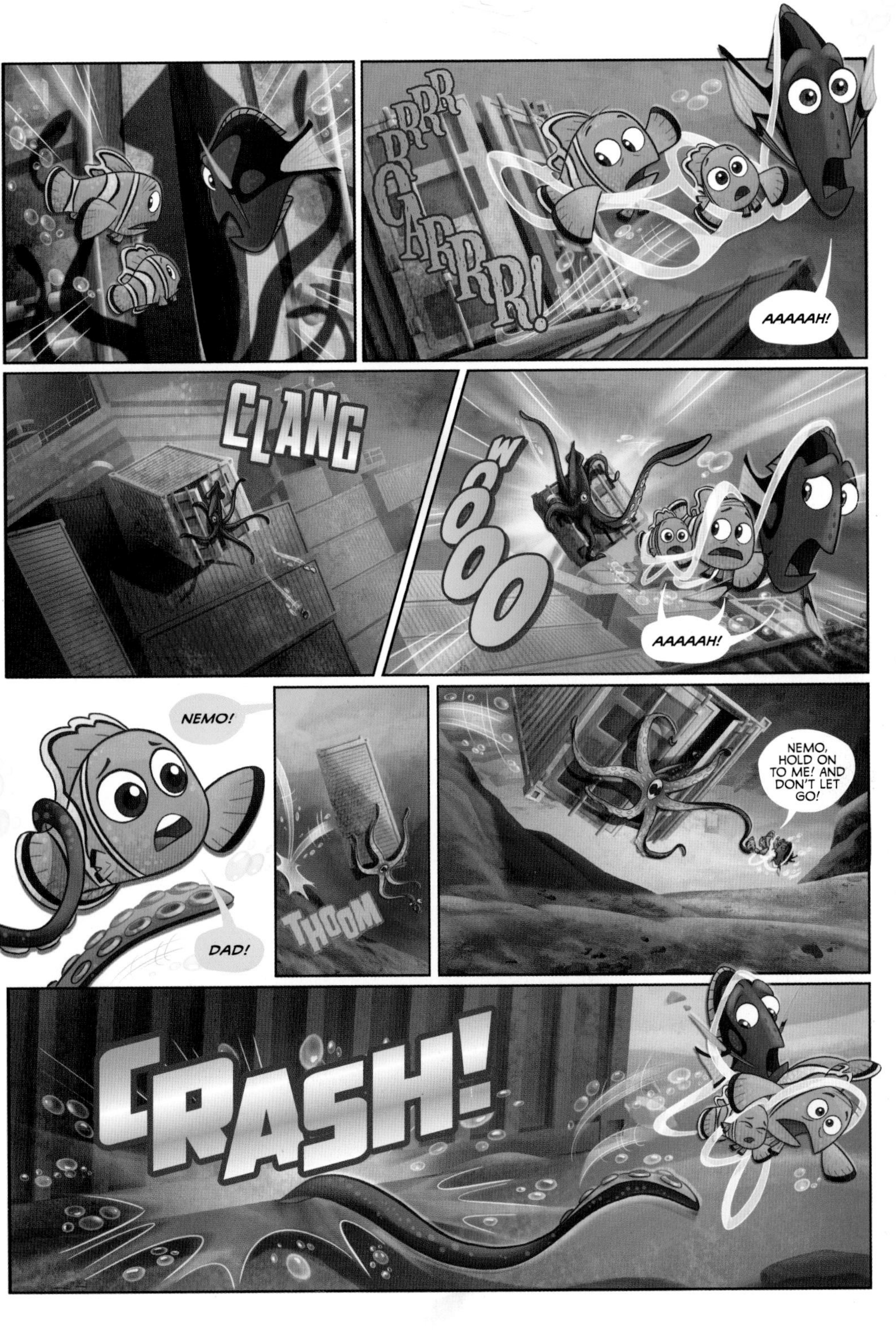

RRRRGARRRR!
AAAAAH!
CLANG
WOOOO
AAAAAH!
NEMO!
DAD!
THOOM
NEMO, HOLD ON TO ME! AND DON'T LET GO!
CRASH!

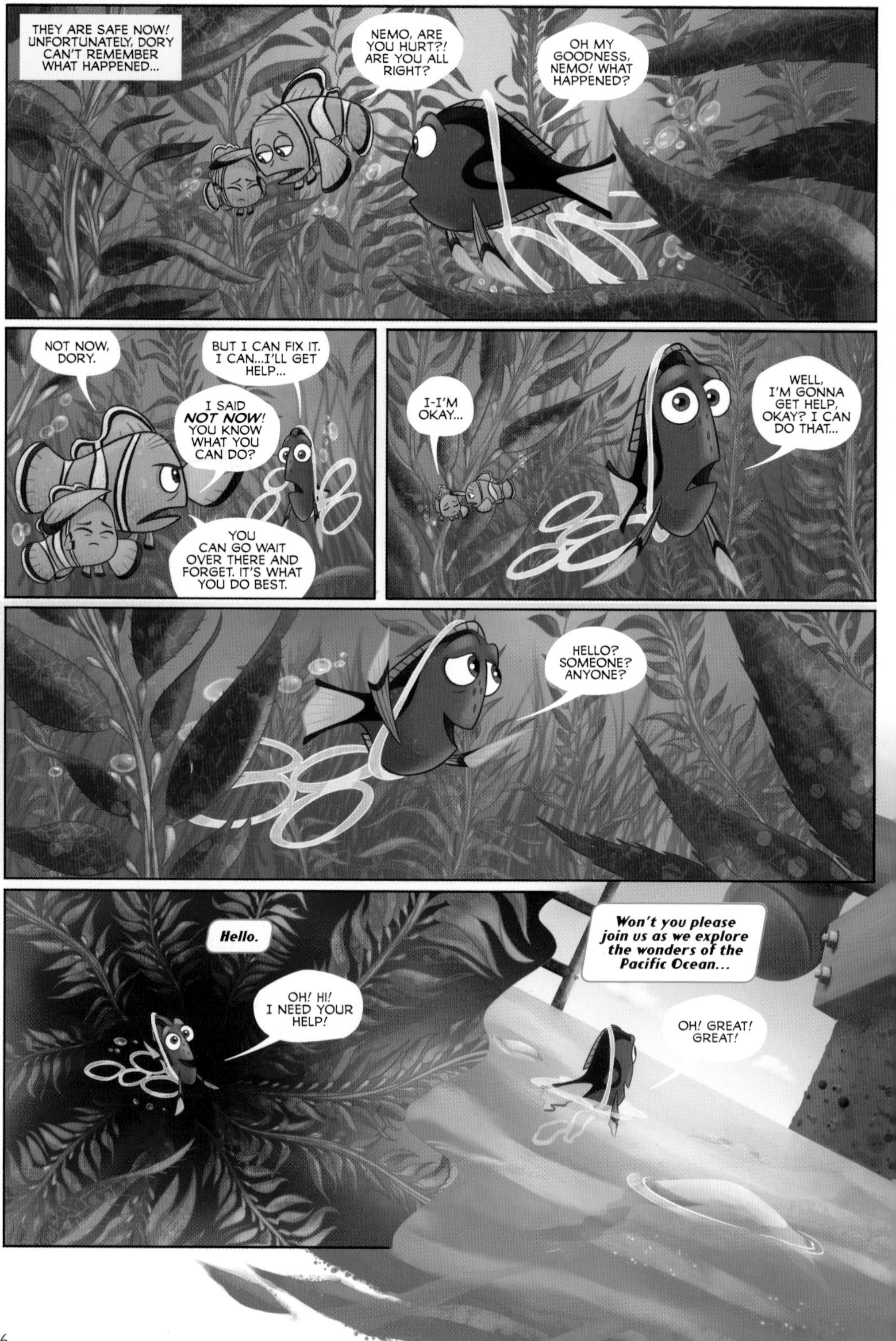
THEY ARE SAFE NOW! UNFORTUNATELY, DORY CAN'T REMEMBER WHAT HAPPENED...
NEMO, ARE YOU HURT?! ARE YOU ALL RIGHT?
OH MY GOODNESS, NEMO! WHAT HAPPENED?
NOT NOW, DORY.
BUT I CAN FIX IT. I CAN...I'LL GET HELP...
I SAID ***NOT NOW***! YOU KNOW WHAT YOU CAN DO?
YOU CAN GO WAIT OVER THERE AND FORGET. IT'S WHAT YOU DO BEST.
I-I'M OKAY...
WELL, I'M GONNA GET HELP, OKAY? I CAN DO THAT...
HELLO? SOMEONE? ANYONE?
Hello.
Won't you please join us as we explore the wonders of the Pacific Ocean...
OH! HI! I NEED YOUR HELP!
OH! GREAT! GREAT!

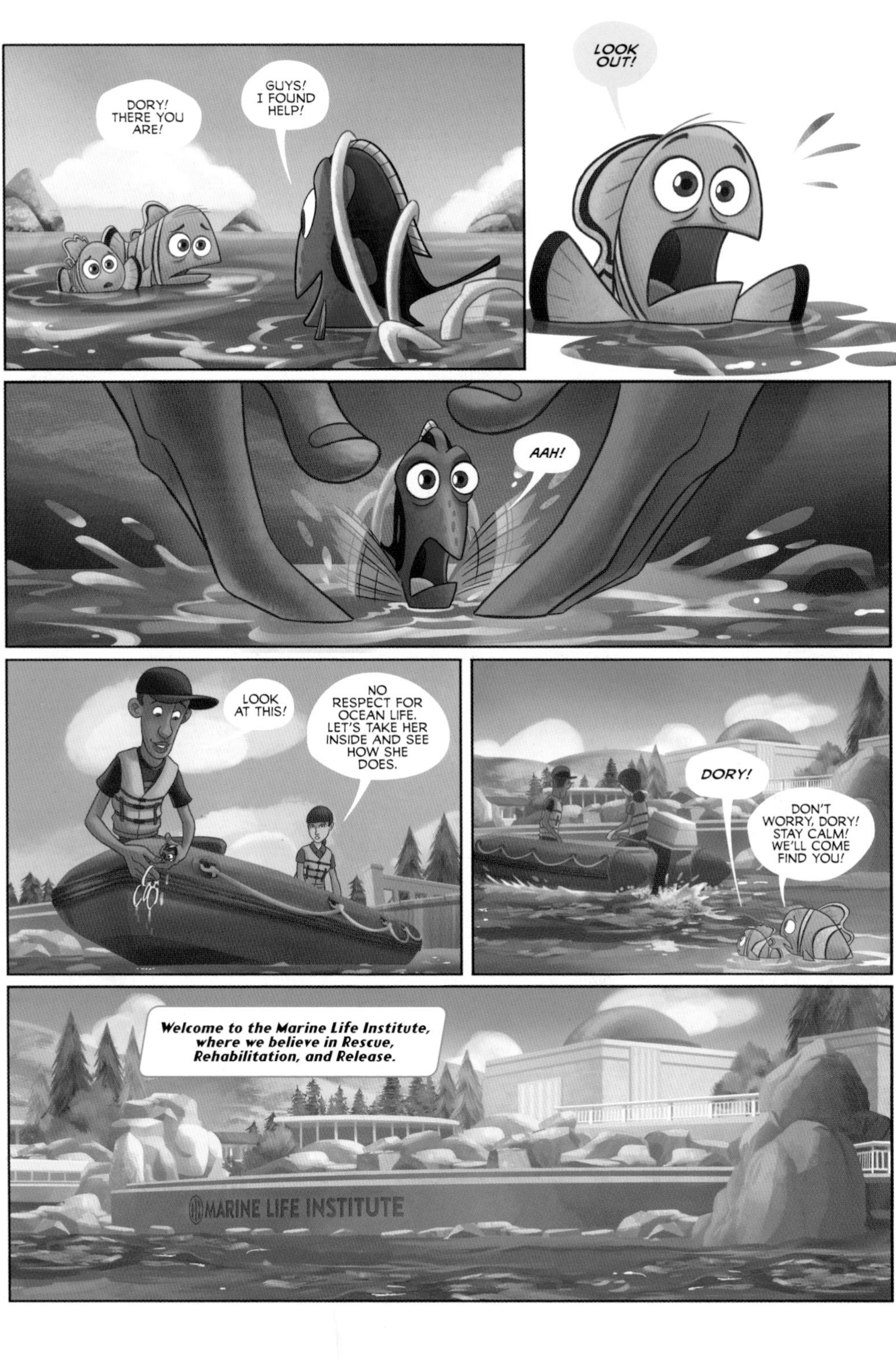
DORY! THERE YOU ARE!
GUYS! I FOUND HELP!
LOOK OUT!
AAH!
LOOK AT THIS!
NO RESPECT FOR OCEAN LIFE. LET'S TAKE HER INSIDE AND SEE HOW SHE DOES.
DORY!
DON'T WORRY, DORY! STAY CALM! WE'LL COME FIND YOU!
Welcome to the Marine Life Institute, where we believe in Rescue, Rehabilitation, and Release.
MARINE LIFE INSTITUTE

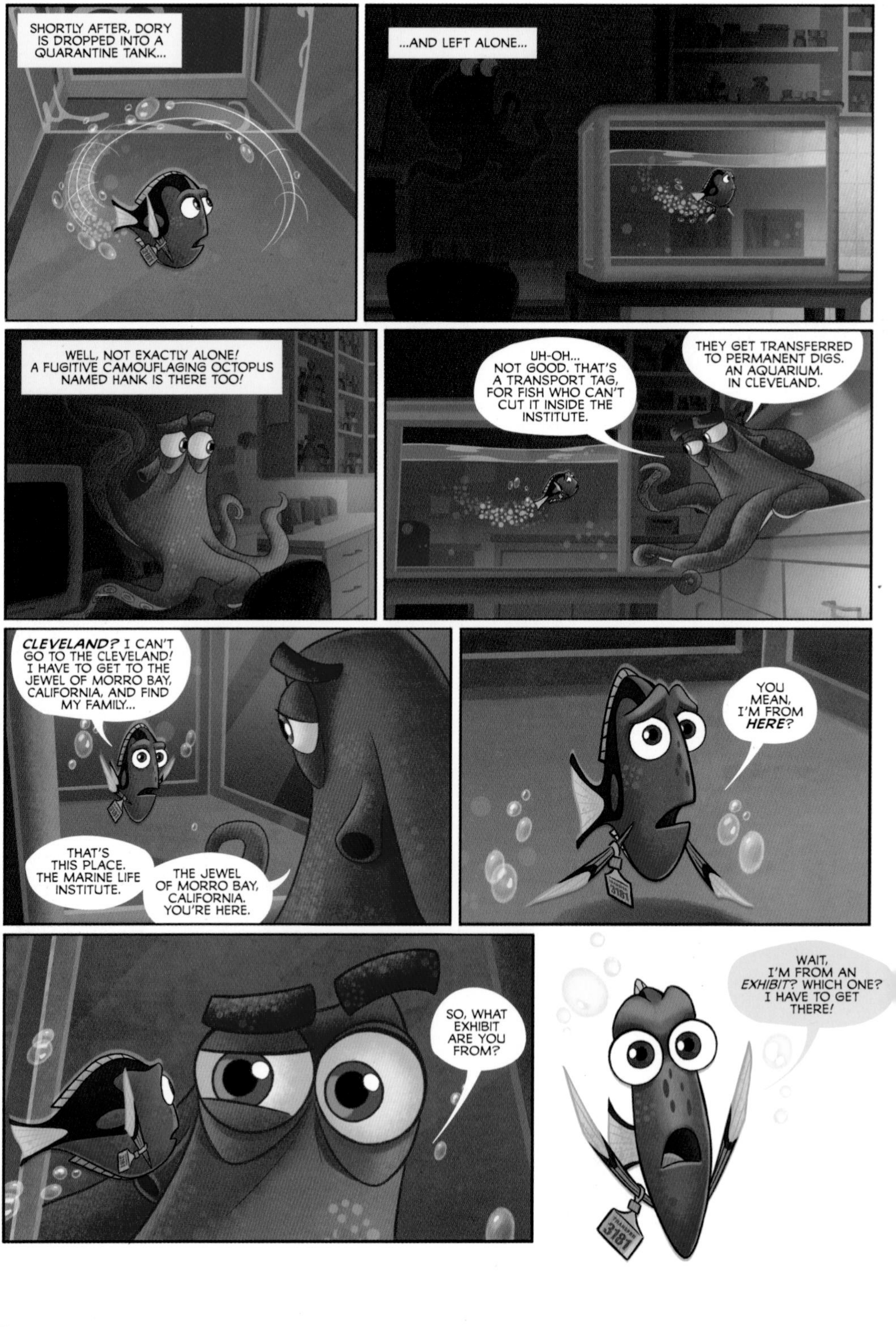
SHORTLY AFTER, DORY IS DROPPED INTO A QUARANTINE TANK...
...AND LEFT ALONE...
WELL, NOT EXACTLY ALONE! A FUGITIVE CAMOUFLAGING OCTOPUS NAMED HANK IS THERE TOO!
UH-OH... NOT GOOD. THAT'S A TRANSPORT TAG, FOR FISH WHO CAN'T CUT IT INSIDE THE INSTITUTE.
THEY GET TRANSFERRED TO PERMANENT DIGS. AN AQUARIUM. IN CLEVELAND.
CLEVELAND? I CAN'T GO TO THE CLEVELAND! I HAVE TO GET TO THE JEWEL OF MORRO BAY, CALIFORNIA, AND FIND MY FAMILY...
THAT'S THIS PLACE. THE MARINE LIFE INSTITUTE.
THE JEWEL OF MORRO BAY, CALIFORNIA. YOU'RE HERE.
YOU MEAN, I'M FROM *HERE*?
SO, WHAT EXHIBIT ARE YOU FROM?
WAIT, I'M FROM AN *EXHIBIT*? WHICH ONE? I HAVE TO GET THERE!
3181

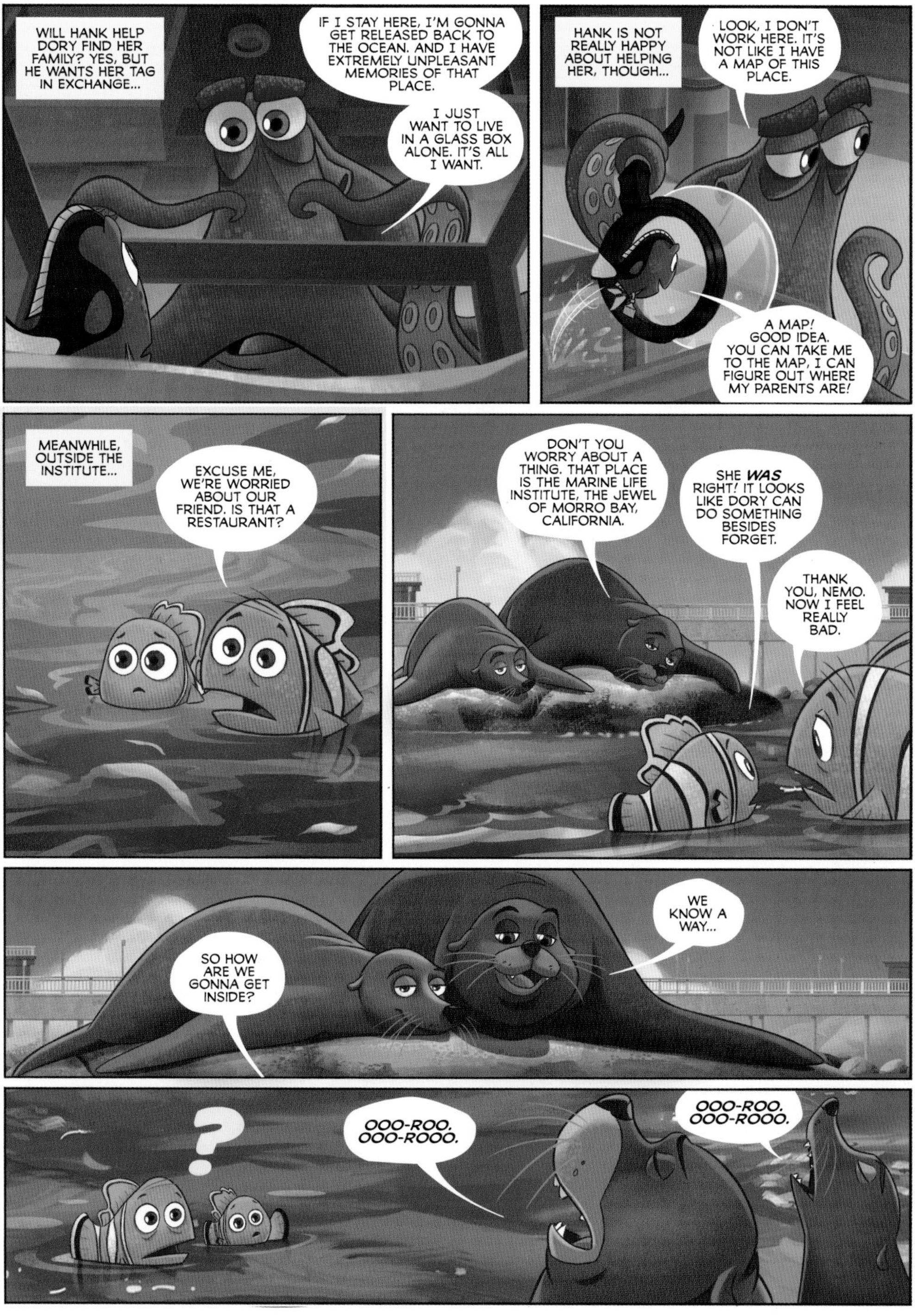
WILL HANK HELP DORY FIND HER FAMILY? YES, BUT HE WANTS HER TAG IN EXCHANGE...
IF I STAY HERE, I'M GONNA GET RELEASED BACK TO THE OCEAN. AND I HAVE EXTREMELY UNPLEASANT MEMORIES OF THAT PLACE.
I JUST WANT TO LIVE IN A GLASS BOX ALONE. IT'S ALL I WANT.
HANK IS NOT REALLY HAPPY ABOUT HELPING HER, THOUGH...
LOOK, I DON'T WORK HERE. IT'S NOT LIKE I HAVE A MAP OF THIS PLACE.
A MAP! GOOD IDEA. YOU CAN TAKE ME TO THE MAP, I CAN FIGURE OUT WHERE MY PARENTS ARE!
MEANWHILE, OUTSIDE THE INSTITUTE...
EXCUSE ME, WE'RE WORRIED ABOUT OUR FRIEND. IS THAT A RESTAURANT?
DON'T YOU WORRY ABOUT A THING. THAT PLACE IS THE MARINE LIFE INSTITUTE, THE JEWEL OF MORRO BAY, CALIFORNIA.
SHE *WAS* RIGHT! IT LOOKS LIKE DORY CAN DO SOMETHING BESIDES FORGET.
THANK YOU, NEMO. NOW I FEEL REALLY BAD.
SO HOW ARE WE GONNA GET INSIDE?
WE KNOW A WAY...
?
OOO-ROO. OOO-ROOO.
OOO-ROO. OOO-ROOO.

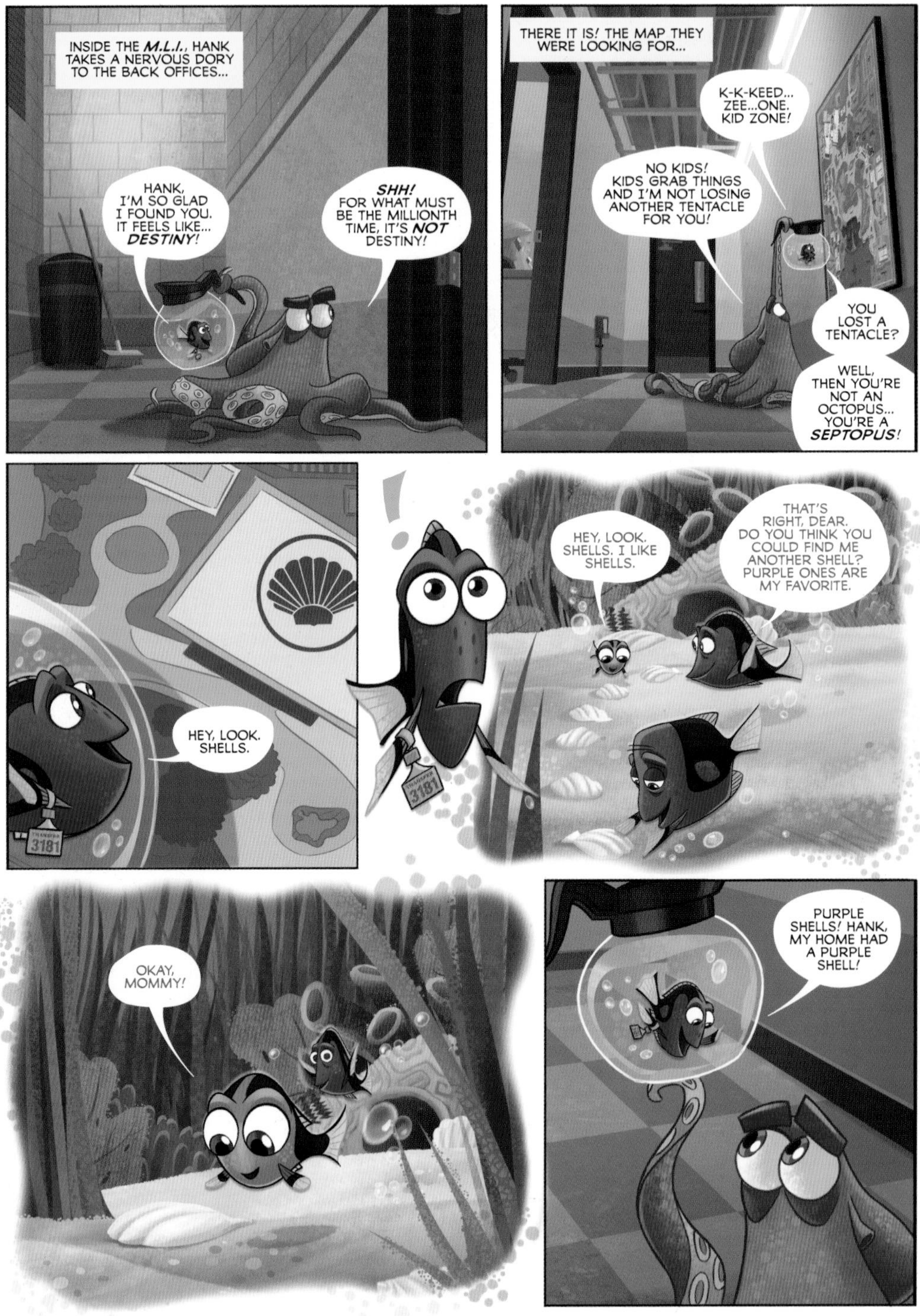
INSIDE THE *M.L.I.*, HANK TAKES A NERVOUS DORY TO THE BACK OFFICES...
HANK, I'M SO GLAD I FOUND YOU. IT FEELS LIKE... ***DESTINY***!
SHH! FOR WHAT MUST BE THE MILLIONTH TIME, IT'S ***NOT*** DESTINY!
THERE IT IS! THE MAP THEY WERE LOOKING FOR...
K-K-KEED... ZEE...ONE. KID ZONE!
NO KIDS! KIDS GRAB THINGS AND I'M NOT LOSING ANOTHER TENTACLE FOR YOU!
YOU LOST A TENTACLE?
WELL, THEN YOU'RE NOT AN OCTOPUS... YOU'RE A ***SEPTOPUS***!
HEY, LOOK. SHELLS.
HEY, LOOK. SHELLS. I LIKE SHELLS.
THAT'S RIGHT, DEAR. DO YOU THINK YOU COULD FIND ME ANOTHER SHELL? PURPLE ONES ARE MY FAVORITE.
OKAY, MOMMY!
PURPLE SHELLS! HANK, MY HOME HAD A PURPLE SHELL!

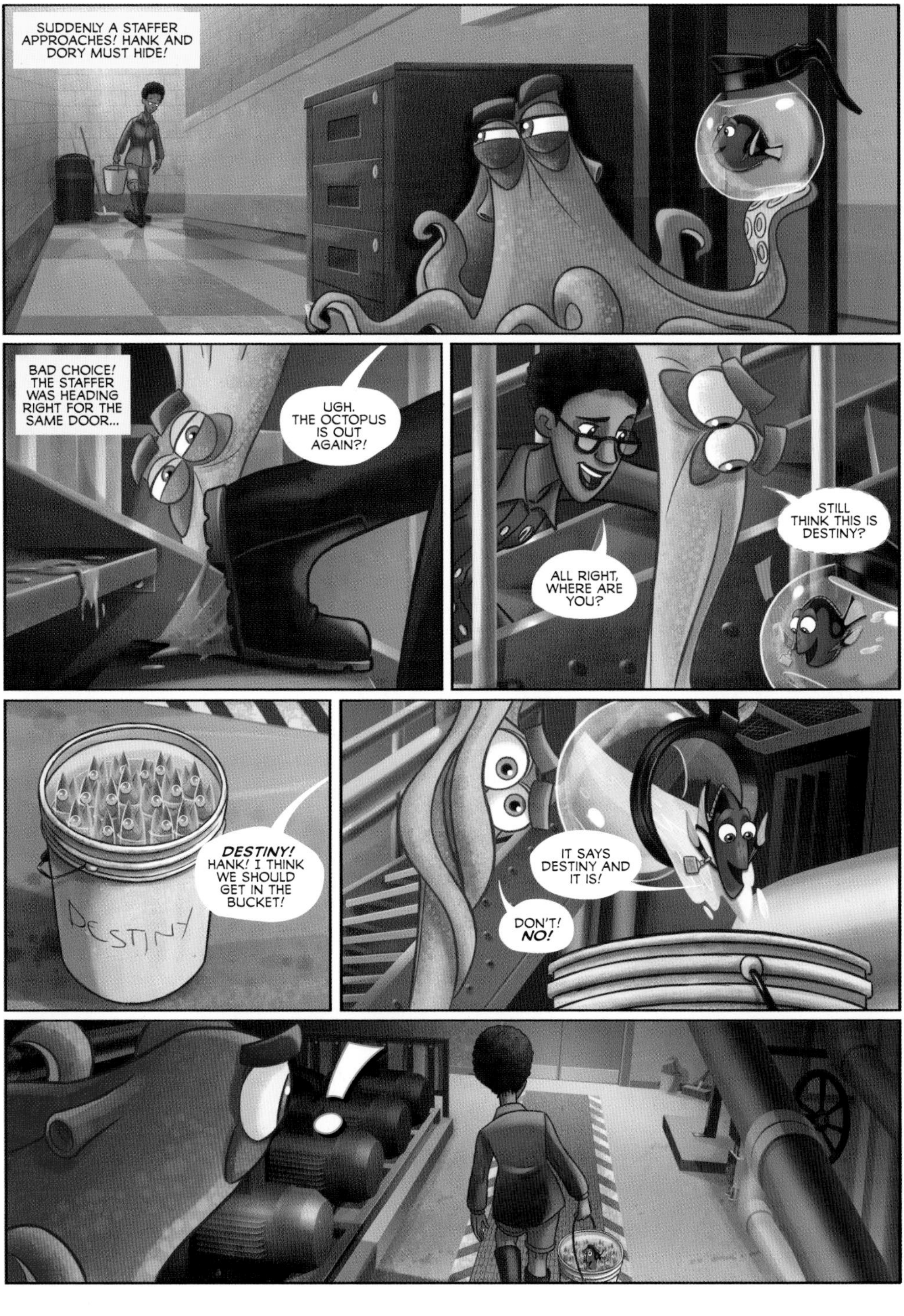
SUDDENLY A STAFFER APPROACHES! HANK AND DORY MUST HIDE!
BAD CHOICE! THE STAFFER WAS HEADING RIGHT FOR THE SAME DOOR...
UGH. THE OCTOPUS IS OUT AGAIN?!
ALL RIGHT, WHERE ARE YOU?
STILL THINK THIS IS DESTINY?
DESTINY! HANK! I THINK WE SHOULD GET IN THE BUCKET!
DESTINY
IT SAYS DESTINY AND IT IS!
DON'T! NO!
!

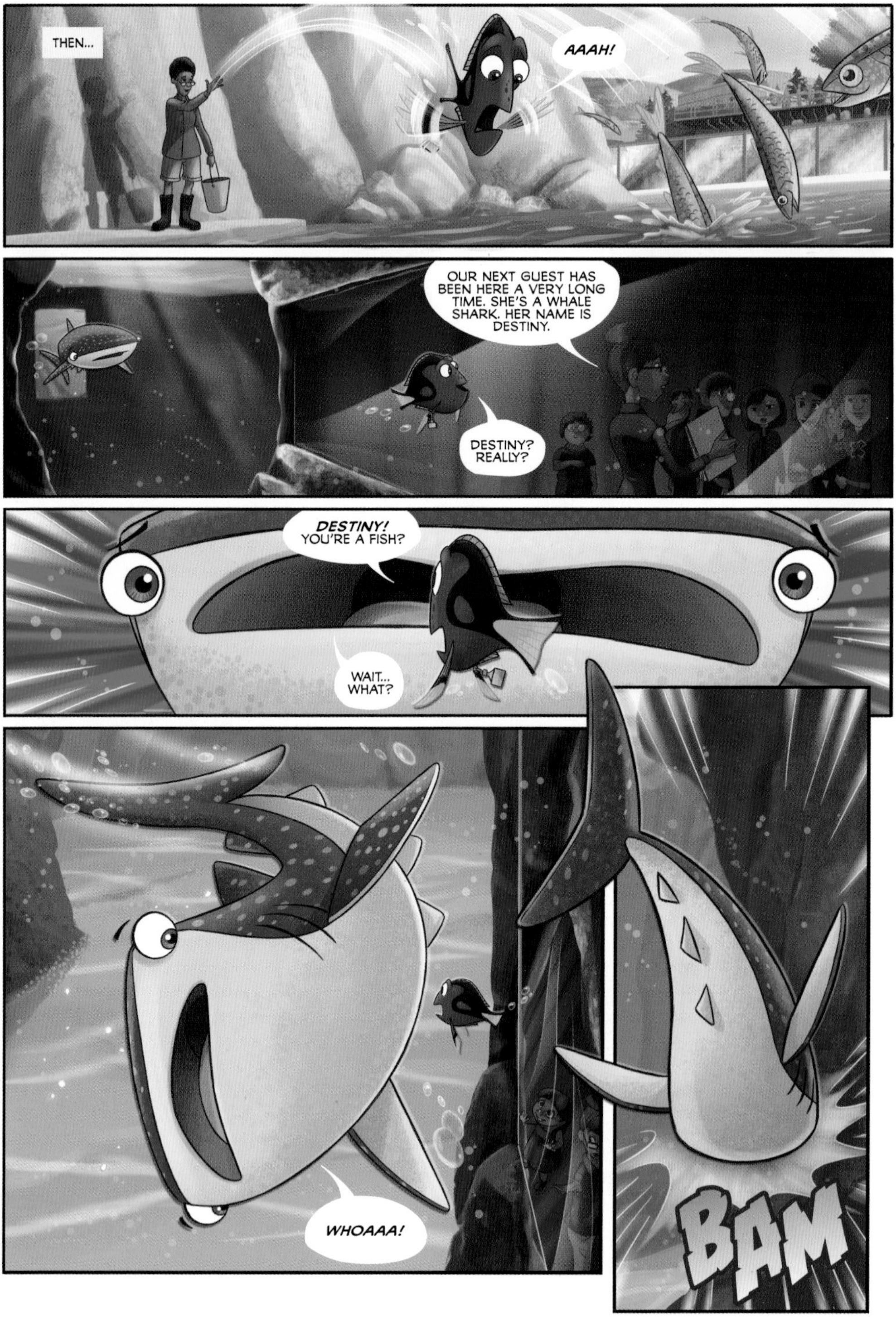
THEN...
AAAH!
OUR NEXT GUEST HAS BEEN HERE A VERY LONG TIME. SHE'S A WHALE SHARK. HER NAME IS DESTINY.
DESTINY? REALLY?
DESTINY! YOU'RE A FISH?
WAIT... WHAT?
WHOAAA!
BAM

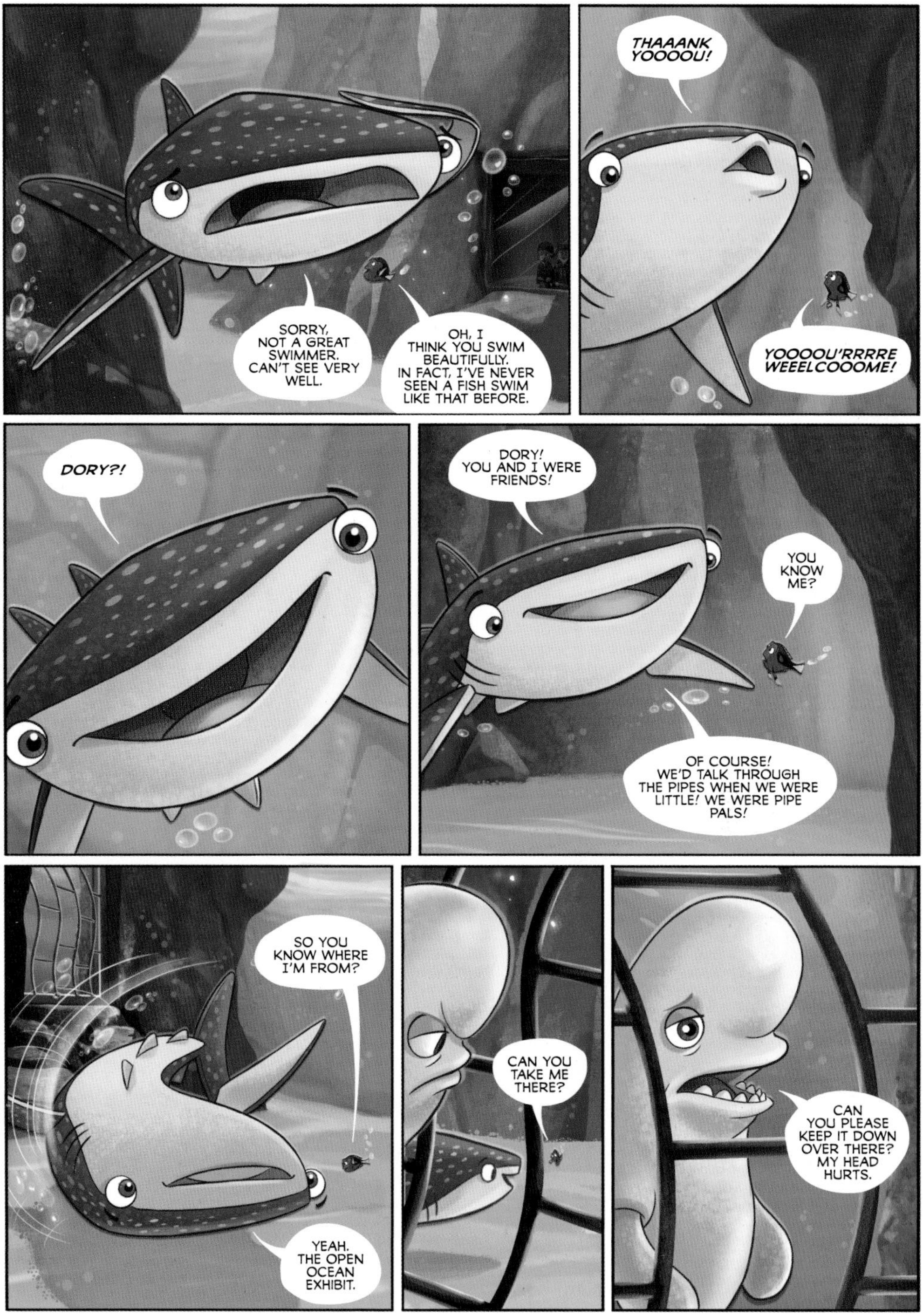
SORRY, NOT A GREAT SWIMMER. CAN'T SEE VERY WELL.
OH, I THINK YOU SWIM BEAUTIFULLY. IN FACT, I'VE NEVER SEEN A FISH SWIM LIKE THAT BEFORE.
THAAANK YOOOOU!
YOOOOU'RRRRE WEEELCOOOME!
DORY?!
DORY! YOU AND I WERE FRIENDS!
YOU KNOW ME?
OF COURSE! WE'D TALK THROUGH THE PIPES WHEN WE WERE LITTLE! WE WERE PIPE PALS!
SO YOU KNOW WHERE I'M FROM?
YEAH. THE OPEN OCEAN EXHIBIT.
CAN YOU TAKE ME THERE?
CAN YOU PLEASE KEEP IT DOWN OVER THERE? MY HEAD HURTS.

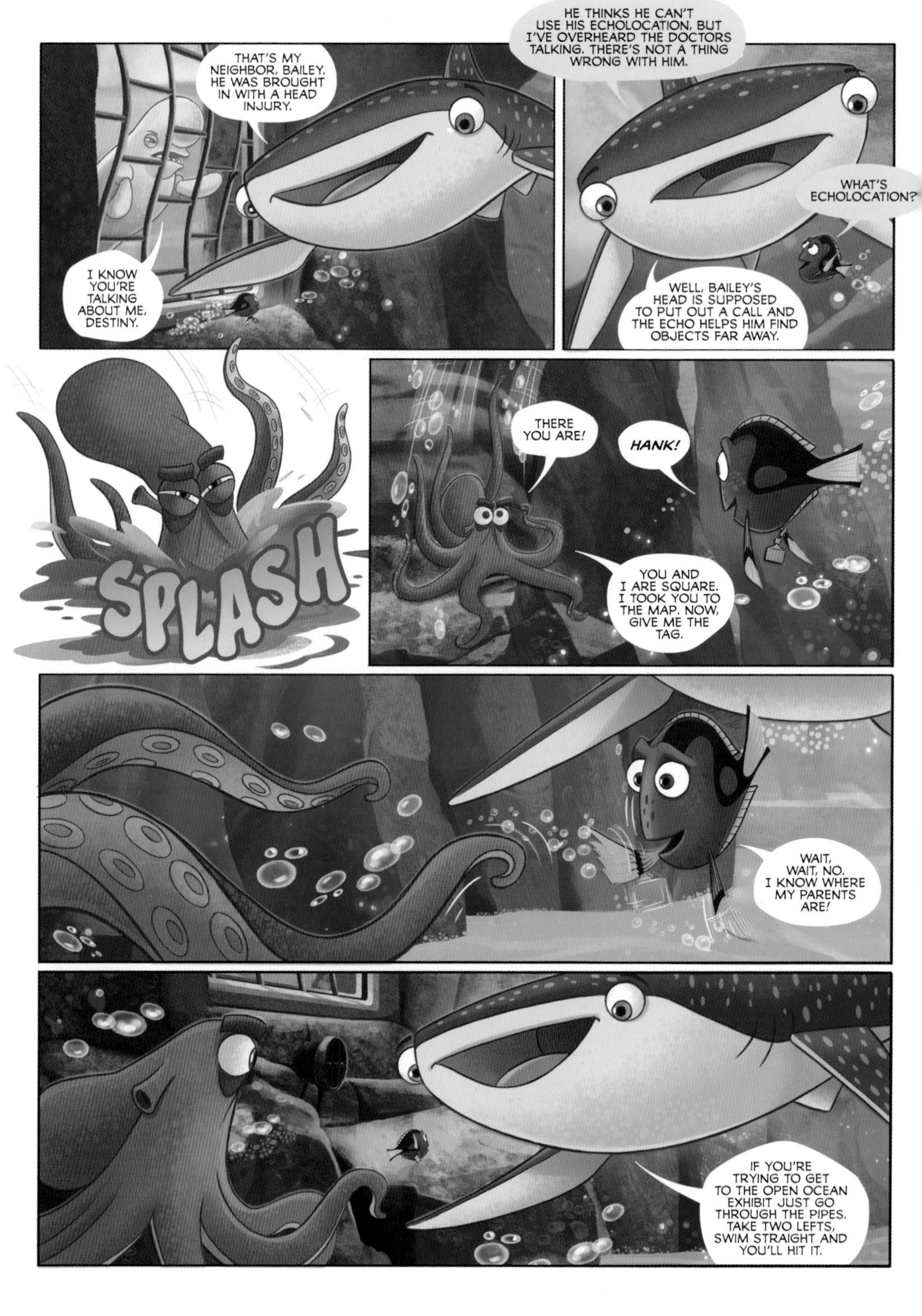
THAT'S MY NEIGHBOR, BAILEY. HE WAS BROUGHT IN WITH A HEAD INJURY.
I KNOW YOU'RE TALKING ABOUT ME, DESTINY.
HE THINKS HE CAN'T USE HIS ECHOLOCATION, BUT I'VE OVERHEARD THE DOCTORS TALKING. THERE'S NOT A THING WRONG WITH HIM.
WHAT'S ECHOLOCATION?
WELL, BAILEY'S HEAD IS SUPPOSED TO PUT OUT A CALL AND THE ECHO HELPS HIM FIND OBJECTS FAR AWAY.
SPLASH
THERE YOU ARE!
HANK!
YOU AND I ARE SQUARE. I TOOK YOU TO THE MAP. NOW, GIVE ME THE TAG.
WAIT, WAIT, NO. I KNOW WHERE MY PARENTS ARE!
IF YOU'RE TRYING TO GET TO THE OPEN OCEAN EXHIBIT JUST GO THROUGH THE PIPES. TAKE TWO LEFTS, SWIM STRAIGHT AND YOU'LL HIT IT.

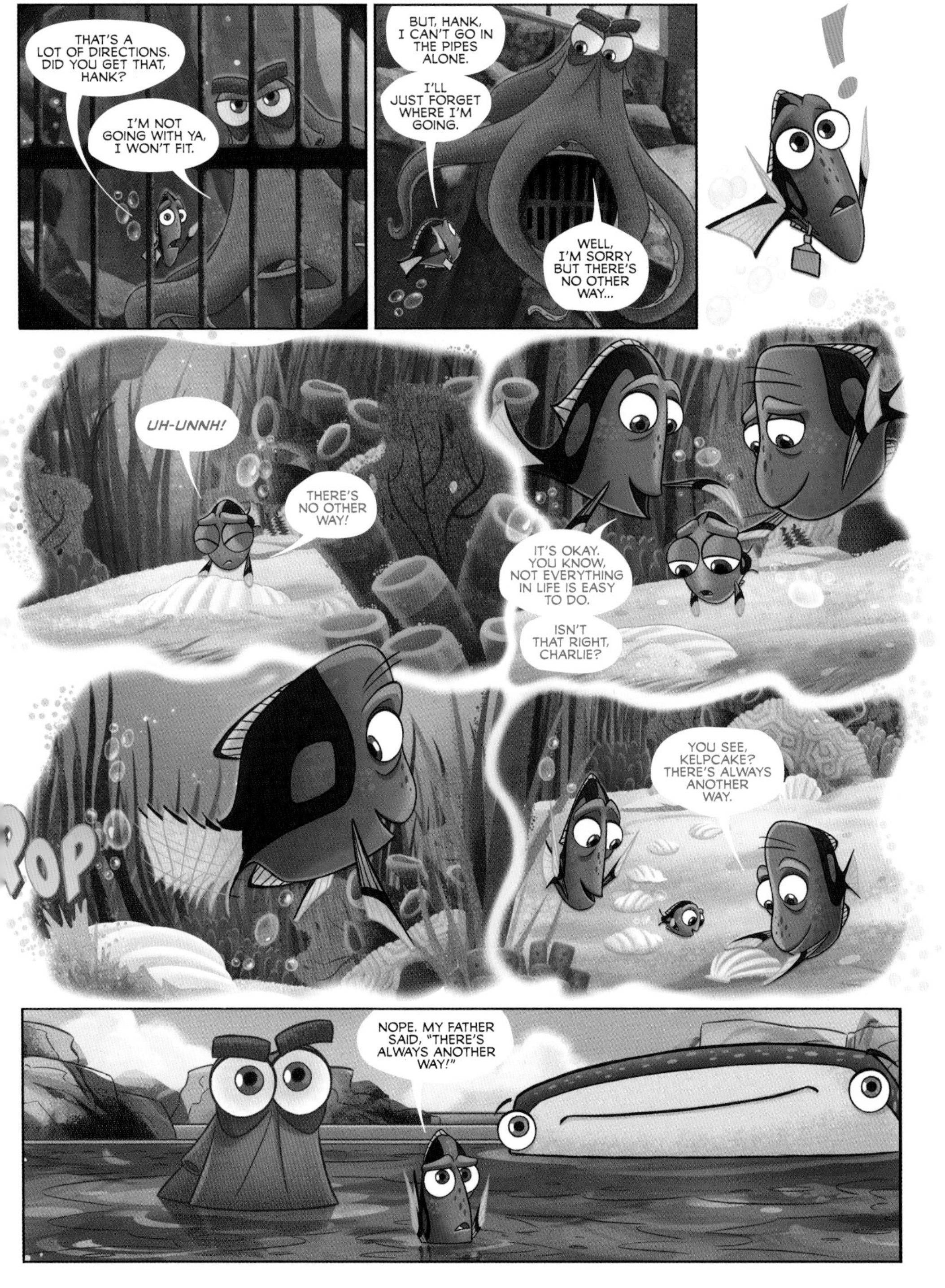
THAT'S A LOT OF DIRECTIONS. DID YOU GET THAT, HANK?
I'M NOT GOING WITH YA, I WON'T FIT.
BUT, HANK, I CAN'T GO IN THE PIPES ALONE.
I'LL JUST FORGET WHERE I'M GOING.
WELL, I'M SORRY BUT THERE'S NO OTHER WAY...
!
UH-UNNH!
THERE'S NO OTHER WAY!
IT'S OKAY. YOU KNOW, NOT EVERYTHING IN LIFE IS EASY TO DO.
ISN'T THAT RIGHT, CHARLIE?
POP
YOU SEE, KELPCAKE? THERE'S ALWAYS ANOTHER WAY.
NOPE. MY FATHER SAID, "THERE'S ALWAYS ANOTHER WAY!"

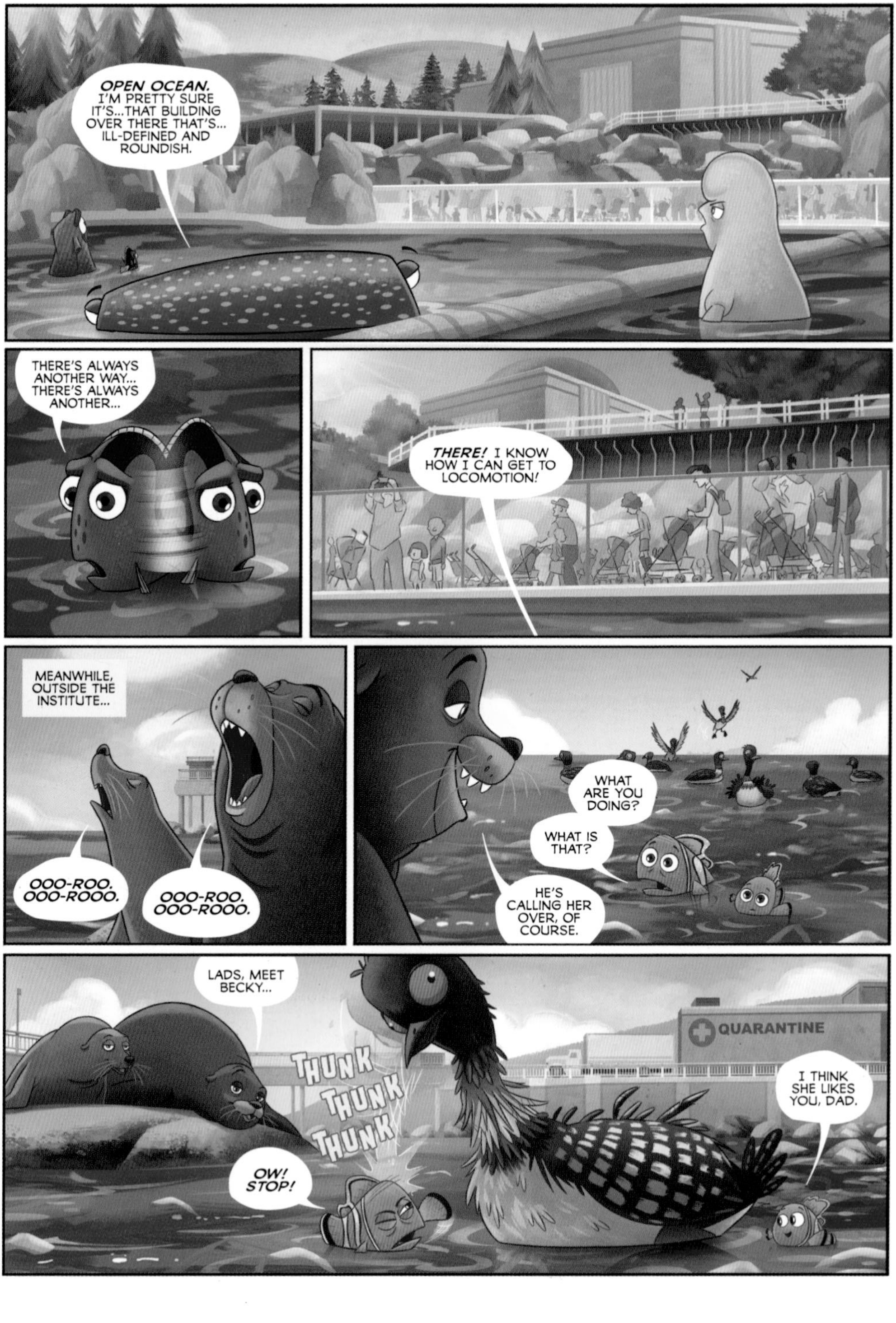
OPEN OCEAN. I'M PRETTY SURE IT'S...THAT BUILDING OVER THERE THAT'S... ILL-DEFINED AND ROUNDISH.
THERE'S ALWAYS ANOTHER WAY... THERE'S ALWAYS ANOTHER...
THERE! I KNOW HOW I CAN GET TO LOCOMOTION!
MEANWHILE, OUTSIDE THE INSTITUTE...
OOO-ROO. OOO-ROOO.
OOO-ROO. OOO-ROOO.
WHAT ARE YOU DOING?
WHAT IS THAT?
HE'S CALLING HER OVER, OF COURSE.
LADS, MEET BECKY...
QUARANTINE
THUNK THUNK THUNK
OW! STOP!
I THINK SHE LIKES YOU, DAD.

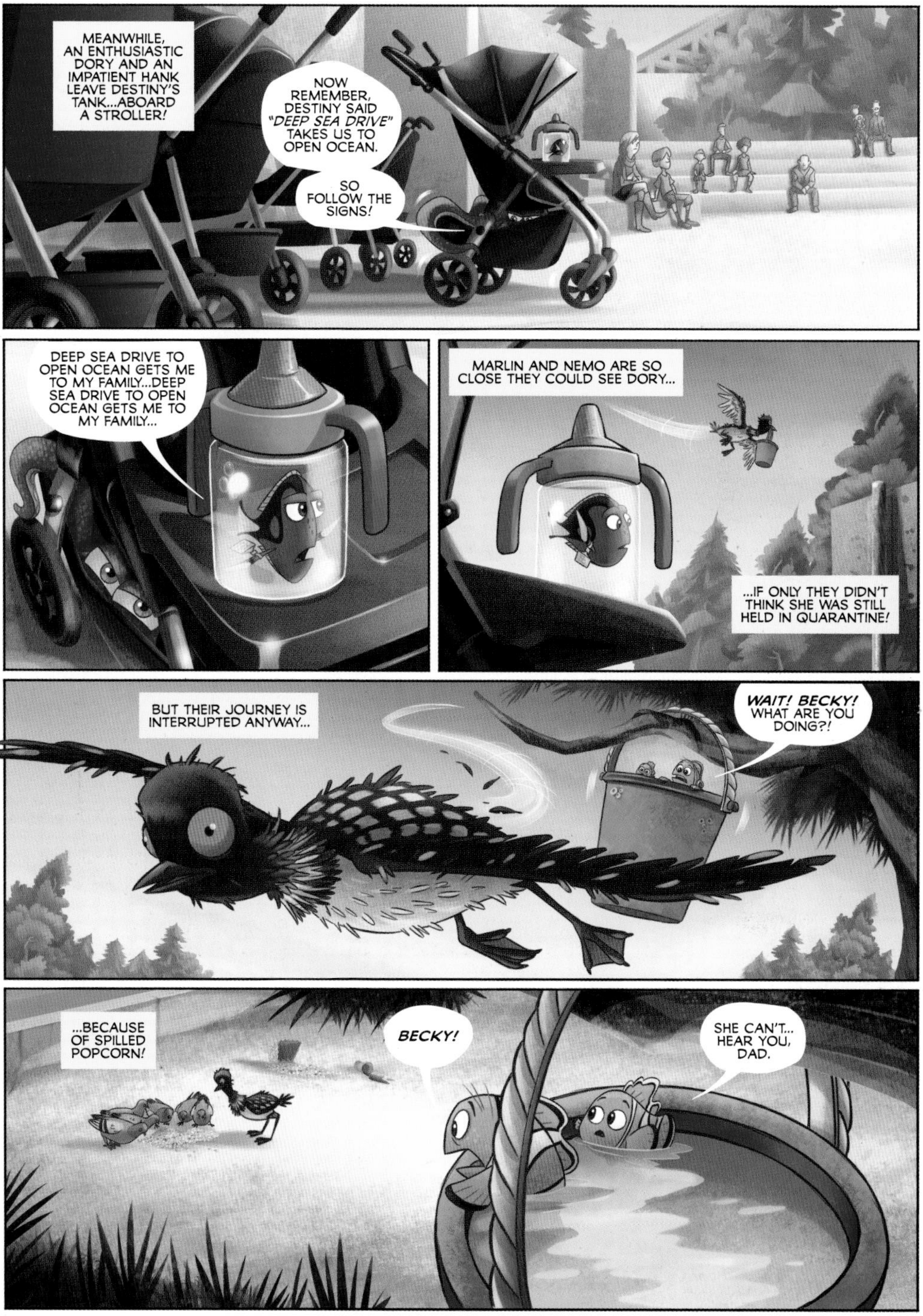
MEANWHILE, AN ENTHUSIASTIC DORY AND AN IMPATIENT HANK LEAVE DESTINY'S TANK...ABOARD A STROLLER!
NOW REMEMBER, DESTINY SAID "*DEEP SEA DRIVE*" TAKES US TO OPEN OCEAN.
SO FOLLOW THE SIGNS!
DEEP SEA DRIVE TO OPEN OCEAN GETS ME TO MY FAMILY...DEEP SEA DRIVE TO OPEN OCEAN GETS ME TO MY FAMILY...
MARLIN AND NEMO ARE SO CLOSE THEY COULD SEE DORY...
...IF ONLY THEY DIDN'T THINK SHE WAS STILL HELD IN QUARANTINE!
BUT THEIR JOURNEY IS INTERRUPTED ANYWAY...
WAIT! BECKY! WHAT ARE YOU DOING?!
...BECAUSE OF SPILLED POPCORN!
BECKY!
SHE CAN'T... HEAR YOU, DAD.

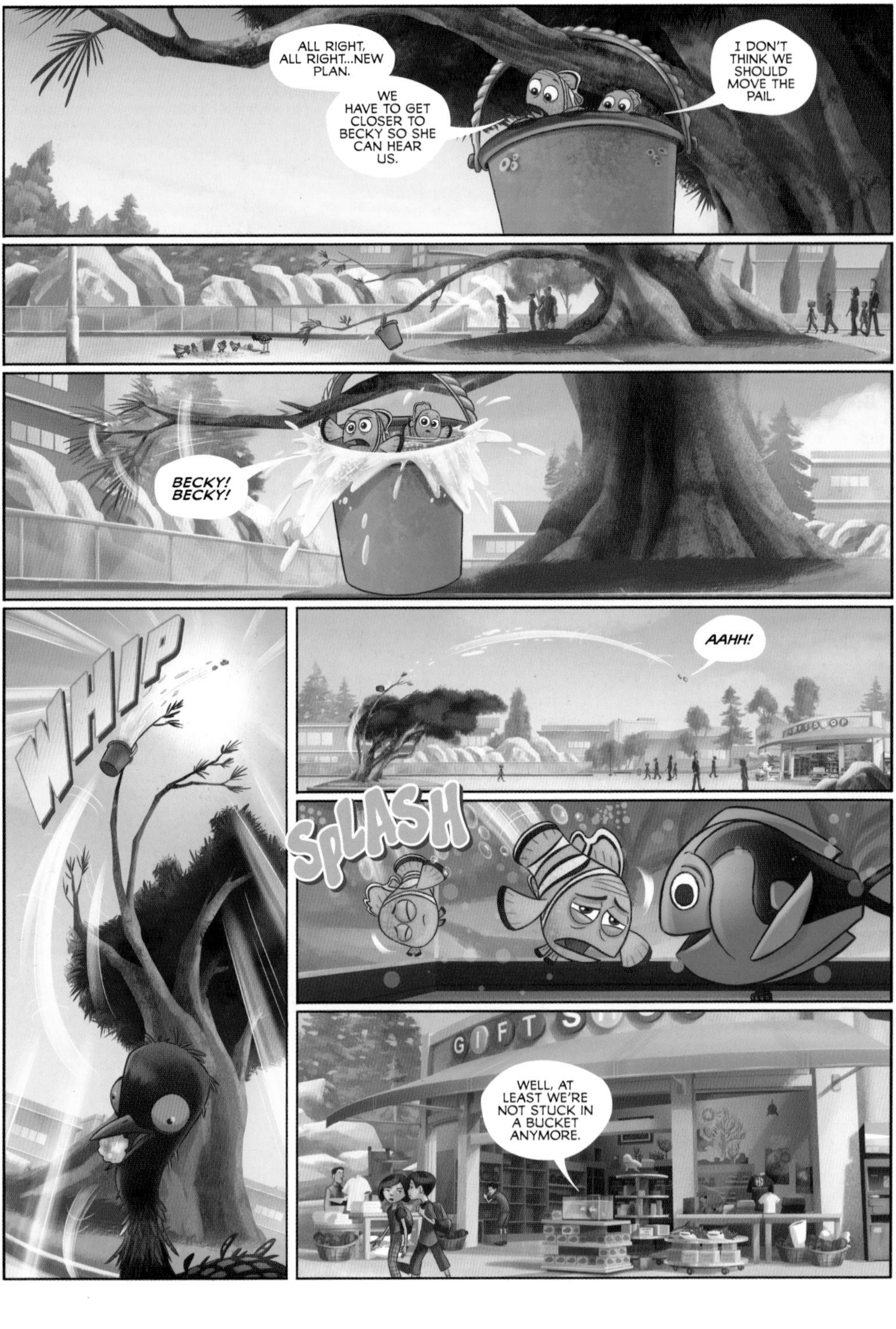
ALL RIGHT, ALL RIGHT...NEW PLAN.
WE HAVE TO GET CLOSER TO BECKY SO SHE CAN HEAR US.
I DON'T THINK WE SHOULD MOVE THE PAIL.
BECKY! BECKY!
WHIP
AAHH!
SPLASH
GIFT
WELL, AT LEAST WE'RE NOT STUCK IN A BUCKET ANYMORE.

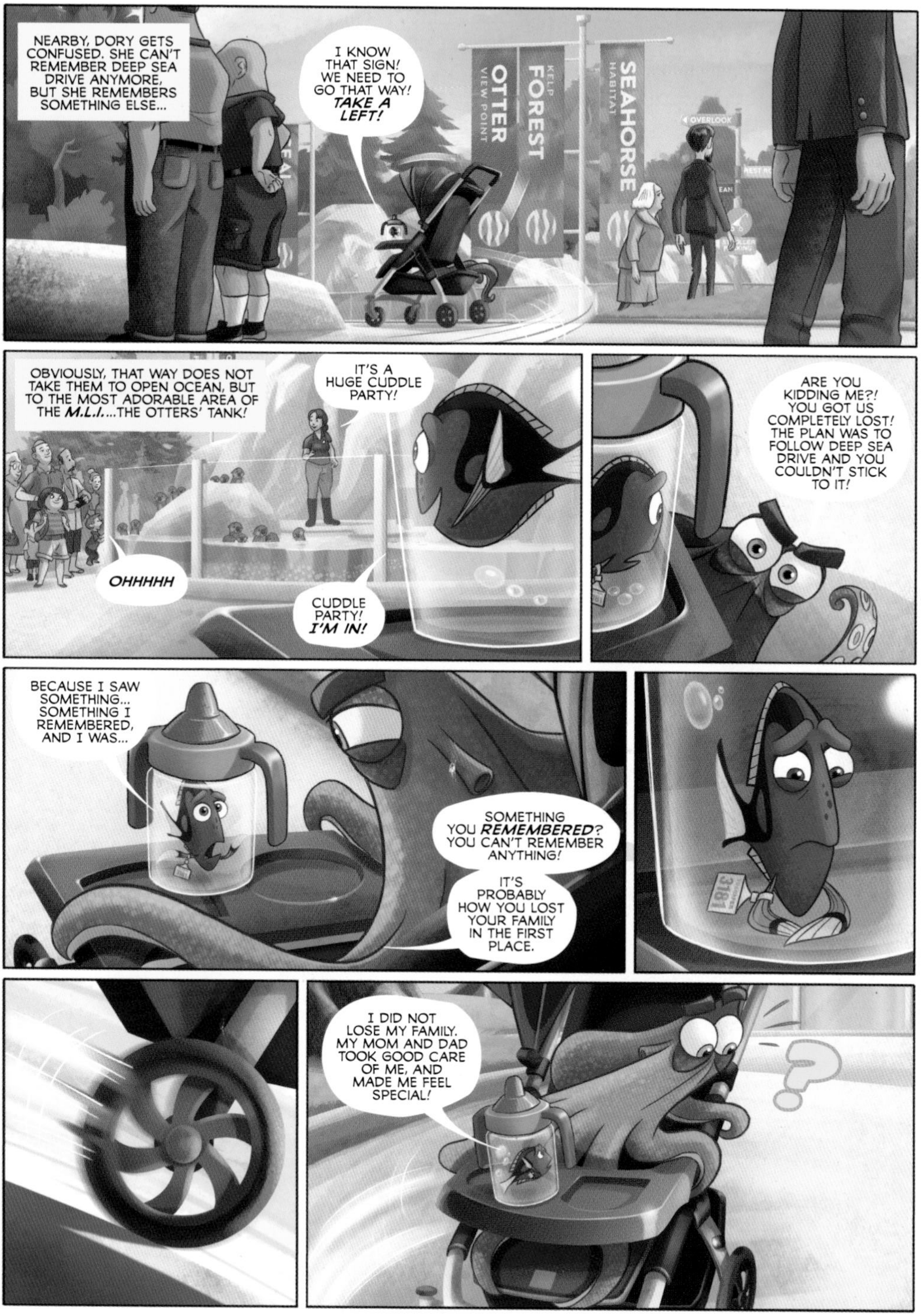

NEARBY, DORY GETS CONFUSED. SHE CAN'T REMEMBER DEEP SEA DRIVE ANYMORE, BUT SHE REMEMBERS SOMETHING ELSE...
I KNOW THAT SIGN! WE NEED TO GO THAT WAY! TAKE A LEFT!
OTTER VIEW POINT
KELP FOREST
SEAHORSE HABITAT
OVERLOOK
OBVIOUSLY, THAT WAY DOES NOT TAKE THEM TO OPEN OCEAN, BUT TO THE MOST ADORABLE AREA OF THE M.L.I....THE OTTERS' TANK!
IT'S A HUGE CUDDLE PARTY!
OHHHHH
CUDDLE PARTY! I'M IN!
ARE YOU KIDDING ME?! YOU GOT US COMPLETELY LOST! THE PLAN WAS TO FOLLOW DEEP SEA DRIVE AND YOU COULDN'T STICK TO IT!
BECAUSE I SAW SOMETHING... SOMETHING I REMEMBERED, AND I WAS...
SOMETHING YOU REMEMBERED? YOU CAN'T REMEMBER ANYTHING!
IT'S PROBABLY HOW YOU LOST YOUR FAMILY IN THE FIRST PLACE.
I DID NOT LOSE MY FAMILY. MY MOM AND DAD TOOK GOOD CARE OF ME, AND MADE ME FEEL SPECIAL!
?

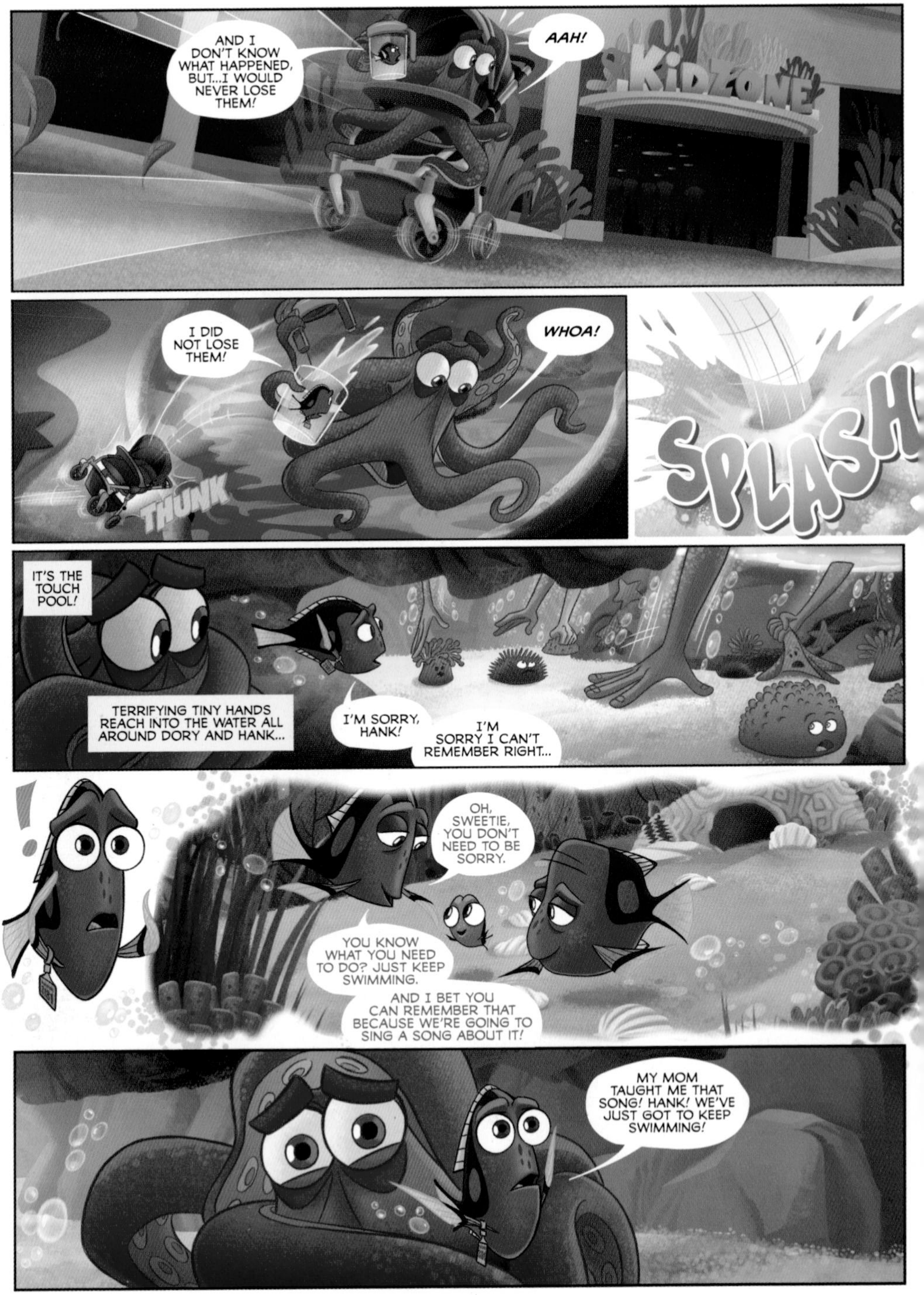
AND I DON'T KNOW WHAT HAPPENED, BUT...I WOULD NEVER LOSE THEM!
AAH!
KIDZONE
I DID NOT LOSE THEM!
WHOA!
THUNK
SPLASH
IT'S THE TOUCH POOL!
TERRIFYING TINY HANDS REACH INTO THE WATER ALL AROUND DORY AND HANK...
I'M SORRY, HANK!
I'M SORRY I CAN'T REMEMBER RIGHT...
OH, SWEETIE, YOU DON'T NEED TO BE SORRY.
YOU KNOW WHAT YOU NEED TO DO? JUST KEEP SWIMMING.
AND I BET YOU CAN REMEMBER THAT BECAUSE WE'RE GOING TO SING A SONG ABOUT IT!
MY MOM TAUGHT ME THAT SONG! HANK! WE'VE JUST GOT TO KEEP SWIMMING!

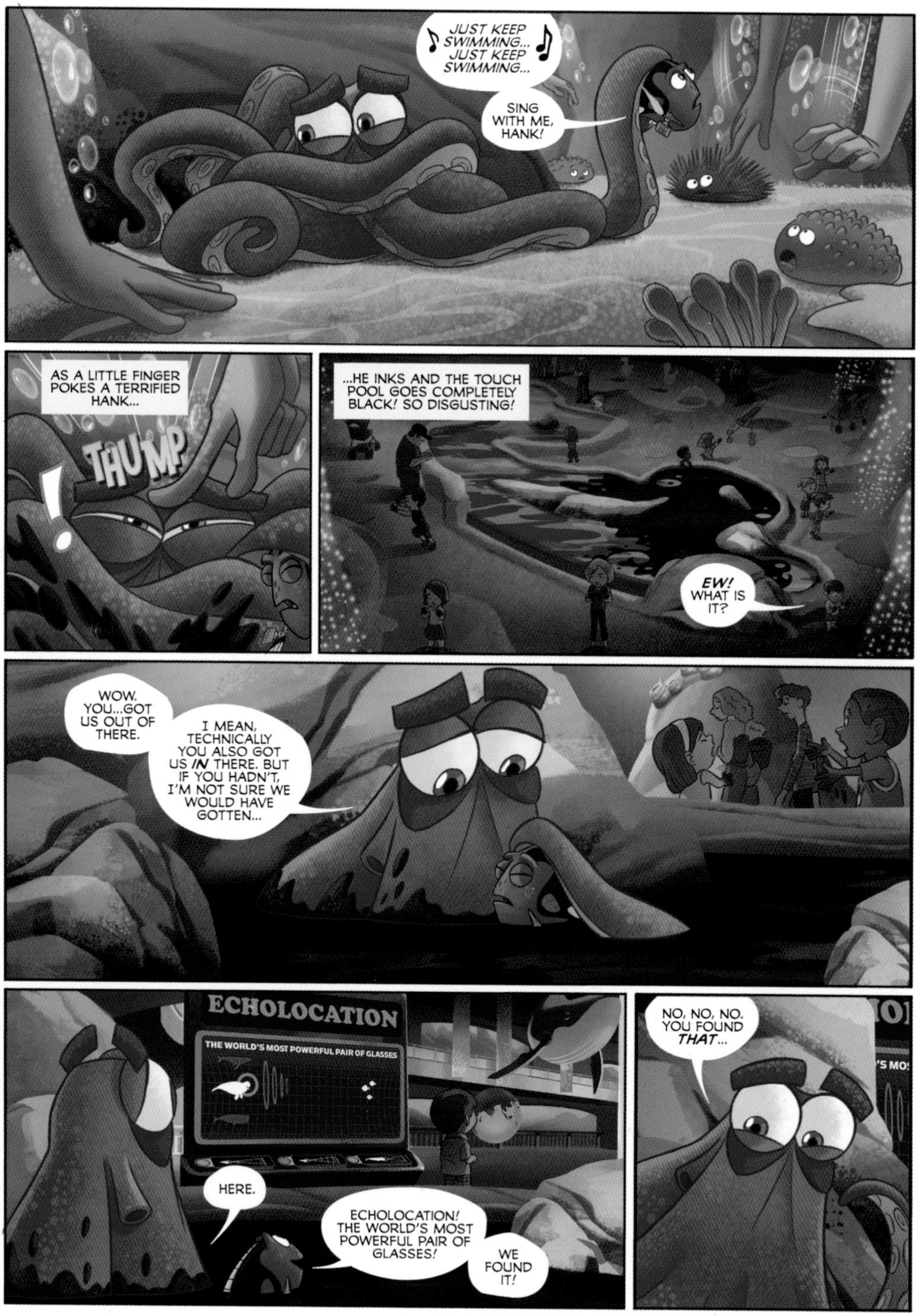
JUST KEEP SWIMMING... JUST KEEP SWIMMING...
SING WITH ME, HANK!
AS A LITTLE FINGER POKES A TERRIFIED HANK...
THUMP
!
...HE INKS AND THE TOUCH POOL GOES COMPLETELY BLACK! SO DISGUSTING!
EW! WHAT IS IT?
WOW. YOU...GOT US OUT OF THERE.
I MEAN, TECHNICALLY YOU ALSO GOT US IN THERE. BUT IF YOU HADN'T, I'M NOT SURE WE WOULD HAVE GOTTEN...
ECHOLOCATION
THE WORLD'S MOST POWERFUL PAIR OF GLASSES
HERE.
ECHOLOCATION! THE WORLD'S MOST POWERFUL PAIR OF GLASSES!
WE FOUND IT!
NO, NO, NO. YOU FOUND THAT...

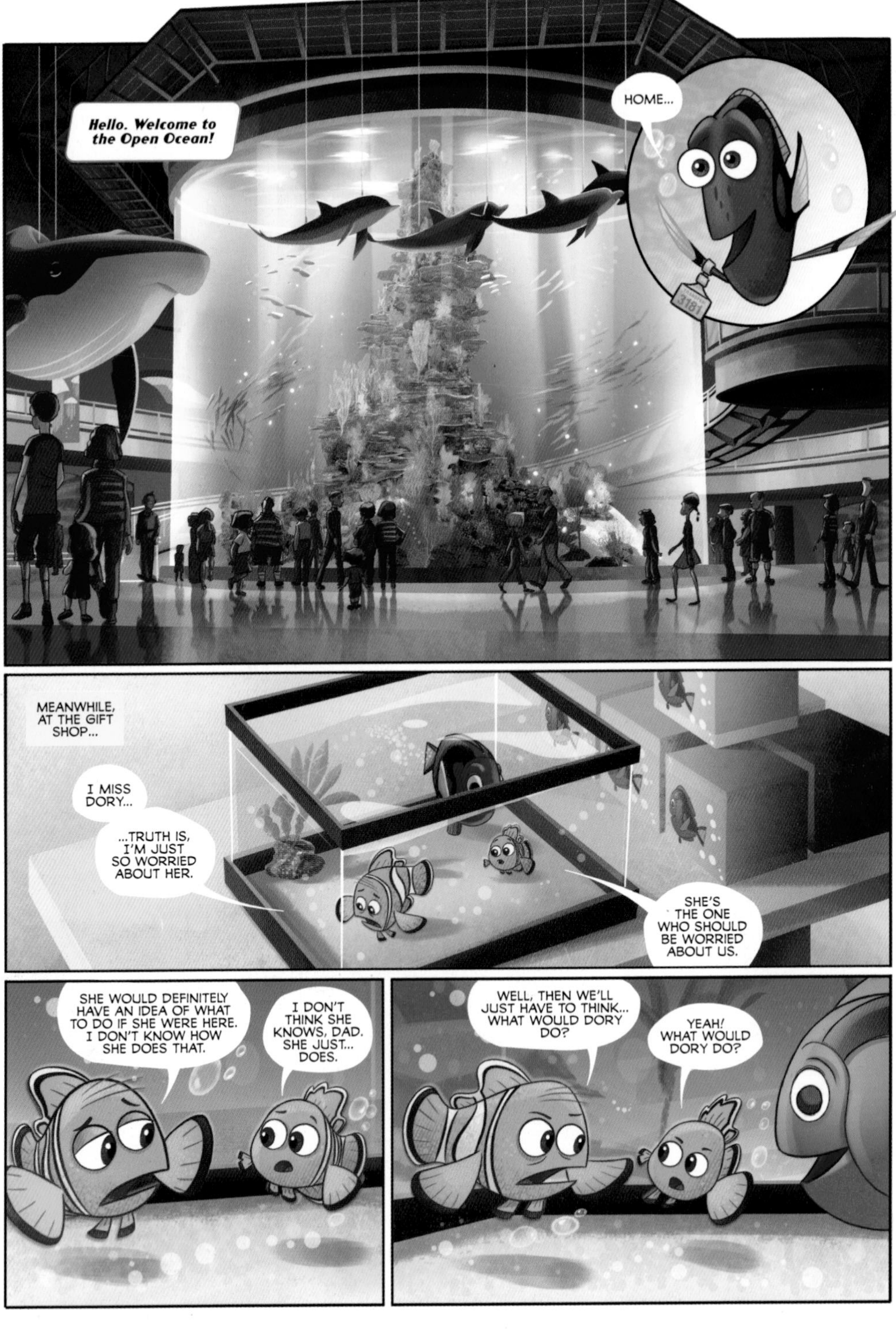
Hello. Welcome to the Open Ocean!
HOME...
MEANWHILE, AT THE GIFT SHOP...
I MISS DORY...
...TRUTH IS, I'M JUST SO WORRIED ABOUT HER.
SHE'S THE ONE WHO SHOULD BE WORRIED ABOUT US.
SHE WOULD DEFINITELY HAVE AN IDEA OF WHAT TO DO IF SHE WERE HERE. I DON'T KNOW HOW SHE DOES THAT.
I DON'T THINK SHE KNOWS, DAD. SHE JUST... DOES.
WELL, THEN WE'LL JUST HAVE TO THINK... WHAT WOULD DORY DO?
YEAH! WHAT WOULD DORY DO?

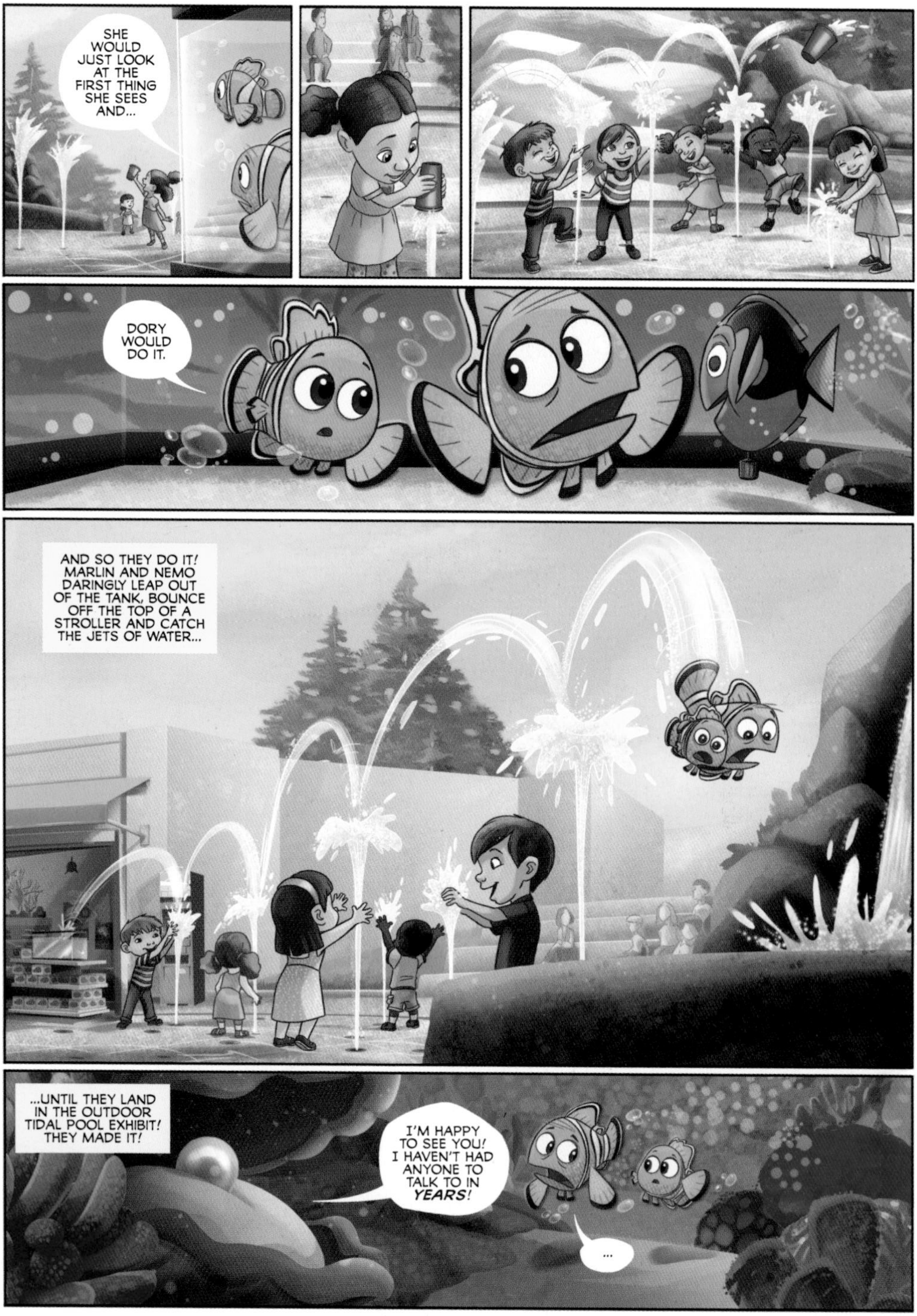
SHE WOULD JUST LOOK AT THE FIRST THING SHE SEES AND...
DORY WOULD DO IT.
AND SO THEY DO IT! MARLIN AND NEMO DARINGLY LEAP OUT OF THE TANK, BOUNCE OFF THE TOP OF A STROLLER AND CATCH THE JETS OF WATER...
...UNTIL THEY LAND IN THE OUTDOOR TIDAL POOL EXHIBIT! THEY MADE IT!
I'M HAPPY TO SEE YOU! I HAVEN'T HAD ANYONE TO TALK TO IN ***YEARS***!
...

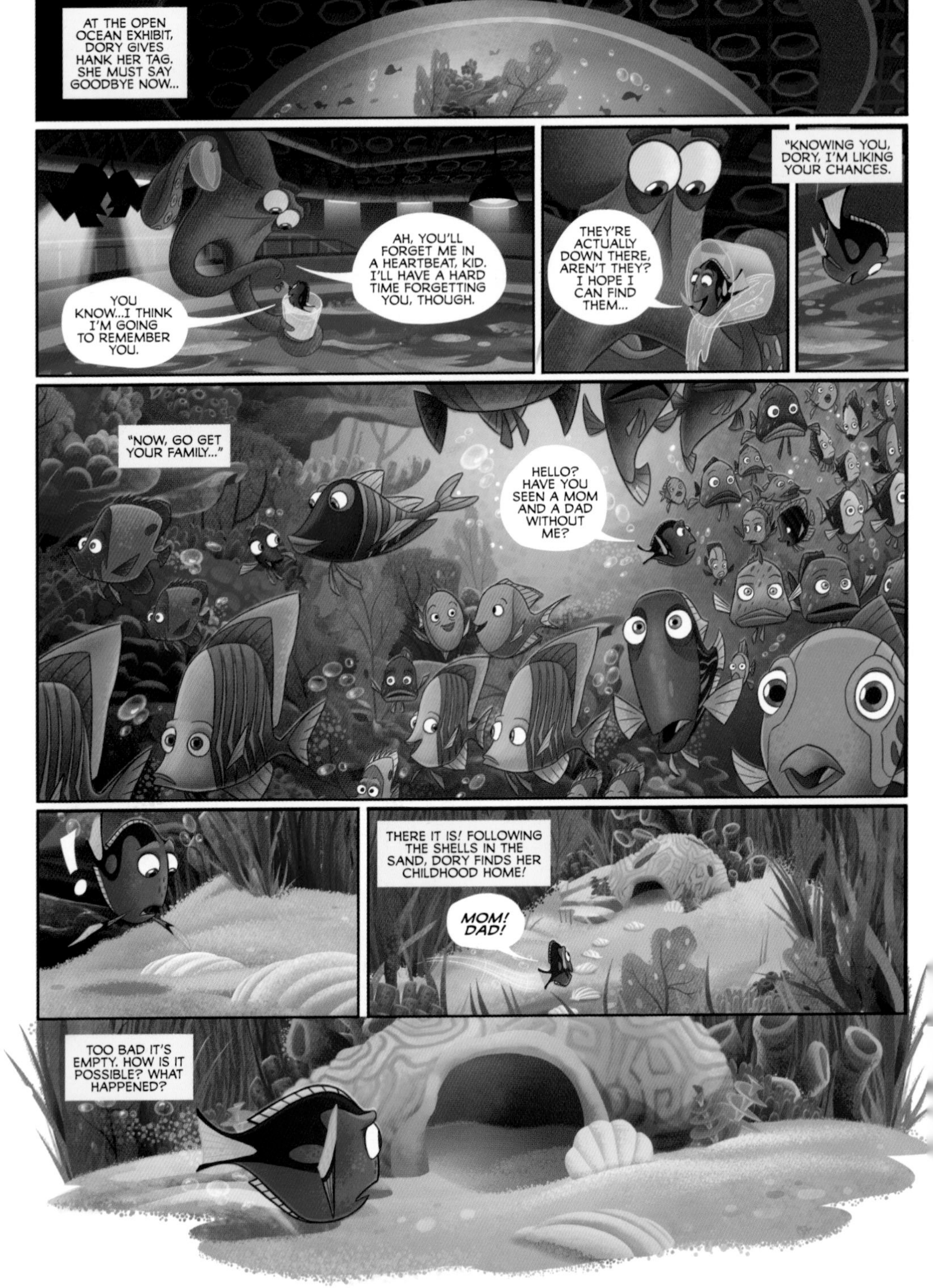
AT THE OPEN OCEAN EXHIBIT, DORY GIVES HANK HER TAG. SHE MUST SAY GOODBYE NOW...
YOU KNOW...I THINK I'M GOING TO REMEMBER YOU.
AH, YOU'LL FORGET ME IN A HEARTBEAT, KID. I'LL HAVE A HARD TIME FORGETTING YOU, THOUGH.
THEY'RE ACTUALLY DOWN THERE, AREN'T THEY? I HOPE I CAN FIND THEM...
"KNOWING YOU, DORY, I'M LIKING YOUR CHANCES.
"NOW, GO GET YOUR FAMILY..."
HELLO? HAVE YOU SEEN A MOM AND A DAD WITHOUT ME?
THERE IT IS! FOLLOWING THE SHELLS IN THE SAND, DORY FINDS HER CHILDHOOD HOME!
MOM! DAD!
TOO BAD IT'S EMPTY. HOW IS IT POSSIBLE? WHAT HAPPENED?

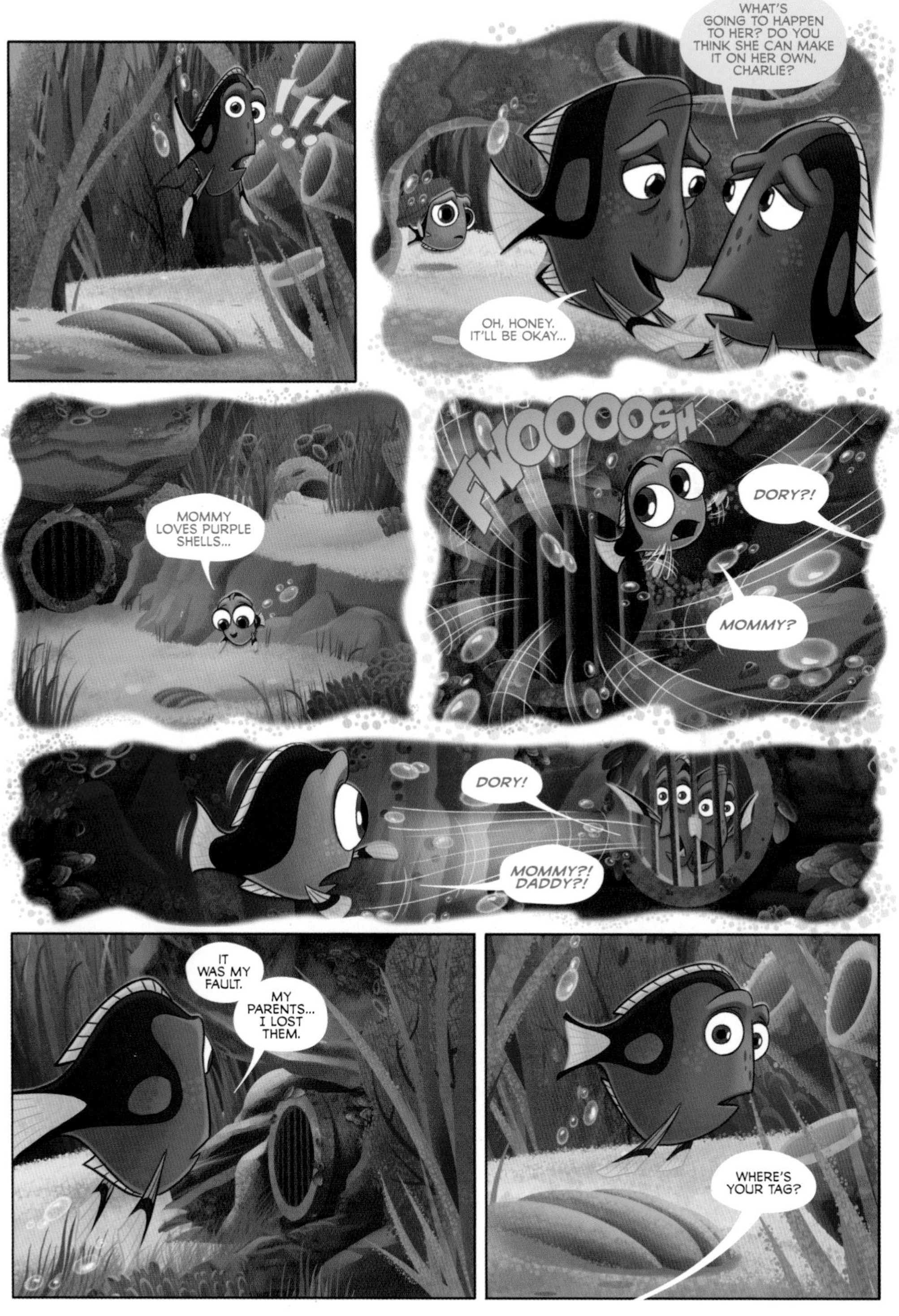
WHAT'S GOING TO HAPPEN TO HER? DO YOU THINK SHE CAN MAKE IT ON HER OWN, CHARLIE?
OH, HONEY. IT'LL BE OKAY...
MOMMY LOVES PURPLE SHELLS...
FWOOOOOSH
DORY?!
MOMMY?
DORY!
MOMMY?! DADDY?!
IT WAS MY FAULT.
MY PARENTS... I LOST THEM.
WHERE'S YOUR TAG?

IT'S MISSING? THAT'S WHY YOU'RE NOT IN QUARANTINE?

QUARANTINE?

THAT'S WHERE THEY TOOK ALL THE BLUE TANGS.

YEP. BEING SHIPPED ON A TRUCK TO CLEVELAND AT THE CRACK O' DAWN.

WHAT? MY PARENTS ARE BACK IN QUARANTINE?!

IT'S EASY TO GET TO QUARANTINE. YOU CAN JUST GO THROUGH THE PIPES, HONEY...

"...IT'S TWO LEFTS AND A RIGHT. SIMPLE."

TWO LEFTS AND A RIGHT.

TWO LEFTS AND A RIGHT.

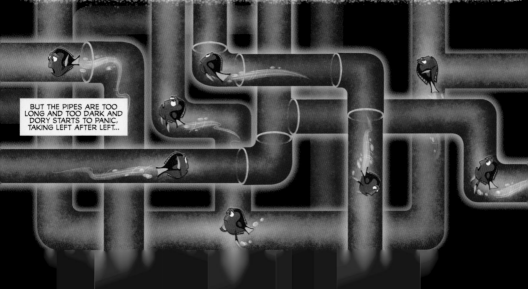

BUT THE PIPES ARE TOO LONG AND TOO DARK AND DORY STARTS TO PANIC, TAKING LEFT AFTER LEFT...

UNTIL...
OH NO... IT'S HAPPENING. I'M LOST. IT'S TOO HARD. I CAN'T REMEMBER!
I'M GONNA BE STUCK FOREVER IN THE PIPES!
THE PIPES! THE PIPE PALS!
DESTINEEE!
DORY?
I'M LOOOST IN THE PIIIPES AAAND MY PAAAAREEENTS AAARE IN QUAAARAAANTIIINE!
HAAANG OOON, DOOORY!
BAILEY! YOU'VE GOTTA USE YOUR ECHOLOCATION!
IT WORKS! BAILEY'S ECHOLOCATION IS NOT REALLY BROKEN... EXACTLY AS DESTINY HAS SAID!
I'M GETTING SOMETHING! I CAN SEE THE QUARANTINE! I CAN SEE EVERYTHING! AND I CAN SEE YOU!
DORY FOLLOWS BAILEY'S DIRECTIONS, SWIMMING FAST TOWARD THE QUARANTINE...

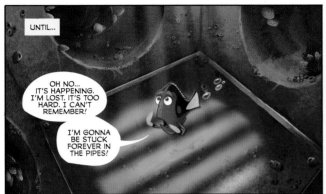

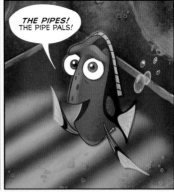

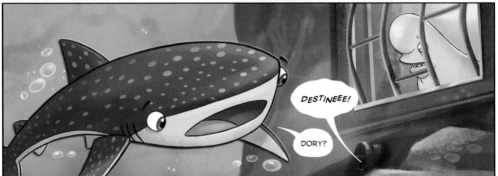

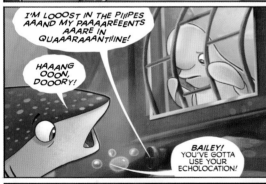

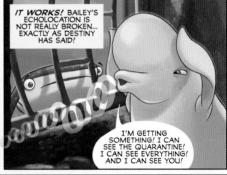

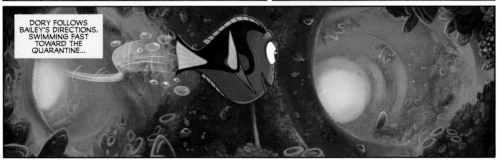

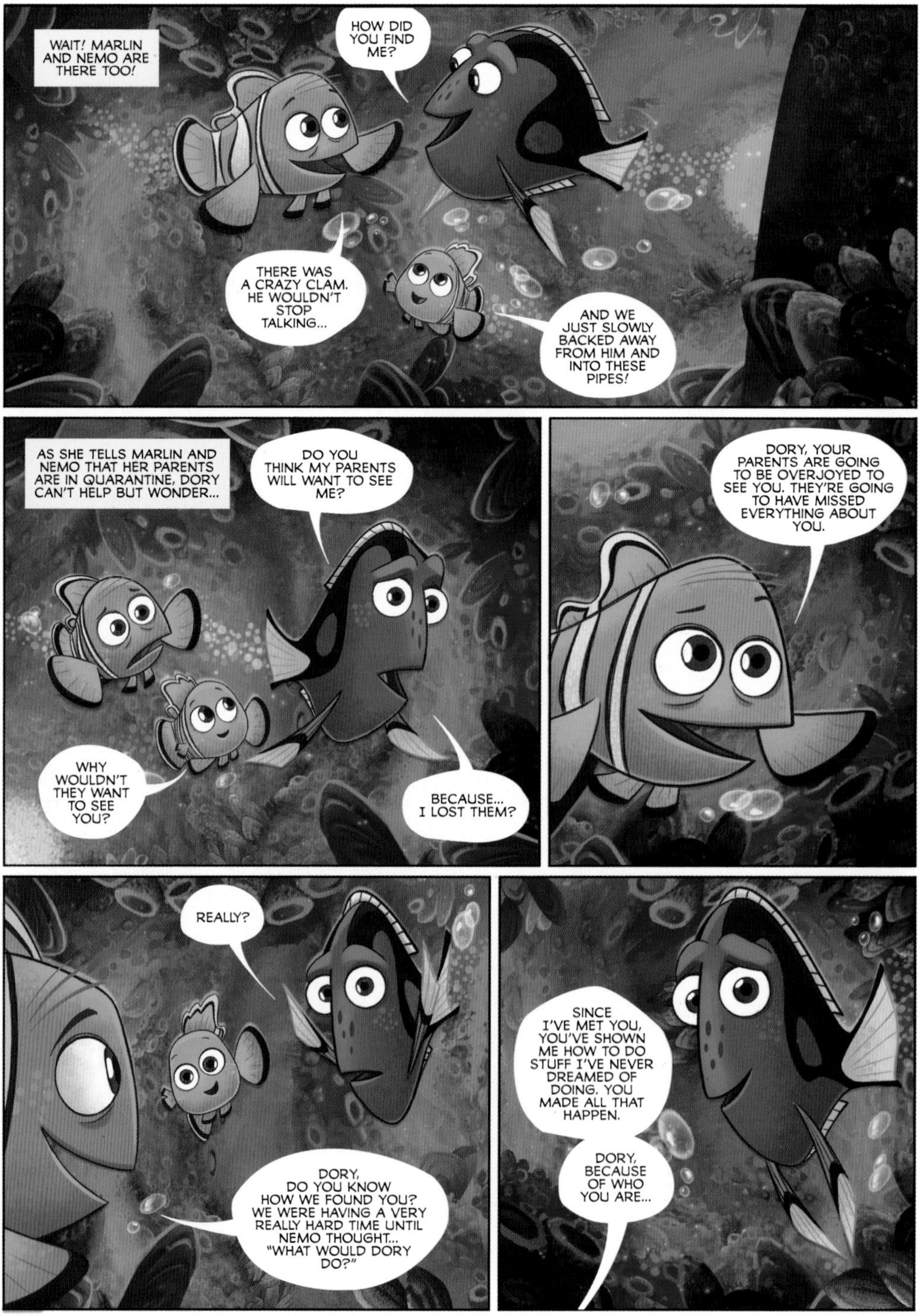
WAIT! MARLIN AND NEMO ARE THERE TOO!
HOW DID YOU FIND ME?
THERE WAS A CRAZY CLAM. HE WOULDN'T STOP TALKING...
AND WE JUST SLOWLY BACKED AWAY FROM HIM AND INTO THESE PIPES!
AS SHE TELLS MARLIN AND NEMO THAT HER PARENTS ARE IN QUARANTINE, DORY CAN'T HELP BUT WONDER...
DO YOU THINK MY PARENTS WILL WANT TO SEE ME?
WHY WOULDN'T THEY WANT TO SEE YOU?
BECAUSE... I LOST THEM?
DORY, YOUR PARENTS ARE GOING TO BE OVERJOYED TO SEE YOU. THEY'RE GOING TO HAVE MISSED EVERYTHING ABOUT YOU.
REALLY?
DORY, DO YOU KNOW HOW WE FOUND YOU? WE WERE HAVING A VERY REALLY HARD TIME UNTIL NEMO THOUGHT... "WHAT WOULD DORY DO?"
SINCE I'VE MET YOU, YOU'VE SHOWN ME HOW TO DO STUFF I'VE NEVER DREAMED OF DOING. YOU MADE ALL THAT HAPPEN.
DORY, BECAUSE OF WHO YOU ARE...

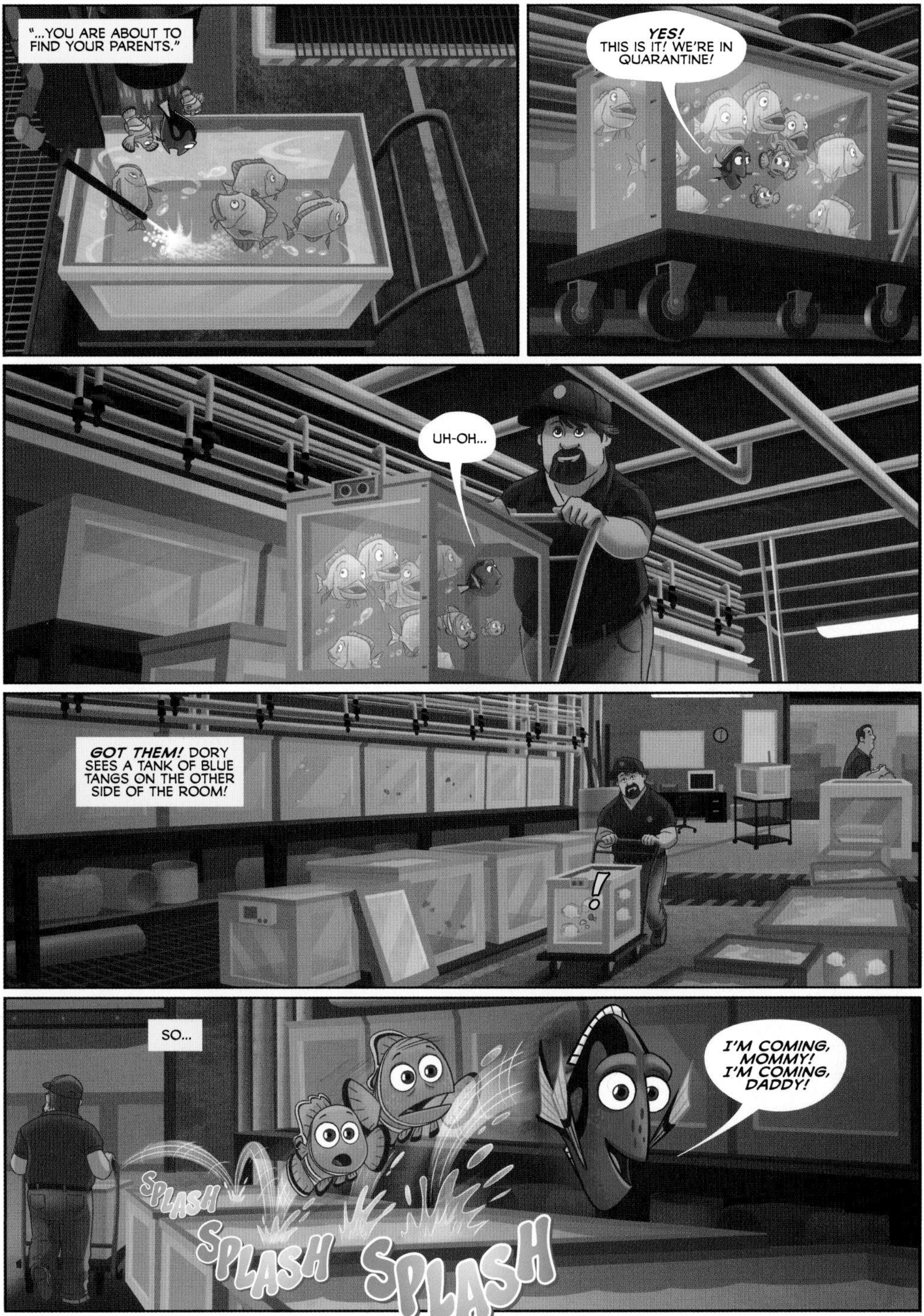
"...YOU ARE ABOUT TO FIND YOUR PARENTS."
YES! THIS IS IT! WE'RE IN QUARANTINE!
UH-OH...
GOT THEM! DORY SEES A TANK OF BLUE TANGS ON THE OTHER SIDE OF THE ROOM!
!
SO...
I'M COMING, MOMMY! I'M COMING, DADDY!
SPLASH
SPLASH
SPLASH

BUT AT THE LAST MOMENT...

SPLASH

SPLASH

MTV 2001

CAUT

WET FLOOR

OH NO!

WHAT DO WE DO?

HANK!

QUIET.

CAUTION

HANK, WE NEED TO GET INTO THAT TANK!

HEY! THAT RHYMED!

LOOK, YOU'VE GOT THREE MINUTES TO GET EVERYONE IN THIS CUP WITH YOU...

...AND THEN I'M ON THAT TRUCK TO CLEVELAND, GOT IT?

GOT IT.

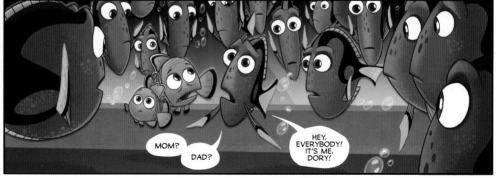

MOM?

DAD?

HEY, EVERYBODY! IT'S ME, DORY!

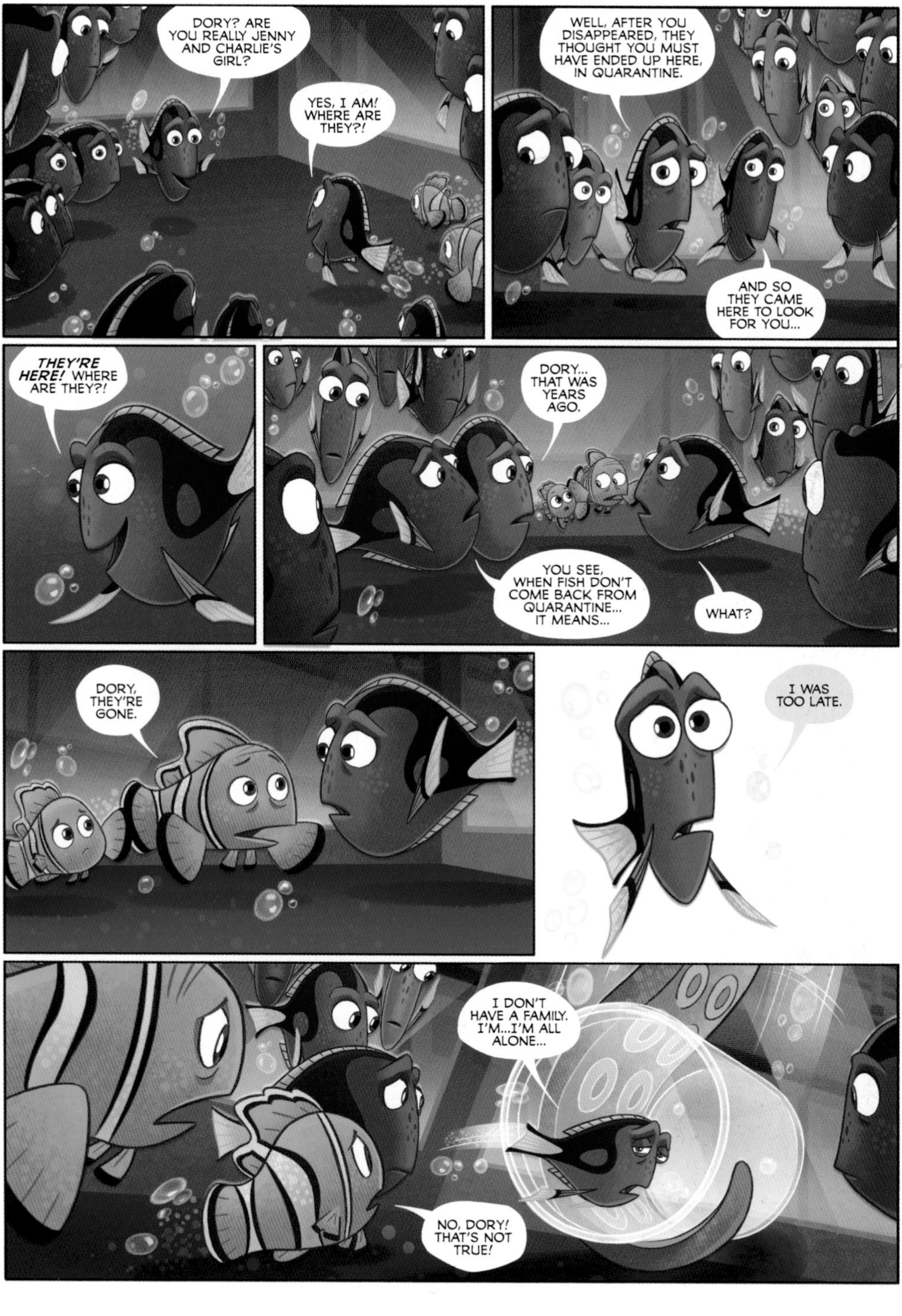
DORY? ARE YOU REALLY JENNY AND CHARLIE'S GIRL?
YES, I AM! WHERE ARE THEY?!
WELL, AFTER YOU DISAPPEARED, THEY THOUGHT YOU MUST HAVE ENDED UP HERE, IN QUARANTINE.
AND SO THEY CAME HERE TO LOOK FOR YOU...
THEY'RE HERE! WHERE ARE THEY?!
DORY... THAT WAS YEARS AGO.
YOU SEE, WHEN FISH DON'T COME BACK FROM QUARANTINE... IT MEANS...
WHAT?
DORY, THEY'RE GONE.
I WAS TOO LATE.
I DON'T HAVE A FAMILY. I'M...I'M ALL ALONE...
NO, DORY! THAT'S NOT TRUE!

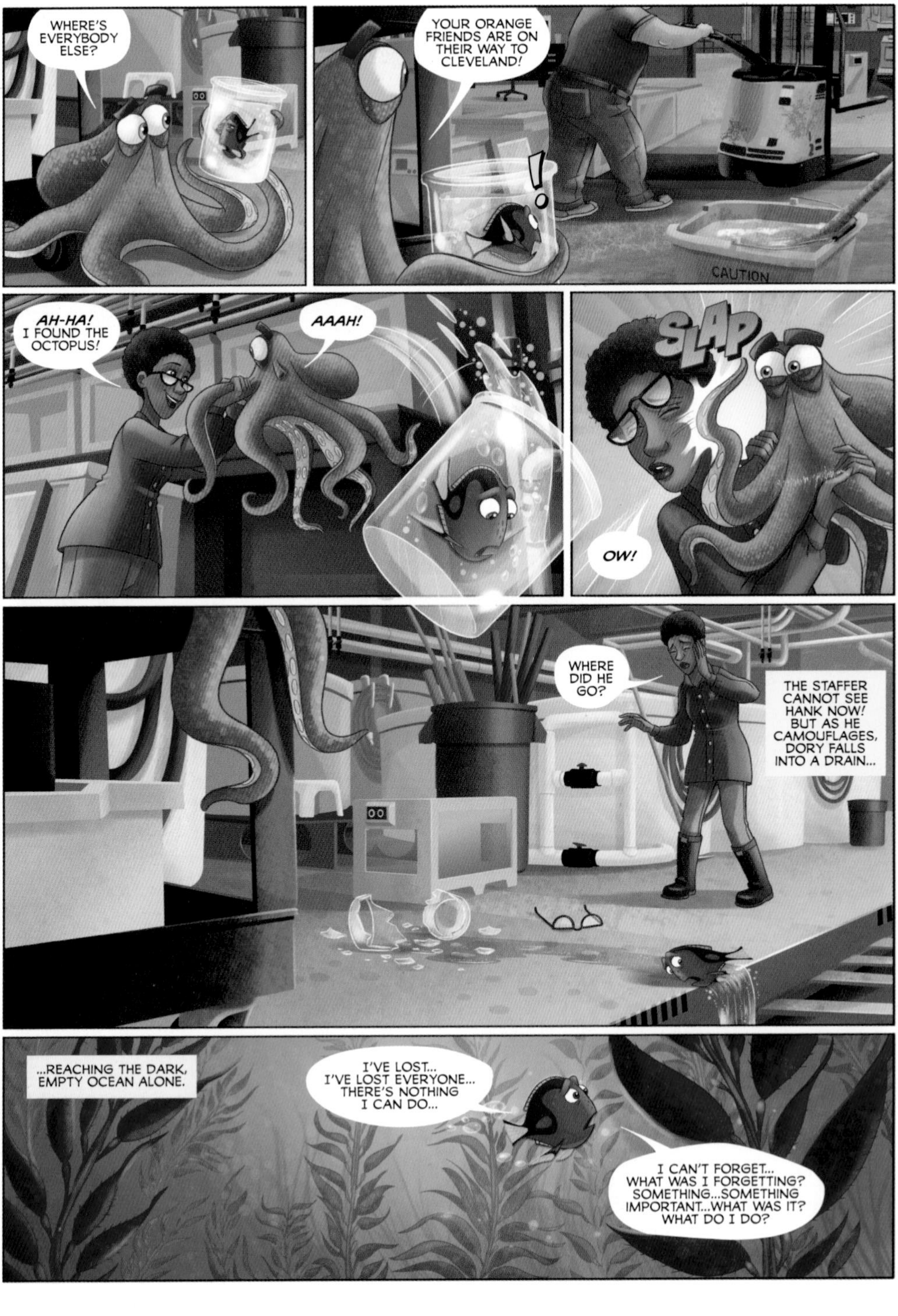
WHERE'S EVERYBODY ELSE?
YOUR ORANGE FRIENDS ARE ON THEIR WAY TO CLEVELAND!
!
CAUTION
AH-HA! I FOUND THE OCTOPUS!
AAAH!
SLAP
OW!
WHERE DID HE GO?
THE STAFFER CANNOT SEE HANK NOW! BUT AS HE CAMOUFLAGES, DORY FALLS INTO A DRAIN...
...REACHING THE DARK, EMPTY OCEAN ALONE.
I'VE LOST... I'VE LOST EVERYONE... THERE'S NOTHING I CAN DO...
I CAN'T FORGET... WHAT WAS I FORGETTING? SOMETHING...SOMETHING IMPORTANT...WHAT WAS IT? WHAT DO I DO?

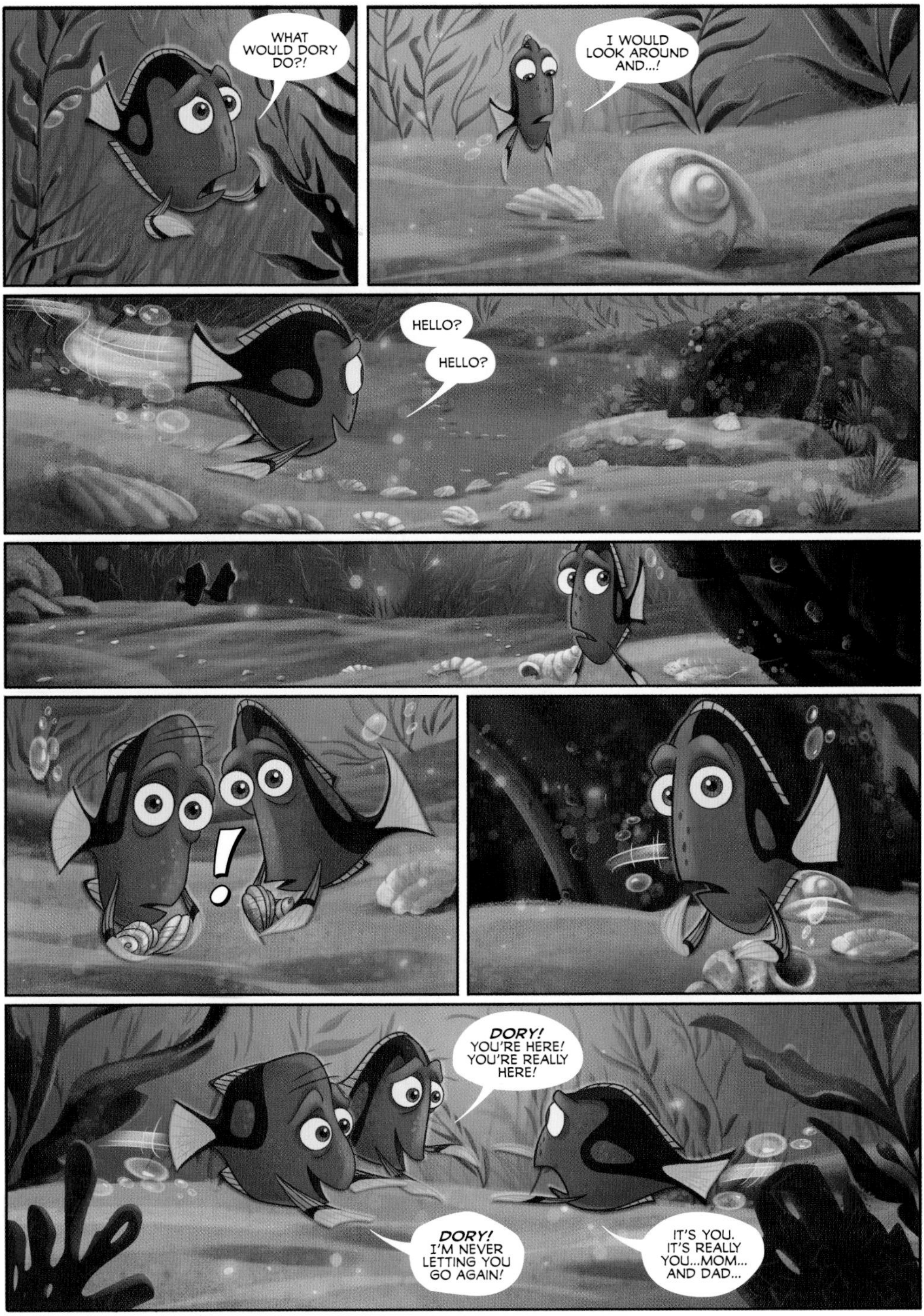
WHAT WOULD DORY DO?!
I WOULD LOOK AROUND AND...!
HELLO?
HELLO?
!
DORY! YOU'RE HERE! YOU'RE REALLY HERE!
DORY! I'M NEVER LETTING YOU GO AGAIN!
IT'S YOU. IT'S REALLY YOU...MOM... AND DAD...

I'M SO SORRY. I KNOW I'VE GOT A PROBLEM AND ALL THIS TIME I WANTED TO FIX IT AND I CAN'T...

DON'T YOU DARE BE SORRY. LOOK WHAT YOU DID! YOU FOUND US!

WE WENT TO QUARANTINE TO LOOK FOR YOU, BUT YOU WEREN'T THERE.

AND WE KNEW YOU MUST HAVE GOTTEN OUT THROUGH THE PIPES...

SO WE DID TOO. AND WE'VE STAYED IN THIS SPOT FOR YOU EVER SINCE.

BECAUSE WE THOUGHT YOU MIGHT COME BACK.

SO EVERY DAY, WE GO OUT AND LAY OUT...

SHELLS!

AND YOU FOUND US...BECAUSE YOU *REMEMBERED*.

IN YOUR OWN AMAZING DORY WAY.

I DID. ALL BY MYSELF.

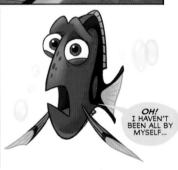

OH! I HAVEN'T BEEN ALL BY MYSELF...

"...MARLIN AND NEMO!"

SLAM

MARINE LIFE INSTITUTE CLEVELAND

NO!

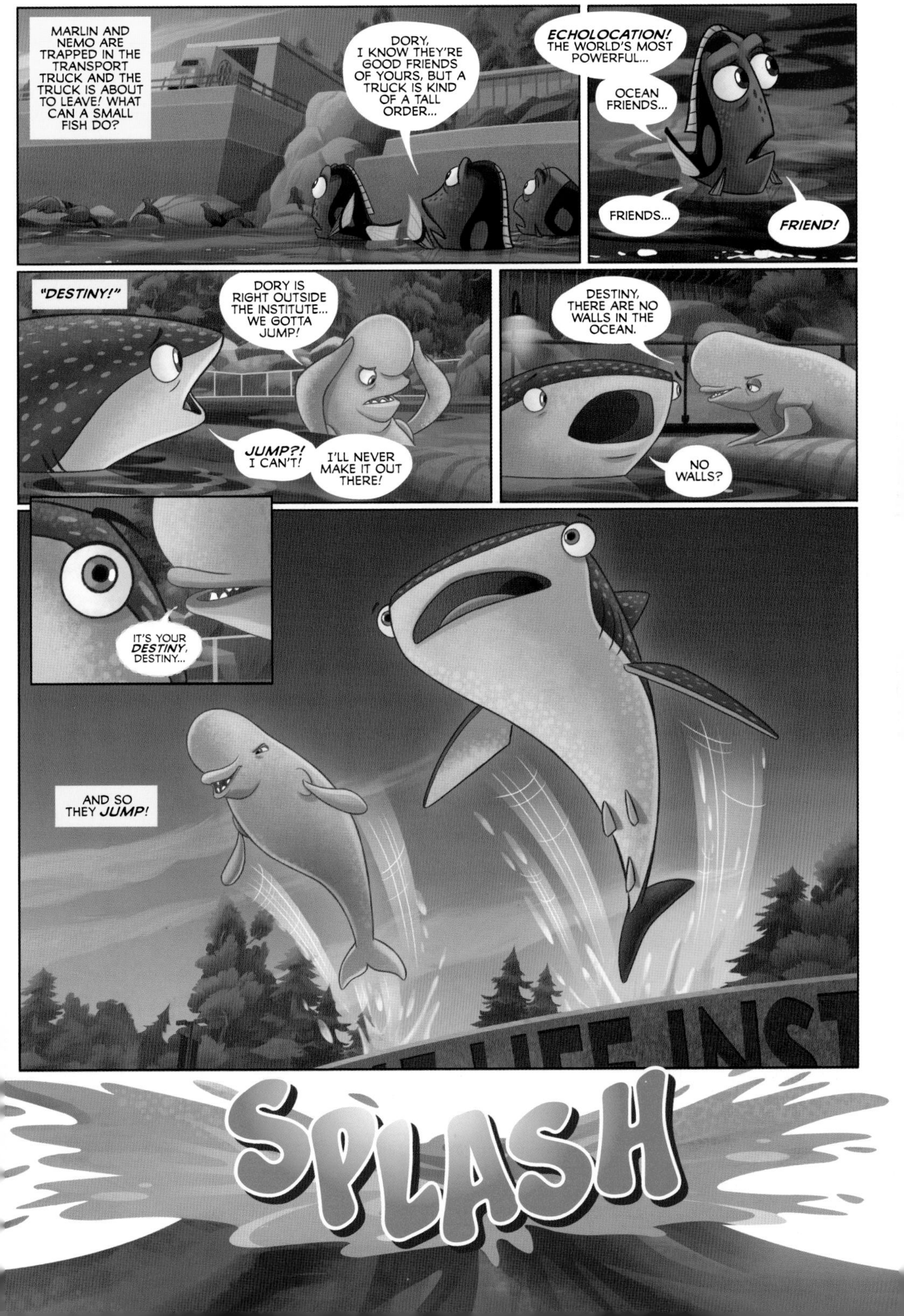

MARLIN AND NEMO ARE TRAPPED IN THE TRANSPORT TRUCK AND THE TRUCK IS ABOUT TO LEAVE! WHAT CAN A SMALL FISH DO?
DORY, I KNOW THEY'RE GOOD FRIENDS OF YOURS, BUT A TRUCK IS KIND OF A TALL ORDER...
ECHOLOCATION! THE WORLD'S MOST POWERFUL...
OCEAN FRIENDS...
FRIENDS...
FRIEND!
"DESTINY!"
DORY IS RIGHT OUTSIDE THE INSTITUTE... WE GOTTA JUMP!
JUMP?! I CAN'T!
I'LL NEVER MAKE IT OUT THERE!
DESTINY, THERE ARE NO WALLS IN THE OCEAN.
NO WALLS?
IT'S YOUR DESTINY, DESTINY...
AND SO THEY JUMP!
SPLASH

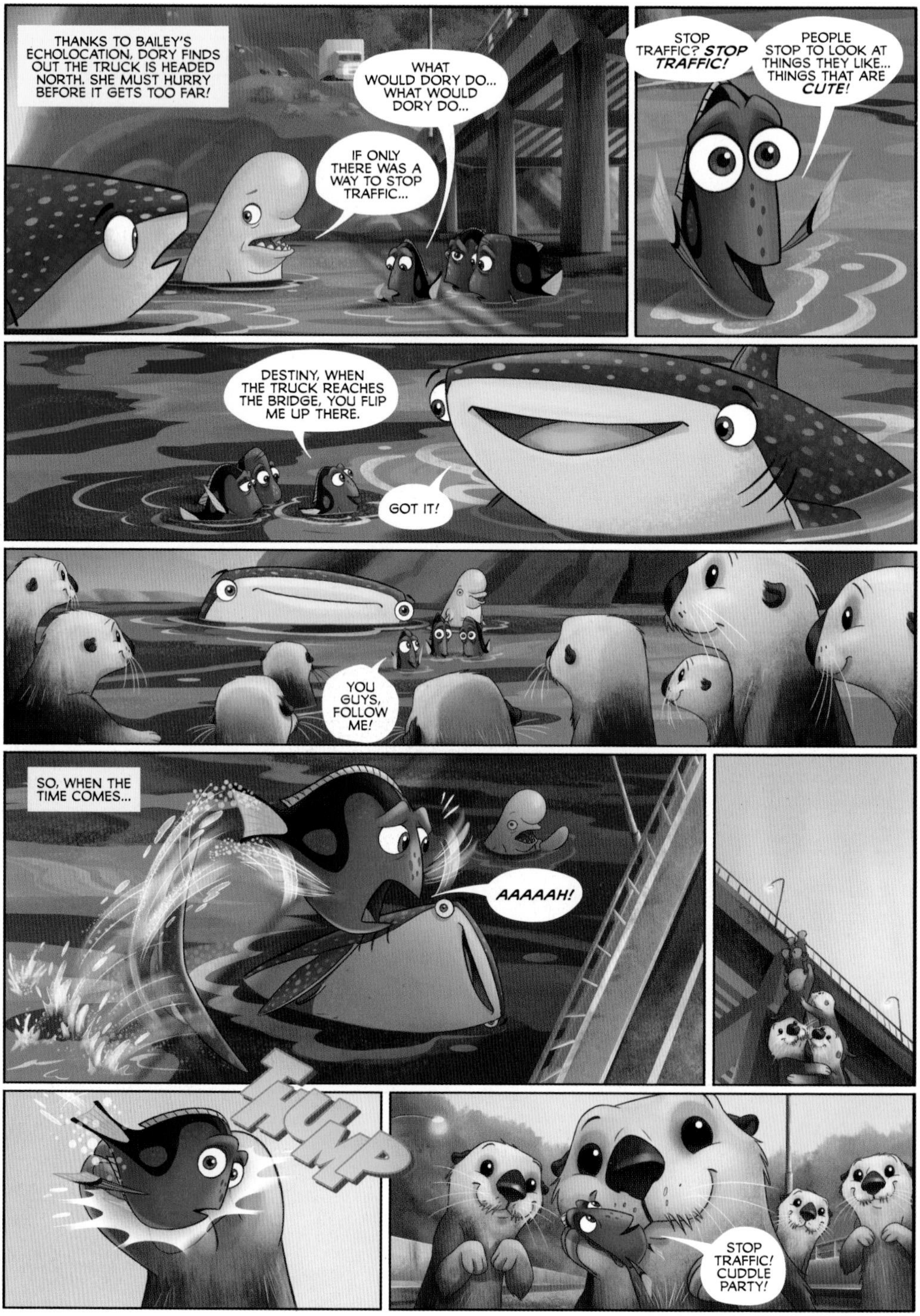
THANKS TO BAILEY'S ECHOLOCATION, DORY FINDS OUT THE TRUCK IS HEADED NORTH. SHE MUST HURRY BEFORE IT GETS TOO FAR!
WHAT WOULD DORY DO... WHAT WOULD DORY DO...
IF ONLY THERE WAS A WAY TO STOP TRAFFIC...
STOP TRAFFIC? STOP TRAFFIC!
PEOPLE STOP TO LOOK AT THINGS THEY LIKE... THINGS THAT ARE CUTE!
DESTINY, WHEN THE TRUCK REACHES THE BRIDGE, YOU FLIP ME UP THERE.
GOT IT!
YOU GUYS, FOLLOW ME!
SO, WHEN THE TIME COMES...
AAAAAH!
THUMP
STOP TRAFFIC! CUDDLE PARTY!

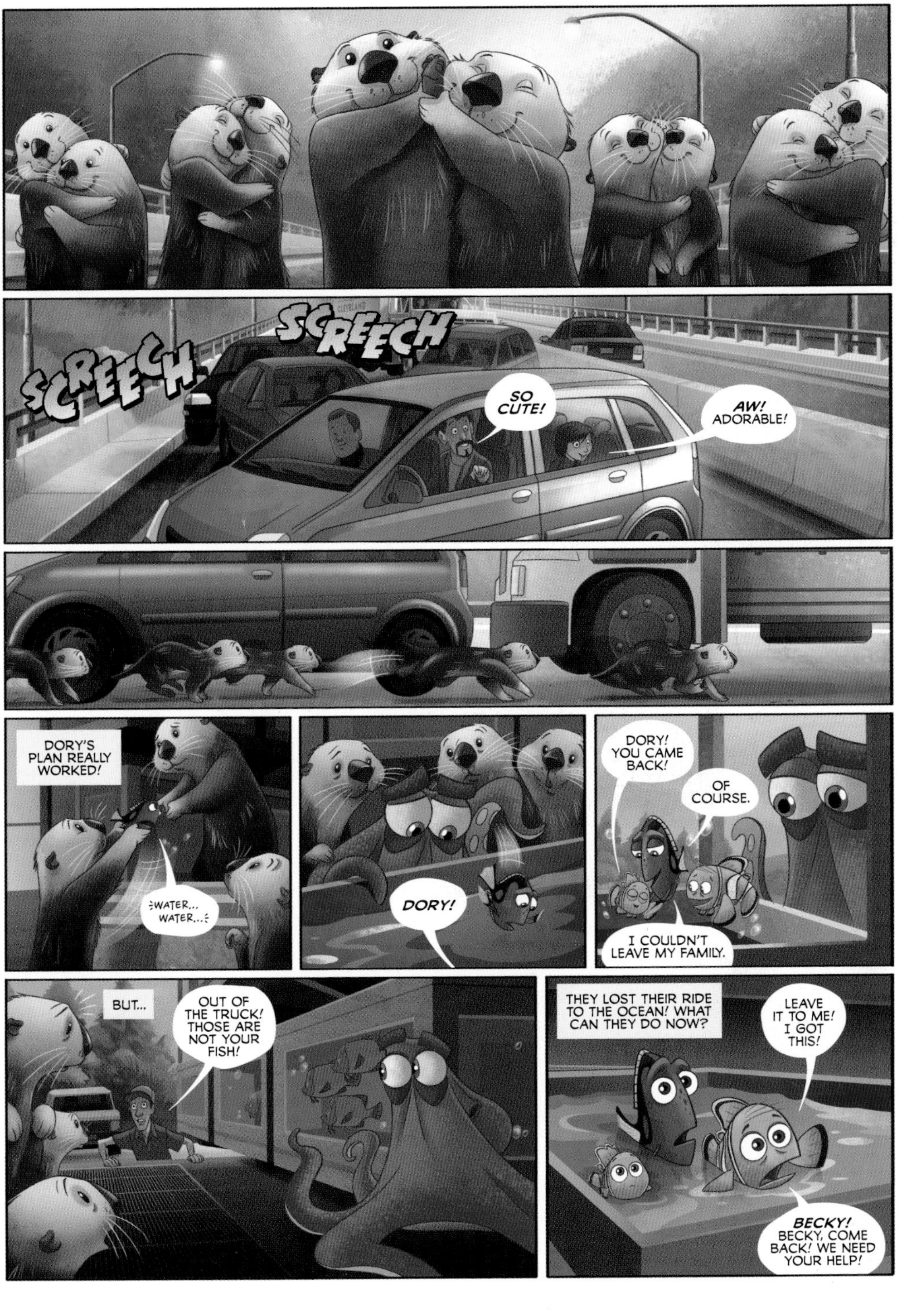

SCREECH
SCREECH
SO CUTE!
AW! ADORABLE!
DORY'S PLAN REALLY WORKED!
WATER... WATER...
DORY!
DORY! YOU CAME BACK!
OF COURSE.
I COULDN'T LEAVE MY FAMILY.
BUT...
OUT OF THE TRUCK! THOSE ARE NOT YOUR FISH!
THEY LOST THEIR RIDE TO THE OCEAN! WHAT CAN THEY DO NOW?
LEAVE IT TO ME! I GOT THIS!
BECKY! BECKY, COME BACK! WE NEED YOUR HELP!

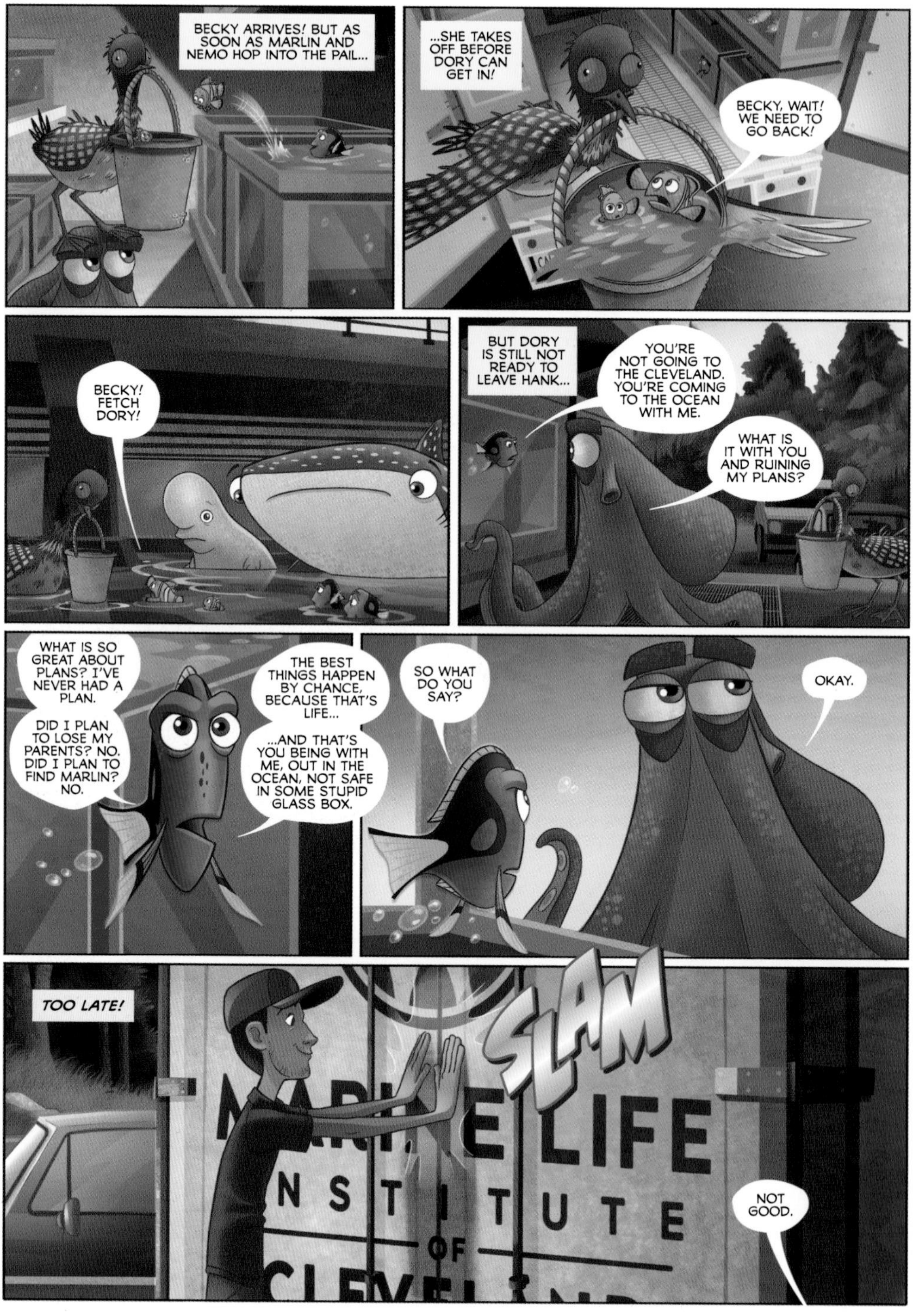

BECKY ARRIVES! BUT AS SOON AS MARLIN AND NEMO HOP INTO THE PAIL...
...SHE TAKES OFF BEFORE DORY CAN GET IN!
BECKY, WAIT! WE NEED TO GO BACK!
BECKY! FETCH DORY!
BUT DORY IS STILL NOT READY TO LEAVE HANK...
YOU'RE NOT GOING TO THE CLEVELAND. YOU'RE COMING TO THE OCEAN WITH ME.
WHAT IS IT WITH YOU AND RUINING MY PLANS?
WHAT IS SO GREAT ABOUT PLANS? I'VE NEVER HAD A PLAN.
DID I PLAN TO LOSE MY PARENTS? NO. DID I PLAN TO FIND MARLIN? NO.
THE BEST THINGS HAPPEN BY CHANCE, BECAUSE THAT'S LIFE...
...AND THAT'S YOU BEING WITH ME, OUT IN THE OCEAN, NOT SAFE IN SOME STUPID GLASS BOX.
SO WHAT DO YOU SAY?
OKAY.
TOO LATE!
SLAM
LIFE
N S T I T U T E
OF
NOT GOOD.

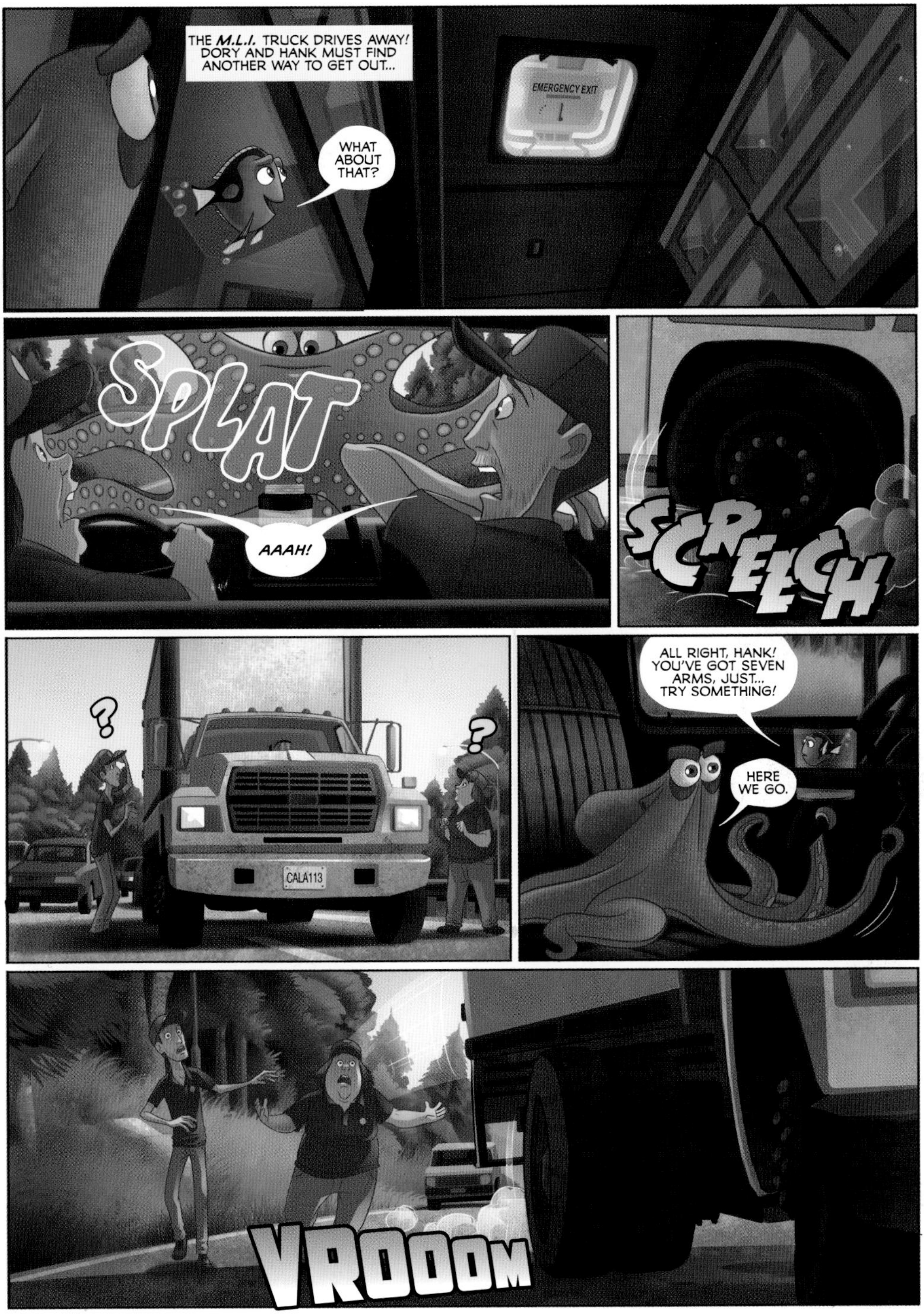
THE M.L.I. TRUCK DRIVES AWAY! DORY AND HANK MUST FIND ANOTHER WAY TO GET OUT...
WHAT ABOUT THAT?
EMERGENCY EXIT
SPLAT
AAAH!
SCREECH
?
?
CALA113
ALL RIGHT, HANK! YOU'VE GOT SEVEN ARMS, JUST... TRY SOMETHING!
HERE WE GO.
VROOOM

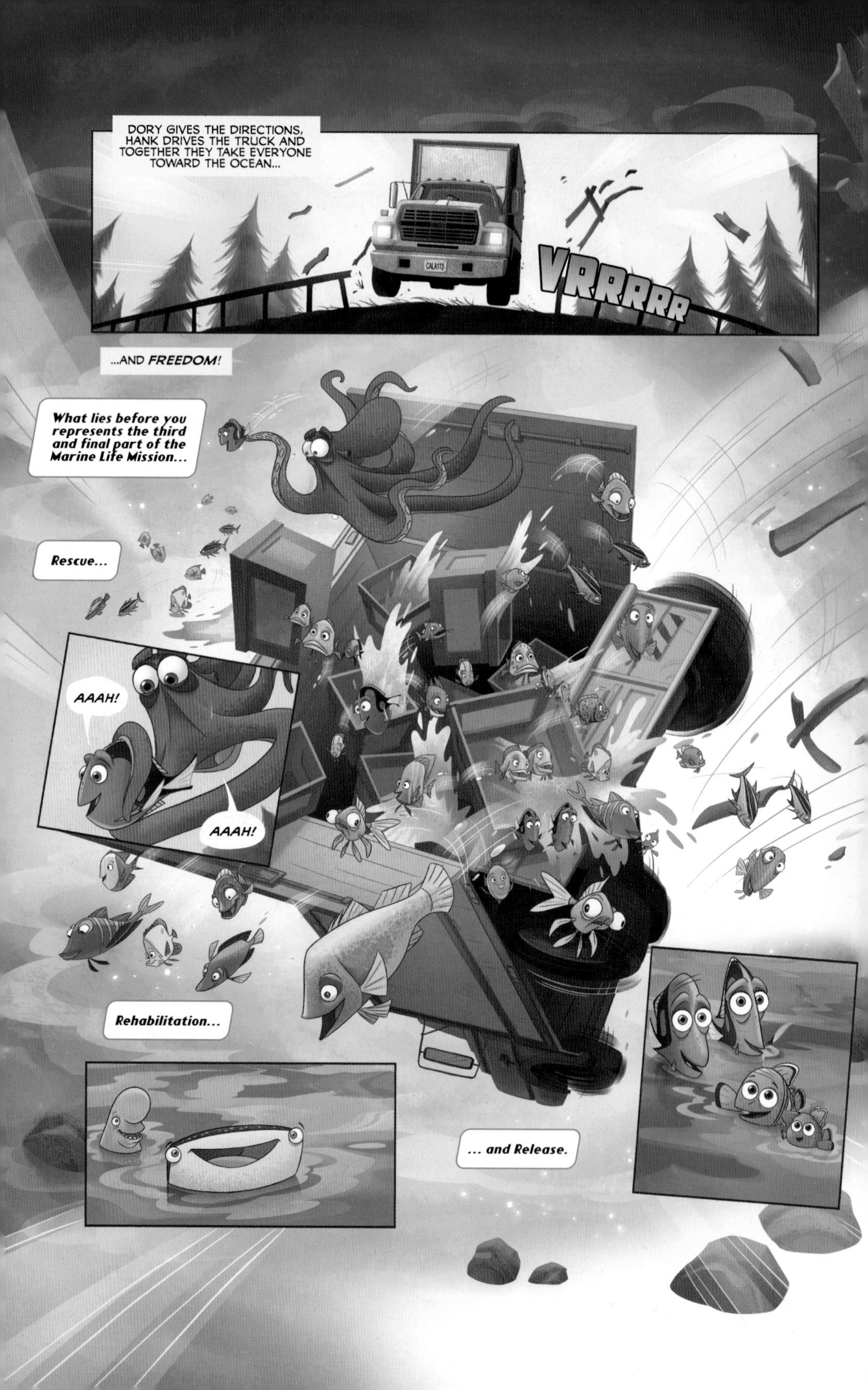
DORY GIVES THE DIRECTIONS, HANK DRIVES THE TRUCK AND TOGETHER THEY TAKE EVERYONE TOWARD THE OCEAN...
VRRRRRR
...AND FREEDOM!
What lies before you represents the third and final part of the Marine Life Mission...
Rescue...
AAAH!
AAAH!
Rehabilitation...
... and Release.

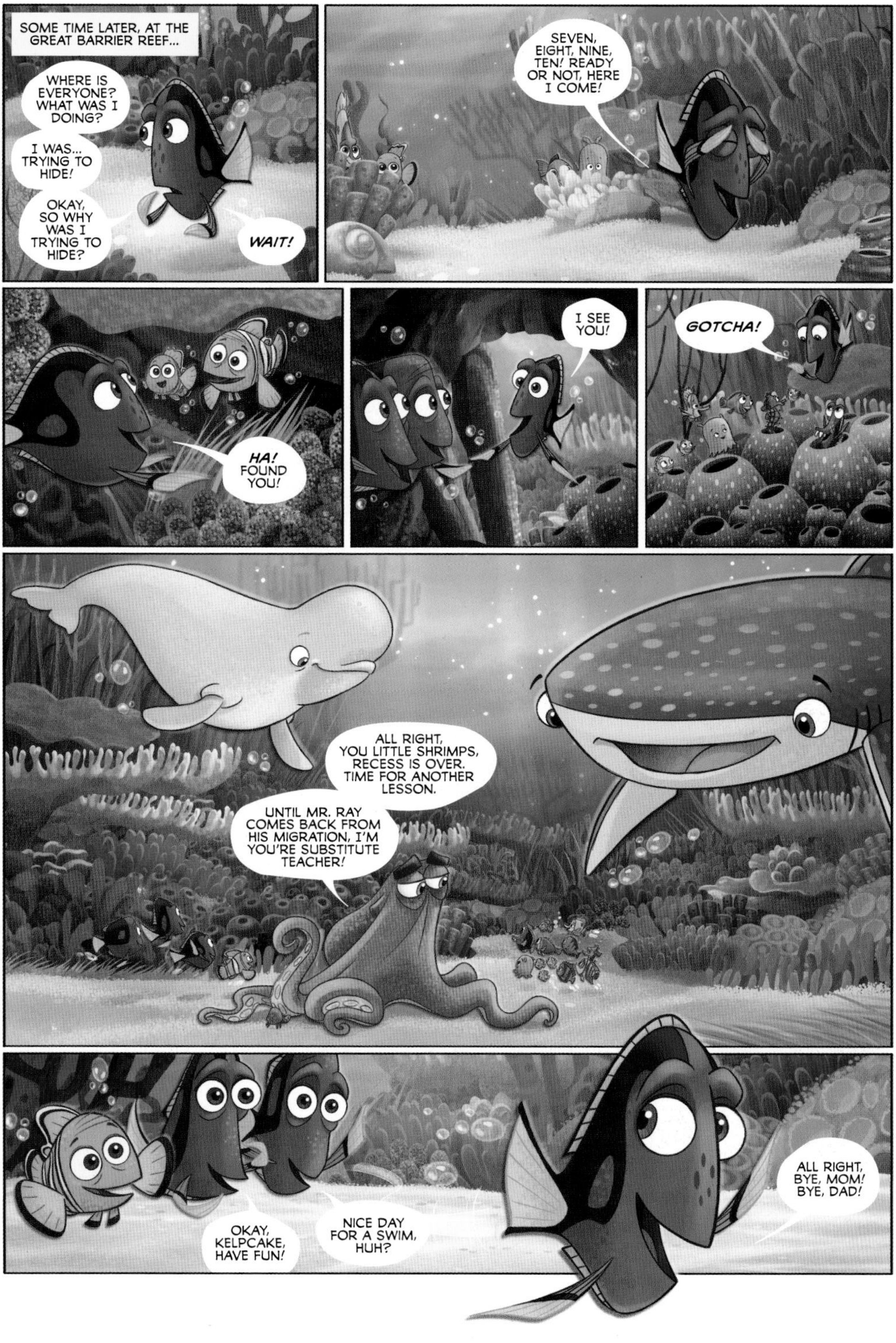
SOME TIME LATER, AT THE GREAT BARRIER REEF...
WHERE IS EVERYONE? WHAT WAS I DOING?
I WAS... TRYING TO HIDE!
OKAY, SO WHY WAS I TRYING TO HIDE?
WAIT!
SEVEN, EIGHT, NINE, TEN! READY OR NOT, HERE I COME!
HA! FOUND YOU!
I SEE YOU!
GOTCHA!
ALL RIGHT, YOU LITTLE SHRIMPS, RECESS IS OVER. TIME FOR ANOTHER LESSON.
UNTIL MR. RAY COMES BACK FROM HIS MIGRATION, I'M YOU'RE SUBSTITUTE TEACHER!
OKAY, KELPCAKE, HAVE FUN!
NICE DAY FOR A SWIM, HUH?
ALL RIGHT, BYE, MOM! BYE, DAD!

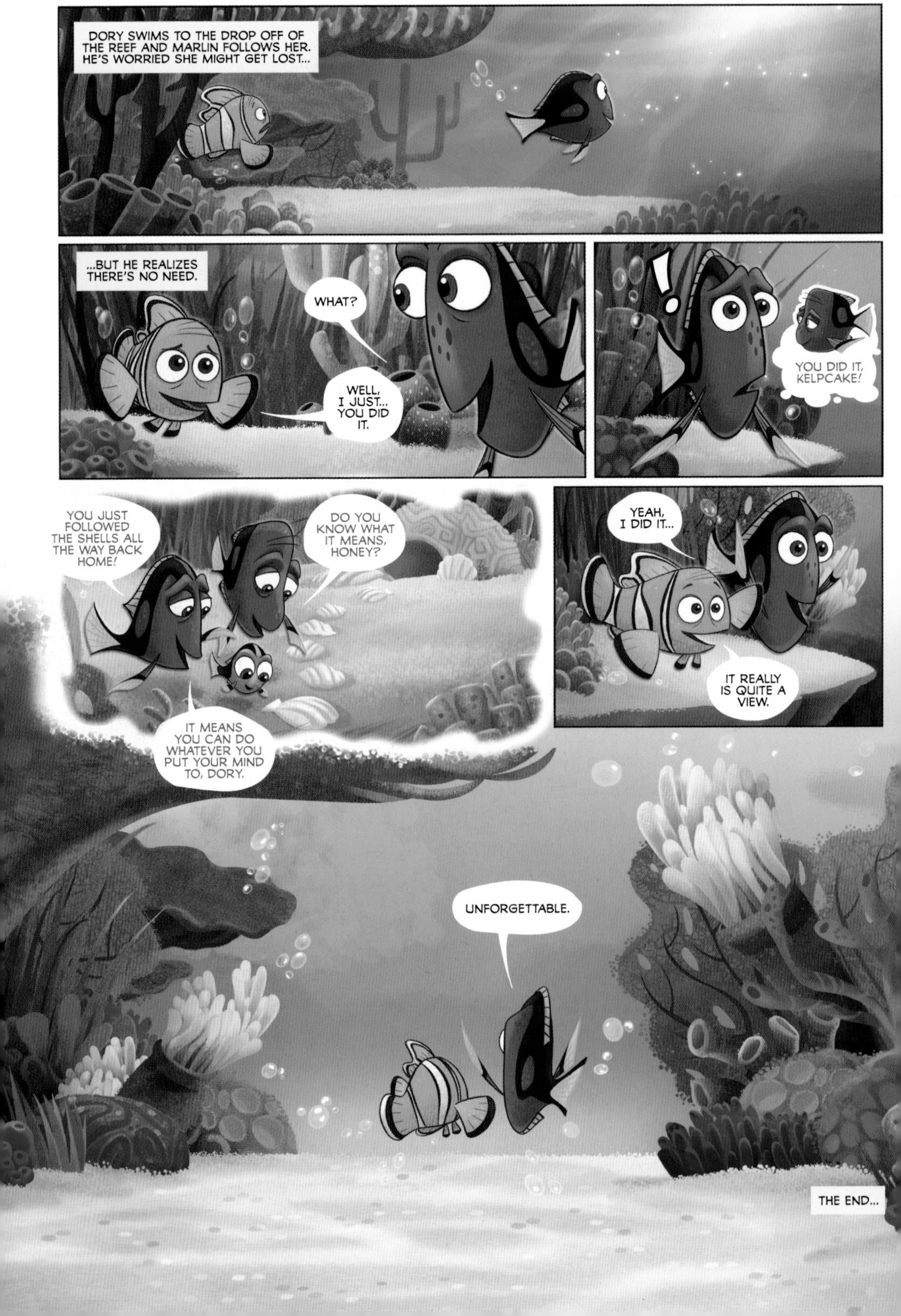
DORY SWIMS TO THE DROP OFF OF THE REEF AND MARLIN FOLLOWS HER. HE'S WORRIED SHE MIGHT GET LOST...
...BUT HE REALIZES THERE'S NO NEED.
WHAT?
WELL, I JUST... YOU DID IT.
!
YOU DID IT, KELPCAKE!
YOU JUST FOLLOWED THE SHELLS ALL THE WAY BACK HOME!
DO YOU KNOW WHAT IT MEANS, HONEY?
IT MEANS YOU CAN DO WHATEVER YOU PUT YOUR MIND TO, DORY.
YEAH, I DID IT...
IT REALLY IS QUITE A VIEW.
UNFORGETTABLE.
THE END...

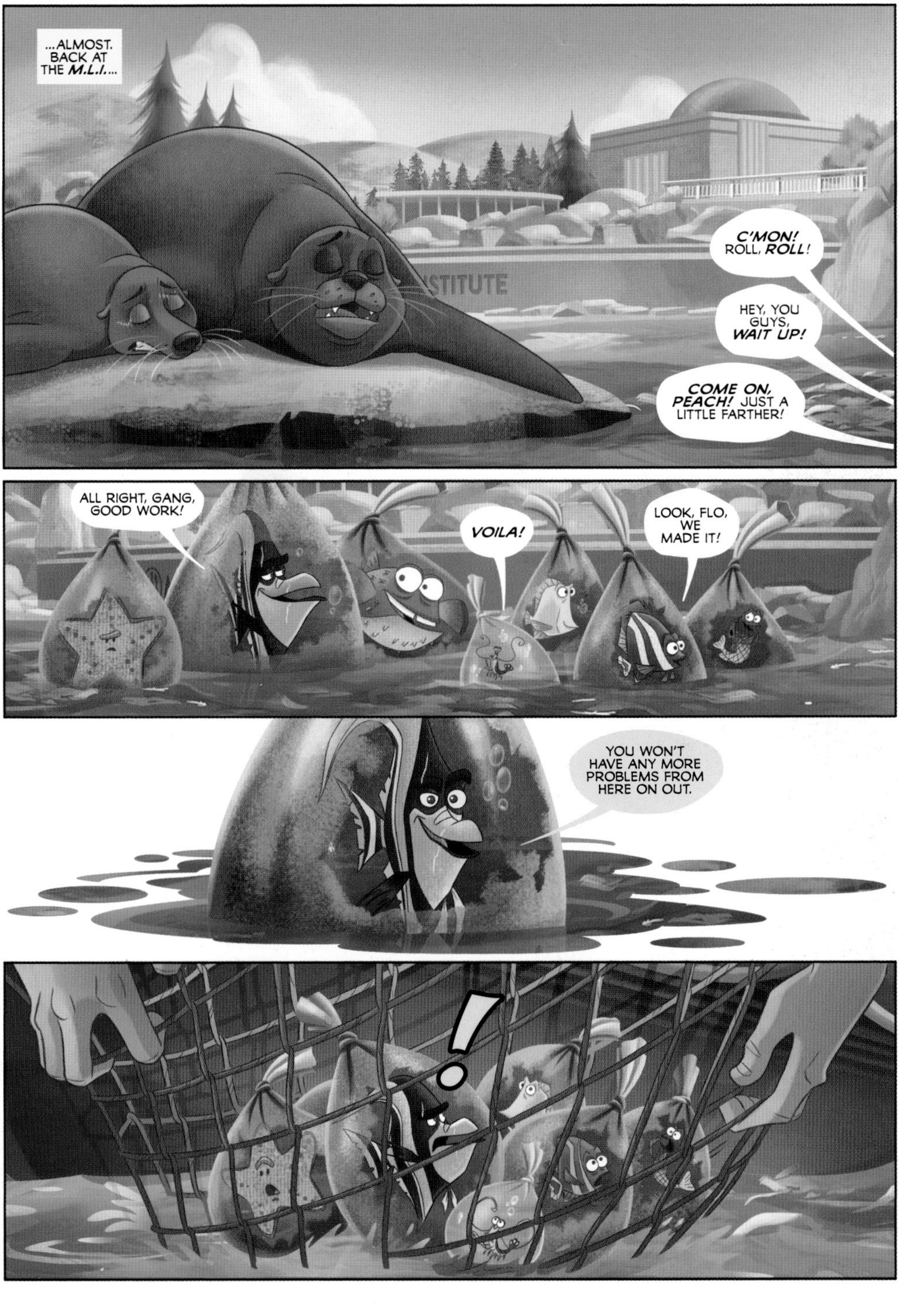
...ALMOST. BACK AT THE M.L.I....
C'MON! ROLL, ROLL!
HEY, YOU GUYS, WAIT UP!
COME ON, PEACH! JUST A LITTLE FARTHER!
INSTITUTE
ALL RIGHT, GANG, GOOD WORK!
VOILA!
LOOK, FLO, WE MADE IT!
YOU WON'T HAVE ANY MORE PROBLEMS FROM HERE ON OUT.
!

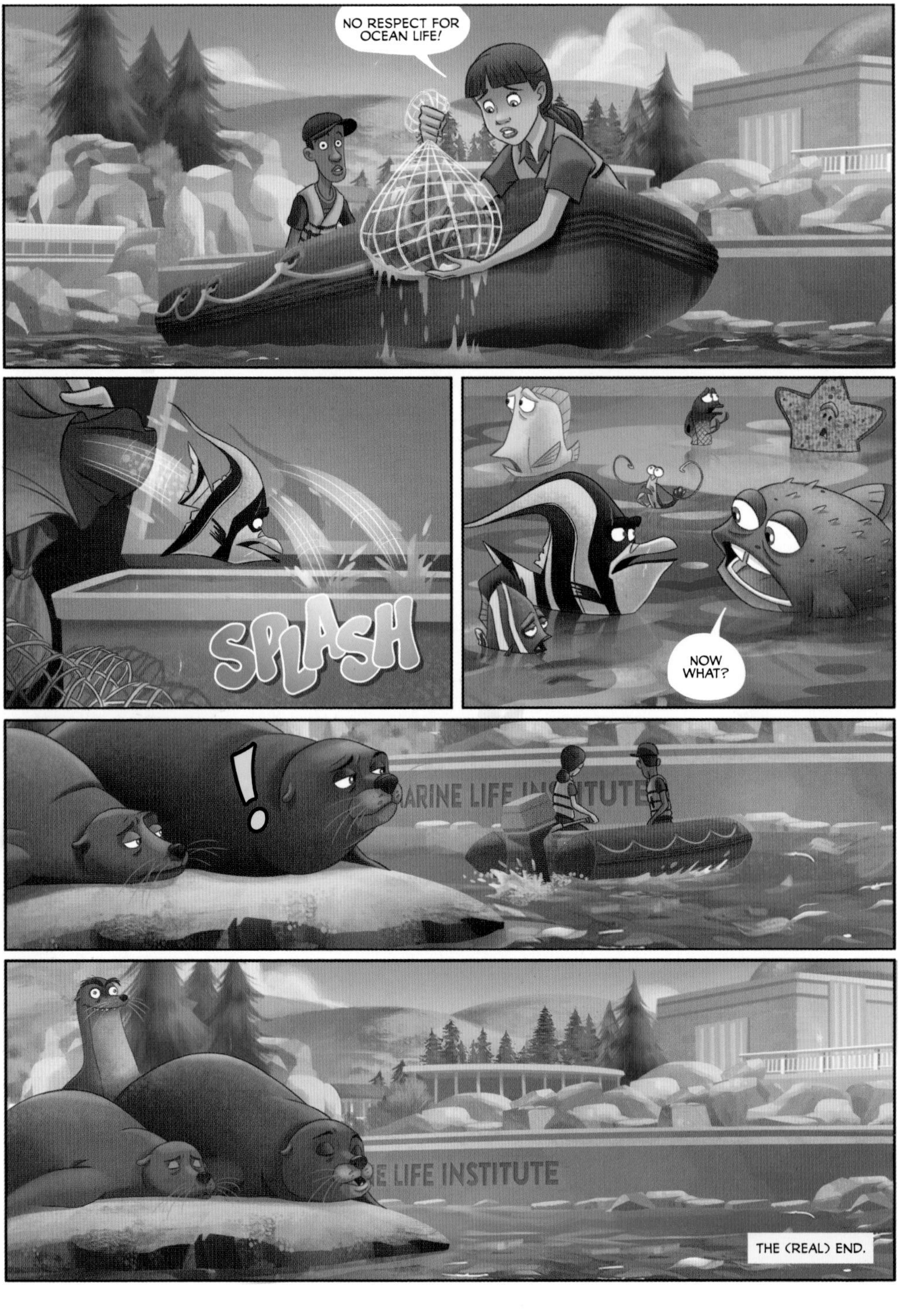
NO RESPECT FOR OCEAN LIFE!
SPLASH
NOW WHAT?
!
ARINE LIFE INSTITUTE
E LIFE INSTITUTE
THE (REAL) END.